"Welcome to Woden"

Books by Jim Ody

Lost Connections

The Place That Never Existed

A Cold Retreat

Beneath The Whispers

...Just South of Heaven

Noah's Lament

Mr Watcher

Mystery Island

Tales From the Coffee Pot

Sweet Vigilante

Bloodline (with ML Rayner)

Hudson Bell Series:

A Lifetime Ago

Come Back Home

Tall Trees Series:

Little Miss Evil

Little Miss Evil 2: Evil Returns

Joel Baxter Series

The Crazy Season

Question Mark Horror Series:

Camp Death

The Brood

The Last Weekend

Jim Ody

Question Mark Horror

This first edition published in 2023 by Question Mark Horror

Question Mark Horror is an imprint of Question Mark Press.

The Last Weekend - Jim Ody. – 1st edition
ISBN: 9798374231878
Cover design by: Elli Toney

The Last Weekend

Prologue

Nothing could quite prepare you for the thick, choking smell of death. It was made no easier when you were shackled and held captive and questioning whether part of the smell was from yourself.

The stench of rotting flesh smothered his nose like an invisible rag, fighting any oxygen that tried to enter his nostrils. His stomach was empty not just from the lack of food, but from the many times he'd vomited, expelling anything he had left inside. His stomach muscles ached from dry-heaving. Old, crusty chunks had hardened on his chin that had passed being stubbly days ago, and his throat was sore, and painfully dry. After the fetid aroma, the second worse thing was the fear of the unknown. He was all alone; the darkness strangled the life out of him. It imprisoned him and he was unable to escape; he was in pain. So much pain.

The summer heat added to his dehydration, and the cool

nights were more painful as aching muscles shivered involuntarily with the drop in temperature.

He was underground below a huge structure created by these animals. A faint glow from a dirty bulb gave him something close to comfort and confirmed he was still alive. But only just.

He'd been left in a crucifix pose. A modern-day Jesus, minus the parlour tricks or superlative social skills, he was still a persecuted and ultimately condemned man. Left to die as nothing but an unwilling martyr. An example of what happens to a man who tries to stand up to them.

His hands were numb from where they'd removed his fingers one by one. They'd grinned at him as he'd screamed in agony. They'd kept his thumbs intact. Not out of pity, but for fear of the cuffs would be able to slip off. If he did escape, at least he'd be able to hitchhike his way home. The gallows humour didn't make him feel any better, but at least his eight stumps no longer throbbed with pain.

His hands were now useless crusty-nubs with thumb-hooks. If he ever got out - and with each passing hour that seemed more unlikely - life would be forever split between before and after the last weekend.

They'd come back soon enough and finish him off. His will to live had dissipated as the endless sorrow became unbearable but, ultimately, his only friend. His soul was packed and waiting to leave, his body just a shell waiting to send him off. Any place would be better than this. Any place at all.

Any. Place.

Today was dark. The humidity had increased, speeding up the decay of his body. He felt a tug and sharp pain in his feet. Something was biting him. Nature knew he was wounded and dying and wanted to consume him there and then. Probably rats. The ugly fucking vermin eating his flesh so they could thrive. Typical. The world was full of them. Some were in human form.

The crack of thunder was loud, and the bulb went out completely, but then, as if trying to recreate lightening, the bulb flashed brighter than it had done before. An electrical surge, that for a split second lit up the room with the horrors within. Another body was hung up like him in a similar fashion, the difference being the guy was a long time dead. His face was gaunt; almost skeletal. His one remaining eye stared off hopefully but no longer saw. His leg had been crudely hacked off, and below him was a dried mess of blood, urine and faeces.

He still heard the laughter from their last assault on him. It had been the worst experience of his life. At first they'd chanted, but then the sound of an old woman cackling sent chills up his spine before they'd set to work on the poor guy.

In some ways he thought his dead roomie was lucky. He was free from this living hell. The monsters stalked around here, drawing you in, before they snatched you and refused to let you go. He'd eaten well and been entertained at first. And then it all went south fast.

Why did he end up here? Did his family know? He hoped to God they didn't. Hope was better than Hell.

He'd stopped believing in God a few days ago. A god would never allow this to happen. He had no passion for being a martyr poster-boy but had won that accolade nevertheless.

He heard laughter. Loud and raucous. And then somewhere on the other side of the room a door swung open with great force. He knew then he was finally about to die.

Running feet, and giggling filled the room. Small hands grabbed at him. Rats screeched with fear and scuttled off.

He was in pain, but that was about to get fatally worse. Flashes of red hoods flooded the room jostling for positions in order to watch the pitiful fool die a painful death.

And then the cackling began.

Chapter 1

Disgruntled office-worker, Jarrod Mathews looked up at the huge glass eye-sore of a building, and wished not for the first time that it would be blown to smithereens. He didn't care about the *who* nor the *why*, and if he was honest, nor did he care whether he was inside the building when it exploded. That was the extent of his feelings towards life. So far it had been a huge anti-climax and nothing on the horizon looked to change that perspective.

No matter how many times he looked up, the building was still there standing strong against a countryside backdrop goading him knowingly that he had showed up like a good little lab-rat once again.

Not that it was unusual, but Jarrod didn't fancy work today. Unfortunately, the thirty-year-old was contractually obliged to frequent the aforementioned building four agonising days a week. It wasn't Friday, so here he was moderately groomed and already counting down the hours before lunch. On Fridays, Jarrod rested at home on the sofa comforted with coffee and Netflix, whilst idly nudging his laptop to fool management into thinking he was hard at work. Not that they were fooled one bit, but his job was as dull as dishwater and to replace him was nothing short of a hard and thankless task, so both parties tolerated the other until the day he was replaced by a bot. Jarrod was good at his job, and it was so technical there would be zero interest in his role should either party finally blink first, and terminate his contract. It was hardly PC to say, but only someone firmly on the spectrum would remotely enjoy what he did. His boss had told him so. It was her idea of motivation. However, Jarrod was not unique in his lack of ambition, nor his general get-up-and-disappear attitude. A fact recently brought to his attention by his ex-girl-fiend when without so much as a warning she walked out on him and took most of his stuff with her. An hour previously, she'd been butt-naked and enthusiastically giving him both a rimjob and handjob simultaneously, before expertly climbing on top of him and bouncing in a determined fashion until he'd exploded inside of her. She'd seemed perfectly happy when she'd rolled off, then kissed him passionately as his fingers finished her off, and her murmurs vibrated on his lips. But a lot had changed in the next sixty minutes, post-afterglow, and he was sure it had nothing to do with the cleanliness of his anus, nor his dexterous finger-wiggling skills, but more an issue with her own long-term perspective of their relationship. The world was full of other men she'd like to arse-tongue, get creampied, and fingered until she lost her voice, and he'd be back to free porn sites for relief, and ejaculating into the dating pool again.

That wasn't the only social boil on his knob, Jarrod hated his work colleagues with a shrugged apathy, too. The only person he got on with was Rick, and he was just plain odd. The guy was even more introverted, and socially awkward than himself and in a way was a bit of an antihero to him. Rick looked like he might be the type of person to plant a bomb at work and happily allow relatives to blame Marilyn Manson for it. Rumour had it Rick was on his final warning. Jarrod knew what that was like. Some days he sat back on his chair willing his boss to finally relieve him of his duties. Let some other dickhead crunch the numbers and check the intricacies of other people's financial transactions. Jesus, the thought of his own job description made him want to run headfirst into the coffee-machine, God-knows what it did to people who actually gave a shit. And now he didn't even have the skills of a woman's tongue to greet him from work. He was munching down anti-depressants and pretending it was completely normal.

Today was Monday, which was a real Debbie-Downer. Only fucking idiots, or colleagues having affairs saw any pleasure in the day. Four fucking mornings and afternoons he'd have to endure with this lot sat in close proximity - albeit divided by large grey, cloth-covered partitions that weren't half as strong as they looked. He knew this as he'd hit his head against them enough times and achieved nothing but the noise of them falling over, and neighbouring departments tutting at him like they were so fucking superior. We're the same fucking pay grade, he wanted to yell, no matter what ass-kissing you're doing. If anyone was superior, it was either the bosses who locked themselves away in their glass power-rooms, or the clever ex-employees who bit the bullet and left for greener pastures. Some so desperate they escaped without another job to go to. This was hardly anyone's vocation of choice. Alongside being a policeman, a footballer, a doctor or a movie star, nobody in the whole of history had ever said they wanted to be a shit-level Financial Analyst. Not outside of a padded cell and therapy. The money was acceptable and it beat watching the sands of time drain from his life's hour-glass whilst at home indulging in house renovation programs on TV, but still there had to be better ways to experience the hours between daylight and darkness, that didn't feel like you were socialising with the mentally incapacitated.

His boss, Keely appeared from her castle, which was a large office that had no business being its over-indulgent size, nor furnished so well. All it did was mock them. She was mid-forties, and painfully attractive in a mature mistress sort of way if she wasn't such a bitch. She was dressed for power. A smart, red dress that was figure-hugging but intimidating at the same time and not even Chris de Burgh would go anywhere near her. She had cougar attributes and rumoured to have an OnlyFans account not that anyone admitted to subscribing. She barely ate, and when not in work had a severe fitness regime that made her body as hard as the main thinking-station of any man in close proximity.

She had Jarrod by the balls, and each day twisted them a little tighter. One call to HR and he'd be flipping burgers at *Burger Me* and blowing men behind the recycling bins to make ends meet. His life's ambition definitely didn't have minimum wage, nor swallowing an elderly man's seed in it.

He hated her, but somehow she bullied her way into his fantasies and that only succeeded in pissing him off further. How was that possible? How could you mutter *fuck you* under your breath and mean it both ways at once?

She would appear at her door, hands behind her back and survey her team accusingly. Just hoping to catch them doing something they shouldn't and ready to explode in a rage Jarrod had been witness to on many an occasion. He wondered how far her dominance ran. It wasn't a stretch to think of her with a cat o' nine tails whip, knee-length boots, and a small leather sheath of an outfit stood in teasing threat stance.

There was a twenty percent new employee retention rate in their department that saw a retaliation of tears (*them*), and raised voices (*her*) before said employee was never seen again.

"*Rick*," she said loudly, making the team slut Eloise jump and expel an audible squeak, and Will awoke from some daydream he thought no one else had noticed while he wiped the drool from the corner of his mouth. Even Dan the ex-army major glanced up from his laptop with a lopsided grin, and quickly went back to his work like the good foot-soldier he now was. He wasn't best pleased taking orders from a woman no matter how good looking she was. To him, world wars hadn't been won by any woman no matter how much they stomped their high-heels and burnt their off-the-shoulder-boulder-holders. Whoopy-fucking-do!

Rick threw Jarrod a knowing glance, rolled his eyes and tried not to look so uncomfortable. Their boss had already gone back into her office so the countdown had started, and now she would be facing him with a well-practised scowl when he walked in. Ready to pounce; the art of intimidation. No one knew what went on but nobody ever reappeared smiling.

"Ooh, called to teacher's office," Eloise taunted, though secretly pleased it wasn't her. Nobody cared what she had to say as she lived in a world of make believe. Rick didn't even glance at her, which only made her clench her jaw tightly. She was a twenty-year-old Insta-girl, permanently late whilst she strove to find aesthetic perfection. In a nutshell, she was a fat girl packaging herself as best she could. Attractive in a cut & paste social media way, but she lived her life like she was in some irrelevant reality-TV show, assuming the rest of the floor to be her audience. Everything about her was false, but carefully planned out. She loved attention and was desperately single because she couldn't afford to be off the market. Her dates were by the hour and whilst at one time she may've dreamed of princesses and romance, she now fooled herself into thinking she was satisfied with being somebody's secret cumbucket. She'd downsized her clothing choices to enhance her curves, but sometimes it only emphasised the rolls of the soft human mattress she could become after a couple of beers. Her legs and mouth were constantly open and begging for attention, and she saw nothing wrong with bringing a travel-vibrator to work should her world of Finance Administration get her too worked up.

The key to Eloise, was to approach her after two beers. She was mildly attractive then. Before that and she was gobby and aggressive, her standards greater than what she offered, but after that she swiftly went downhill, forgetting about her appearance and hygiene as her knickers were stuffed in her handbag, her eyesight blurred and her standards only required a naked body, preferably with a cock but she was happy to snog anyone. It was a shame her head was so full of shit, probably numbed by the various chemicals that straightened, unfrizzed and dyed her hair, plus whatever bronzed her skin to such an unnatural colour. If she was stripped down and attacked with a power-hose, she'd be completely unrecognisably plain. She'd stopped flirting with Jarrod since he fucked her two beers in behind a bar called Capers. It wasn't a memorable event for either of them, but both assumed it not to be something worth repeating and quickly changed the subject each time someone brought it up.

Jarrod watched the numbers on his spreadsheet move around. It happened sometimes. His eyes were going wonky on him. He'd dry swallowed more than his allocation of tablets for the day so there was a danger that he might go a bit weird later. The truth was he felt slightly better each time he upped the dosage. He could stop whenever.

He couldn't be less up for tax calculations today if he was asked to do it covered in marmite, especially since seeing an email appear marked ***Team Building Event***. If there was another thing he hated even more than his work, *and* his colleagues, it was Team Building. An age-old excuse for bosses to make their minions squirm with impossible tasks designed to force them in close proximately to each other whilst psychologically profiling them on invisible clipboards, analysing their every move, and pushing buttons to get a reaction. It felt like one of those Japanese gameshows where contestants were forced to do awful things until they submitted, and were ultimately just ridiculed by the presenters. Here, however, it would be a handful of paragraphs hidden away in an HR file, and used as evidence of grounds for dismissal. *And he'd be back to burgers and blowjobs.*

There was no date, and no venue, which was even worse. If Jarrod didn't know exactly what he was letting himself in for then his anxious mind would conjure up something awful and liable to leave him with PTSD.

Jarrod idly flicked the clock on his monitor hoping in some way it would jump forward to when it would be acceptable to venture from his desk in the guise of a break.

Keely had sent him a threatening email. It sat there in his Outlook in-box. It was cleverly written, vague and in code except he knew what the clandestine message was. She was turning the screw and inserting her power on him. She had one of his balls in her pocket and she was determined to get her hands on the other.

A few minutes later Rick appeared, and shuffled back to his desk. His face held its usual blank expression. He could've got a pay rise, or his P45 and he'd wear the same non-committal look on his face.

"You still got a job?" Jarrod tested him. They both knew he did. His job was just as shit as his own albeit more admin-based. Besides, Keely would be stood over him sweating his every move to make sure he didn't steal any corporate secrets as he logged out and took the one way walk of shame out of the office forever. Others had trodden that path before him, and statistics suggested others would follow after him, too. But not today. His job was safe.

Rick shrugged. "Worse. I've got a task."

Jarrod pulled a face. Nobody wanted to be called into the office and gifted a task. Nothing good ever came of it. Essentially it was always something shit that trickled down from above. If you succeeded in the task you'd hear no more of it, but should you fail, any thoughts of a bonus would be found on American milk cartons, forever a cold case.

"I have to come up with the Team Building event." His face looked like he'd been asked to strip in front of the whole department, and it was only Eloise who'd be remotely interested in doing that. Although she'd probably try to charge, a pointless move as a lot of the men in the office had fucked her more than once.

"That's not so bad, is it? At least you can control what we do, right?"

"What the fuck do I know about team building? She said if I fuck up I'm out and she'd make sure the only references I got were bad, and incredibly unfavourable. Besides, I just have to come up with an idea, she's too much of a control freak to allow me full reign on a final decision."

"Makes sense. Then let's do something she'll hate, but that you wouldn't know she hated. This could be fun." Jarrod was doing his best to put a good spin on it. It was a tough gig. Fun work was an oxymoron.

"Fun?" Rick was shaking his head and trying to choose between a 2B and a 2H pencil to bury deep into his eye-cavities. He wanted to die. Jarrod wondered whether he should send him links to trench coats and Japanese assault rifles. Get the ball rolling so to speak. There were instructions on bomb-making online. He could send those links, too.

"Yeah. We got this."

"It's alright for you," Rick said with something snide attached to the tone. "She likes you." That seemed unlikely. Rick appeared to hate her as much as he did, but never mentioned any sexual attraction. Not that he was outwardly telling Rick he'd fuck her in a heartbeat given the unlikely chance.

It was the pills talking. He was becoming fidgety and his mind was all over the place.

"Well, maybe it's time to get her back." He looked around. "In fact, get them all back!" Rick smiled. Not the normal subtle twitch, but one that started off modest and increased rapidly into a full-blown expression of amusement.

"Just keep a handle on reality, buddy," Rick said in a lowered voice. Jarrod knew what he meant. Of late, his mind had taken him on many journeys, it was a defence mechanism the doctor had said, before idly scribbling out a prescription for the pills to mask the problem. They'd lasted a week. He sourced replacements. Stronger replacements. He liked those better.

"Yeah, yeah," Jarrod responded dismissively, noticing the office killjoy, Verity, taking an interest. She worked hard at looking plain and by all accounts was married to a man she hated – that seemed typically a middle-aged issue. Although, she detested most people and drew pleasure in pointing out a list of a person's failings as soon as she met them. Jarrod glared at her before looking back at his monitor.

His balloons burst as he noticed another email pop into his mailbox just as the blinds were being drawn in his boss's office.

Meeting. Now. it said in the description. Nothing in the body. No pleasantries. No fucking people skills that one.

Rick noticed. "Someone's in trouble," he sighed. "Try not to get booted out. *You* need to help me."

Jarrod got up. "You and I both know I have no control over that," he replied.

"And fucking act normal for once."

The pills made him feel like dancing so Rick was right to worry. He continued to walk the green mile towards the office, doing his best not to add a Saturday Night Fever twirl as he got to the door. He felt numb inside but buzzing. It was like being pissed.

"Shut the door behind you," she barked, her default mean-bitch expression on her face. "And take a seat."

He sat down; his heart was beating fast. He could never relax when he was in this office and the chemicals in his body made him twitchy. How could a woman like her become so scary? What happened to her in her past to make her so bad? A dark movement of paranoia crept out from the corner of the office. He didn't like it. This was not the time for that side-effect.

She glanced over at him. She was scowling in a way that on other people would look awful but on her it was just a slight dent in her attractive façade, which was annoying.

A designer handbag hung from a coat rack like a medal. It was small and pointless but impressive to all the right people. Jarrod wasn't one of them. His ex-girl-fiend only had to get a whiff of a Gucci and she was wetter than a weekend in Wales. He didn't see the attraction. Surely a bag was just a fucking bag?

She got up and walked carefully around her desk refusing to look at him. It was a deliberate tactic so he couldn't read her face. She walked to the door and quietly engaged the lock. With deliberate steps she returned. *Shit just got serious*, he thought as his fingers tapped nervously on the armrest. For a second, he thought she might punch him in the face, like she fancied herself as a wannabe mob-boss. Knuckle dusters and all. Gain some respect from the grunt.

"It's been brought to my attention there have been a few more episodes of insubordination," she began. "Is this correct?" There was no right answer. If he lied then he was calling the whistle-blower a liar, and if he agreed then he would be at the bins by the weekend, kneeling in drunkard's vomit and being face-fucked by a closet homosexual.

"No," he said automatically – too automatically - but in his mind, he could think of many. He gulped. A guilty schoolboy in front of the headmistress. His stomach sunk to the floor. He was really opposed to giving men blowjobs.

"Really? You've forgotten? Or you're choosing to lie to me?" She seemed amused by his defiance. It was a game to her. The lioness and the field mouse.

"I really don't know what you've been told," he began, which in part was correct. He'd done a few things so to be asked to narrow it down was nigh-on impossible, and he certainly was in no position to list them off one-by-one. His mind was skipping and he was struggling to focus. Everything around the room and about her was screaming for attention.

She held up her hand. "I don't want to hear it. Let's cut the bullshit, Jarrod."

There was a deathly silence. A game of chess. Power moving around. His discomfort was her foreplay.

"I warned you the first time. It's not just a matter of losing employment. It's illegal. You could be arrested. You don't want that, do you?"

He felt sick. He knew and she knew. His eyes darted around the office as if it might be his last glance ever.

Her hair was pulled back into a bun. Her make-up was perfect, and a small silver chain sat delicately on her neck, with a diamond hung from it towards her plunging neckline.

"You have an insatiable need to undermine me and question me. I can only assume it's because I'm a woman." He didn't follow. She'd started on a new tactic and he had no clue where she was leading him. But he didn't like it. Ignorance was weakness.

"Do you hate me, Jarrod?"

Her question was unexpected. His eyes zoned in on hers. "No," he said. "Not at all." He no longer believed himself.

She placed her hands on her thighs and slowly wiggled the bottom of her dress up to her waist, exposing small red underwear. All the time her eyes were locked on his, drinking up how shocked he was and the willpower used to not lower his gaze.

"What are you doing?" he stammered, caught in a bizarre cocktail of fear, regret and something else. Something more primal, and sexual.

"You're free to leave whenever you want," she said playfully, and grinned knowingly. She twisted and made a play for her phone, all the while the flash of red was still exposed. "I'll just ring HR, and they can contact the police, okay?"

"No," he said, almost raising from his seat, and unable to take his eyes off her naked thighs. Things had changed. Something was happening in their relationship. A huge #metoo step further.

"No, indeed," she replied, and sat there on the desk and slowly widened her legs expectantly. His heart was galloping inside his ribcage and his face was burning.

Jarrod couldn't believe how bold she was. Outside of this power-room, a large open-plan office was filled with witnesses, any one of whom could knock on her door at any moment, and here she was sat flashing her underwear without a moment of fear, and it was he who felt rigid, and unable to move. She was a fantasy he'd fallen into, and he wasn't sure what it meant. A dumb man caught in the honeytrap. He could never say he hated it, but he disliked being forced to comply by her. Forever bowing to her commands. Now he just felt like a useless pervert staring at her and fumbling with his hands in front him.

"Don't just sit there," she said, her hands slipping to her knickers and pulling them to the side in a slow and sensual manner. "Let's not pretend this isn't something you've thought about…" Jarrod's mouth was open when she added, "Come on. I'm not going to fuck myself."

He stood up awkwardly, and took a deep breath.

"Jarrod! Look at me!" She demanded, and when he did she was there on the desk but her legs were very much closed. He cleared his throat and sat back down.

"What was that?" she demanded. "You were looking at me funny."

"Sorry," his head was bowed with embarrassment. "I…"

"It's nothing," she said and her voice softened. Whatever had happened it had worked in his favour. She felt sorry for him.

"Things will be changing," she said. "You're an important member of the team, remember that, Jarrod, right?"

He nodded but didn't trust himself to look up at her. His eyes would wander over the office at best, and at worst they would come to rest on her breasts or thighs. Then the fantasies would begin. He clenched his left hand feeling the nails bite into his palms. A trick some NHS-appointed specialist had taught him when he couldn't afford to go private.

"You look like you need a break. You got any holidays left?"

He nodded. He still had the week booked when he had meant to be in Spain on a shagfest with his girl-fiend. A week on his own was hardly going to be the same. If he wasn't careful he'd end up with Eloise, watching the second beer kick in before he took her hand and marvelled the PAWG view, as he bent her over the empty barrels until he was done. He’d decline her wishes for him to finger her in place of a vodka that would erase the act from her memory as he slipped off into the night. He wasn’t proud of doing it but it was a thing. Or he’d sit with his friend Paige and they could continue their long-term game of sexual tension as neither wished to make a move on the other, but happily talked about everything else.

Jarrod focused on the image of the picture sat proudly on her desk. She and her husband stood arm in arm wearing some stupid fancy-dress outfit. He looked like some Nordic Viking with a huge beard and wearing a hood, and she in a figure-hugging dress. Neither of them smiling. Perhaps they knew about his recurring fantasies of ejaculating into Keely’s mouth.

“□Do you need help?” Keely was asking.

He shook his head even though he’d not heard her question. Nobody ever admitted to requiring help. Who wanted to talk about themselves to a stranger? Not him.

He muttered, “No,” as she looked like she required an answer, and she appeared satisfied.

Jarrod didn’t trust himself to speak and felt like the world knew his dirty little secrets. He glanced once more at the picture, and then up at his boss, who appeared unmoved by the whole situation. She reached out and brushed her hand against his arm in an uncharacteristic way.

Jarrod was so confused with what had happened, and what that meant.

She stood up and took a step towards him. She pulled him in for a hug. It was for a few seconds and she held him tightly. He carefully held her back and felt like he was in heaven. But then she moved her mouth to his left ear and whispered:

"Tell anyone, and you're finished. Not just here, but in life." He nodded as she walked confidently towards the door, unlocked it and swung it open. Her whole demeanour changed back to what it had been before he'd entered her office.

"By tomorrow," she said in an authoritative voice. "Or we'll have to have another chat!"

"Okay," he replied feeling genuinely confused and trying to control the chemicals whizzing around his body, and he walked out. No one looked up. No one gave a shit. If he'd been female, and she male then the situation would be completely different. But he wasn't, so he had to take it on the chin. That's what men did.

He hated himself for all the fantasies that filled his mind with useless scenes of unlikely filth. He hated the drugs and the bottles of alcohol he used to numb the pain. He hated the prostitute he'd organised and then told her to leave when she arrived. The reality of rock bottom hit him hard.

Things had to change here, and he couldn't completely rule out planting a bomb and blowing the whole bloody place up himself; one huge great explosion! It was sad when the only way out included blowing everyone up in a huge fireball.

But at least he'd be somebody.

Chapter 2

With the sixth sense of another unhappy employee, Rick understood the abnormality of the meeting between Jarrod and Keely. There was something strange about it. He got special treatment. It was twenty minutes before he raised the point. He may've been wrestling with it for a while.

"You get a task, too?" Rick asked, sitting back in his chair and lacing his fingers over the top of his head trying to look calm. He was barely twenty but acted like he was older. Jarrod just took a deep breath conflicted in what response he could give. The whole sea of irrelevant people around him just made him feel worse. It didn't help that his mind and body couldn't decide whether his mood was up or down.

"A new project," he lied, and deliberately failed to expand on that. Even as colleagues, Rick and Jarrod shared very little of their lives. Their common ground was their hatred of their job coupled with their weakness and inability to do anything about it. They also were devoid of family; both only ever admitted to vague notions of abandonment and left it at that.

"Project? On what?" Rick pushed, but was shushed by Di, a woman in her late forties who huffed and puffed in a seat just in front of them. She hated the world too, but for different reasons. At one time she might've entered other people's fantasies but she'd not been thought of in that way for a long time and it really irked her.

"I'm trying to concentrate," she said, her gravelly voice abused by years of smoking. If you covered her face she looked to be in her twenties. Her diet was water and rabbit-food, and she over-compensated her years of self-abuse by over-exercising in any free moment she had now. Di was the survivor of three marriages, with a bad attitude towards men and a determination to stay youthful. Her hair looked perfect, but her face looked prematurely old and haggard. Dehydrated lines carved her skin, and frown lines drooped at the edges and looked themselves to be unhappy. How she'd found three husbands was beyond anyone. The first probably got in there before she rapidly went downhill, whereas the others were probably entering into a relationship version of self-harm.

"Sorry, Di," Rick muttered, and Jarrod tried to hide his smirk.

"It's nothing to laugh at," she said looking up. "If I fuck up, we lose business, and if that happens, I'm telling Keely it was you!" She'd amounted to be a fucking tell-tale-kiss-arse.

Keely the boss. The head honcho around there. His fantasy woman. He wondered how shocked Di would be if she knew. She hated Keely for being slightly younger, and very much more attractive and successful, but still sucked up to her at any chance she had. Women's Lib was in full effect. At a push she'd side with the sour-faced Verity, but then again, they both saw each other as a threat and secretly hated each other. A total Avril Lavigne situation where life could be simple but they had to go and make things so complicated.

The rest of the day slipped by. The mundane routine continued in its standard clockwork fashion. Columns of numbers appeared busily on spreadsheets sent by dickheads who asked how you were but couldn't give a shit as long as you did their work for them. His eyes scanned over the figures as he checked total calculations, abnormalities and even on auto-pilot was about to spot trends, and patterns.

He was definitely coming down. The bottle of pills were calling him from his pocket but he had to fight the urge. He knew bringing the whole pack to work was a mistake.

He just needed something to take the edge off.

Keely refused to even acknowledge his existence since their physical-contact-meeting and he found himself distracted, and getting jealous when he saw her laughing with other males. What the hell was wrong with him? It made him so mad. A weak male caught up in the black widow's web. Arachnid limbs pushing his emotional buttons and silently toying with his future.

She knew what she was doing.

He just had to find out why.

She was walking around a lot with one of the directors called Martin. A guy in his late forties who smiled too much for someone of his power. He thought of himself as one-of-the-guys. The guys thought of him as one-of-the-knobs.

When the clock hit the acceptable time to escape, Jarrod nodded a goodbye to Rick and escaped, whilst he daydreamed the whole lonely walk back to his one-bed house in a crime-riddled but low-rent part of town.

His standard routine had him sat lonely on his beaten-up sofa. A single portion of chips now gone and with a plate smeared in the remnants of ketchup and grease. He looked at his phone, and before he knew it had scrolled down the numbers until he stopped on his long-term friend Paige.

She was a more acceptable choice ahead of Eloise. Or another embarrassing red-light rendezvous She was socially awkward but bordered on outgoing when with Jarrod. They often watched movies together, and on the rare occasion they went to a pub and drank, they'd fool around and never talk about it the next day. They had invisible boundaries they never talked about but the limit was clothing liberation. Both of them teased buttons, zips and clasps, but neither took the leap to the next level, and it was often the cue to end the night on a high. He'd known her longer than anyone else still in his life, and she would be the outlet he needed after the day he'd had. Not that he'd tell her, of course.

Twenty minutes after he'd called her, there was a knock at his front-door and Paige stood there smiling but unable to make eye-contact with him. They were just a pair of rejects.

"You look weird," she said, walking in and slumping down onto the sofa. Her long black hair had been straightened and her eyeliner, like her lipstick was black. She wore a superhero T-shirt that was tight across her chest, and a pleated skirt, finished with knee-high socks, and a pair of Converse trainers that were considered well-worn a year ago. She'd embraced the alternative look which had evolved from her previous geek-chic as her fashion choices got bold. He liked it and in his awkward way had told her so.

She always forgave him when another woman came in and out of his life and their time together was put on hold. She got jealous, although would never admit it, and they both knew the honeymoon period of a new sexual plaything only lasted a few weeks before it abruptly ended. Perhaps that was why they refused to go that extra step. Their relationship actually had some substance.

"What d'you mean?" he said, not liking the way she could read him so easily. She was very literal and said exactly what was on her mind. He handed her a glass of vodka and coke which she grabbed like he might take it back. She liked drink like he liked taking pills. She was an alcoholic-intern well on her way to being full-time.

She half-smiled and nudged past him. They sat down, and he picked up his bottle of beer when said replied, "I dunno. You look different. Has something happened? Have you just masturbated?" He almost spat out the cheap-as-piss alcohol. She had no filter and said what she thought.

"What? No!" He sat next to her – not too close. The news was on in the background and judging by the tone it was filled with doom and gloom. He clicked it over to Netflix. "Just work," he said. "Same old shit." The throwaway, and overused, line was out before he could reign it back in.

"You ever think about leaving?"

"Every *fucking* day."

"So do it. What's stopping you?" She turned slightly in her seat towards him. She either spoke or remained funereally quiet. When she engaged in conversation she liked to fully commit. Then she'd remain tight-lipped for an hour like they were two strangers who happened to be in the same room. It was strangely comforting. Small talk was for people who had nothing to say.

"What else would I do? I analyse numbers and write reports. If you haven't noticed, I have few social skills."

Paige snorted to prove hers were worse. Not her most attractive feature, but it was what she did when she laughed. "And yet you line fuck-buddies up like take-aways."

"I'm not a nice person when I drink. I lose my anxiety and get horny."

"You're always horny." He dismissed the comment. It might've been a joke but her face was straight. She didn't understand deadpan. A joke had to be obvious to her.

She took another sip. "I'm hardly Miss Sociable! Remember my first job interview when I peed myself!"

He remembered. She'd been mortified, but she'd told him. In graphic detail. That's how they were.

"Paige…" he didn't know how to begin. He went for the Elastoplast approach. "I often think of ending things." He looked away from her. After the day he'd had, he didn't want to see the disappointment in her face.

She surprised him. "I know," she said like he'd just admitted to liking cats. "So do I."

"What?" He turned back and saw she was serious. It took the wind out of his sails even though he knew that was selfish. He was meant to have shocked her not the other way round.

"Don't look so stunned, Jarrod. You're not the only one who has no place in this world."

He went to speak, but stopped. His words now appeared inconsequential as she'd trumped him. There was a deep sadness in her eyes he'd grown used to. He hadn't stopped to wonder exactly what was behind them, and instead had on some level enjoyed her vulnerability. As usual he was too wrapped up in his own self-pity to ask. She was a complex creature packaged nicely, but still slightly odd.

"I really have shocked you, haven't I?" The words came out in a strangely soothing way. A whisper, that made him want to protect her. "I've thought a lot about taking my own life. It's not scary to me."

He nodded. "I guess I didn't really think you felt that bad… I…" He was stumbling over his words now. They didn't come naturally for him at the best of times.

"Well, it's true." He leant over and hugged her. She squeezed him back in a show of affection they rarely shared. As a rule, she didn't like to be touched by people other than Jarrod. For him, she'd always been welcoming for it.

"Don't do it, Paige. You've so much to offer." Empty clichéd words he'd clipped from various media sources. He knew only a couple of people would miss her. She was hardly Princess Diana.

"Thank you… but…" And she knew it, too.

"It's not enough, is it?"

"Would it make a difference if I told you not to end it either?"

Jarrod sat back, and held Paige's hand with an uncharacteristic tenderness. "I don't know," he replied, and with his spare hand tapped his skull. "Everything is so messed up in here."

The moment was broken as Jarrod felt his phone buzz. He pulled his hand from Paige's and swiped his phone.

His stomach sank as he saw it was a group message from his boss to his team:

Confirmation. Team building this weekend. Leave Friday and return Monday. Mandatory.

"Shit," he said, and showed Paige the blunt words.

"You've got to go to this?"

"*Mandatory!*" He boomed in a mock growl.

"Can they do that?"

He nodded. "My boss is a bitch."

"Then do something," she said, looking at him deeply. He'd mentioned his distaste for Keely to her on a number of occasions. "If she's the cause of so much of your pain, then she has to pay, right?" He couldn't tell her about what had happened in her office. She'd never understand. *He* didn't understand.

"You're right," he said, picturing Keely kneeling in front of him. Eyes locked deep into his whilst she moved her head back and forth. He felt broken imagining things weren't right, let alone likely to ever happen. Why was he so obsessed?

Paige nodded towards the TV, and grinned. "Let's stick some gruesome horror on!" He agreed, relieved he could forget about work, Keely, and the fucking weekend away for a little while longer.

A couple of hours later, and Paige was snuggling into him as the final credits rolled, and Netflix tried to get them to watch something else. It was nice. She made a cute pillow. *The calm before the storm*, he thought knowing he still had three more days of the office to endure.

Jarrod got up off the sofa, and Paige followed him silently as they walked into the kitchen and placed their empty glasses onto the sideboard-graveyard with the last few days' worth of potential washing up. They'd both had more than the normal morbid-openness of their conversation and had required lubrication. Both were feeling drunk.

"Imagine," Paige said, pulling her hair back tight into a ponytail, "sneaking into your boss's room whilst she slept and slitting her throat - just like in that movie. The blood trickling down her neck as her eyes shoot open and look at you in utter disbelief!"

"Yes," Jarrod agreed, and placed his hands on the side of her head. "Or grabbing her like this and snapping her neck! Crack!" He pretended to move it, but gently pushed it back to expose her throat.

"Oh no!" she pretended in a little-girl voice. "You're too much for me!"

"No, I've had enough!" he played along.

"Ooh," she said, and leaned forward and kissed him on the cheek. "I like that!" He looked at her with her hair now pulled back and her legs bare. Her face flashed to morph into Keely's. Her smile swapped to the stern face of his boss. He leaned in and kissed her back. Mouths opened and tongues danced together. Neither pulling away.

And then completely uncharacteristically of their platonic relationship, he was reaching under her skirt and she was placing her arms around his neck, silently allowing him to do so. His hands brushed her underwear. They were large and comfortable, but soon tugged down her thighs. They stopped kissing momentarily, as he looked for affirmation of his intentions. She stepped out of them awkwardly and desperately pulled him towards her again, not wanting the spell to end.

In his mind he was back in the office. Paige's thighs were larger as he grabbed them, lifting her onto the counter, and his own trousers were now crumpled around his ankles. She fumbled to help him slip inside her with ease though she barely acknowledged it.

It was much different to how he'd imagined it. Not as intense. A fuller-figure and sloppier kisses. He still pictured

Keely and her straight face, and pumped harder, and faster. This was soft, easy and he hated being the one in control.

And then he pulled out, needing more.

Paige looked unsure what was going on, as he guided her down on her knees, but she wasn't ready for it. He was being a complete dick. She held him but nothing more.

"No," she said, offering an apologetic smile. She stood up carefully, and all the while she still held his manhood. They kissed with less passion as she tugged him to climax, its evidence splattering the lower part of her T-shirt and some of her skirt. And all he felt was an overwhelming feeling of disappointment, then a flood of embarrassment. It wasn't Paige's fault. It wasn't just the lack of fear versus what he'd wanted with Keely, it was that he wanted something he could never have. He hated himself even more for wanting it, too. And not just that either.

It was more.

It was everything. His life. It was all one huge let down.

Tears were streaming down his face, as he pulled up his underwear and trousers. Paige was nuzzling into him and thinking this was the start of something wonderful, but inside he just wanted to die. They'd overstepped the friendzone. *He'd* over stepped it with a residual feeling from earlier. One he still struggled with.

This weekend would be everything, and he knew there was more than a possibility he might not make it back alive.

Her goodbye kiss lingered for too long.

Two friends with suicidal tendencies and his semen still wet on their clothes parted for what could well be the last time ever.

Chapter 3

Like the old seventies rock song by Lynyrd Skynyrd, Tuesday was *gone with the wind.* It breezed by like a standard non-event the way most days did to Jarrod. Keely was out all morning, and in the afternoon, was busy in meetings throwing her managerial weight around in the ball-breaking style she'd become accustomed to. She got results and earnt respect though most thought it her rough-tactics, and the fear she instilled in others. She had an endless wardrobe of power-suits with matching heels and a faint aura of a whorehouse madam about her. It wasn't always a bad thing, and in fact was confusing to the poor simple male brain, Jarrod of course being one of them.

"You with me this weekend, mate?" Rick said, like it was a coded message. "Whatever happens and shit?"

"Of course. Fuck this place." Rick nodded approvingly, and Jarrod wondered exactly what he had up his sleeve. It was better to be on the side of a crazy person organising something than against them. Rick was a loner who acted like he had nothing to lose and they were often the most dangerous.

Di was MIA from her desk, and Eloise was serenaded by the smooth-tongued chat-up lines courtesy of the team Beefcake Will - a rugby player with a lot more confidence than his flat nose, cauliflower ears and no neck should allow, but standing over six feet tall and a bulk of fat and muscle, he was able to make some of the women in the office flutter their eyelids and blush on cue. He was in his twenties but had a rugged look that made him seem older. Will also stepped up to the plate to do battle with Dan for the superiority rights of team Alpha male. A position both Jarrod and Rick would happily give up before any sort of challenge began. It seemed to them both to be a pointless accolade, and one that came with a lot of expectation that came with risk. If you think of all the dangerous people in the world, very few were gym-rats flexing muscle around.

"You better get ya' stuff done or y'all be in trouble!" Eloise said with a little giggle to Will and wiggling her boobs like he was too blind to notice them. Both enjoyed the flirtation and neither really wanted anything from it.

Will nodded towards Keely's office, "She ain't around, is she?"

"Big boss stuff!" Eloise laughed back sarcastically. "Collecting balls and nailing them to the office wall! She's been sniffing around Martin most of the week."

"It's like a playground in here sometimes," Verity huffed and went back to pecking at her keyboard. Smiling didn't come naturally to her at the best of times, and she considered her role to be more important than everyone else's.

Then all eyes fell on Iain, a non-descript guy who could be anywhere between thirty and mid-fifties, it was really hard to tell. He wore small round Harry Potter glasses, was skinny but with a potbelly that made him look like he was pregnant and beginning to show. He always wore a striped shirt and a plain tie – only the colours changed with the day – and he was staring at a woman in another team. Really staring. Like stalker, follow-you-home-kill-your-cat sort of look. Bundy eyes without the handsome charm. The victim was incredibly normal looking and it was unknown what attracted Iain to her so intently.

Maybe she looked like his mother when she was young.

He passed up looking at Beth, the office hottie, and instead had fixated on this poor woman who would probably never know the danger she was in until one night when she regained consciousness and found she was hog-tied and about to have her throat slit from ear to ear.

"Weirdo!" Will called, glancing back at Eloise to emphasise how funny he was. Iain didn't even notice nor blink. Will balled up some paper and lobbed it at him. It hit him in the chest, and Iain looked over immediately with Charles Manson eyes, and a face that remained blank. A beloved family pet in his street would probably die as a result.

"What's got your attention?" Will asked him with a knowing and sly grin.

Iain picked up the paper, and carefully ironed it out as best he could whilst still staring. Will could snap him in two but Iain showed no fear. That in itself made him scarier than Will.

"Insubordination," Iain stated enjoying the wave of syllables rolling off his tongue. His voice was calm and even, and although the words were quoted from Keely, whom he idolised, they'd never been delivered in such a sinister way. Then he held up the paper and through gritted teeth, added, "This is a waste of office resource. Although from you, I expect nothing less."

Eloise laughed, and Will grinned. He looked over at Jarrod and Rick. "What are you two benders looking at?"

Rick looked at Jarrod, and was about to say something when he decided against it. It was probably a wise move.

"You got no come back?" Will looked at Eloise for affirmation, then continued, "I suppose I should finish up. Especially with this fucking weekend thing – where I'll be the best at everything! Again. As per fucking us-u-al!"

Rick smirked to himself, and turned back to his laptop and Jarrod wondered exactly what was going to be in store.

Verity made a noise of displeasure at the interruption, frowned at everyone and looked back at her screen. "Some of us have work to do!"

Will nodded to Eloise again, and turned back to type out a load of bullshit in the form of an email.

Jarrod got his head down and let the sands of time trickle out. It was another day closer to death, that was the only positive.

That night Paige had asked to come round again.

Jarrod knew it was on account of what had happened the night before. Lies of sickness flowed from his mouth like the well-rehearsed salesman's patter. He felt really bad about the situation between them and needed to process it. They'd kissed before. Drunk, lip locking and a bit of tongue action, and even hugging, but that had been it. He'd never even seen her boobs, and yet for some strange reason he'd thought it okay to just remove her knickers and fuck her unapologetically in his kitchen. He didn't know what had come over him. He made a move to pop another Mother's-Little-Helper before his mood dropped further.

The reality was, the two of them would probably have fallen into being a couple. They'd slip so easily from sharing their snacks and watching their favourite movies, to swapping bodily fluids and recording themselves having sex. It would not be the worst thing in the world. But Keely touching him in a way that was a bit Harvey Weinstein, had thrown him the curviest of curve-balls, and it had hit him square in the groin. The man-eater had known she could act that way and he'd responded in the predictable, and submissive way he had. He was left with mixed feelings of wanting more, and being anxious about it happening again. The aforementioned black widow spider killed its sexual partner and ate them. He pictured his head on a silver platter with an apple wedged in his mouth and Keely stood laughing at him.

He also knew he was reading heavily between lines that weren't even there. But fuck it. If you don't believe then you don't achieve. Or some such bullshit.

Paige had been disappointed in his rebuff and that hit him hard. He needed time. He had to reflect on what was going on. He wanted to see what Keely's next move was.

The next day, work dragged like a heavy weight had attached itself to the hands of the large office clock. The oversized eyesore that had cost the company silly money for a mix of practical time-keeping and some abstract artistic ejaculation for the whole office to see.

Keely had taken the day off which meant the office turned into a schoolyard. Will and Dan argued constantly, and their banter towards each other had begun light-hearted and with rapid speed escalated to heated words, and threats with barbed wire wrapped around them. It finished a little short of the two of them offering each other a fight in the car park like it was fucking *Tom Brown's School Days*. Eloise was on a self-esteem building mission, popping open one button too many on her blouse, and interjecting herself into male populated areas of the business, much to the disgust of Di who uttered the words, "Whore," in her Mariella Frostrup voice (although none of the youngsters knew the reference when Dan suggested it), whilst bothering the buttons on her own blouse. Nobody wanted to see her plain M&S undergarments and would happily button her back up.

Iain sat picking his nose, and wiping it under the desk. He also wasted many minutes staring at his own female obsession. Sometimes he held up his phone and Jarrod suspected him of taking pics. His voyeurism held no boundaries and he probably had a dedicated shrine of her that he'd pound his meat to in pure ecstasy by candlelight. She'd die if she knew he pleasured himself over her. Sometimes at home. Sometimes at work undeterred by the straining wheeze, and the plop and splash from the next cubicle.

Rick kept to himself, and Jarrod tried to concentrate on an important report that was needed by the next day. Most of his reports were like that. He fucking hated how mundane his life was outside of the sexual highs that had somehow inadvertently gate-crashed his banality. Even with his recent ex, sex had become routine and passionless. Minimal clothing removal, repetitive and singular-position with eyes closed and fluids remaining with its owner and no longer shared. Until the day she announced she was gay and moved out. He was left lost, lonely and feeling like a great opportunity had been missed. Now at the cost of two beers, his conquests were mostly humping bare-buttocks over beer barrels. Okay, he admitted it. Eloise was his booty call as she was for a lot of people.

He looked around the office and hated everything about the place. Other employees had been moulded and merged into robots looking and acting the same. He felt so out of place as an introvert smothered by extroverts that he wanted to just scream whilst spraying bullets from a Japanese assault rifle.

He texted Paige throughout the day, laying down the foundations of why he couldn't see her again that night. He pretended he was well enough to go to work but had gone downhill as the day matured. He tried to pad out the small talk to disguise it being just that. She bought it, and somewhere along the line kisses had attached themselves to the messages. She was probably thinking about how black her wedding dress would be, and how many kids she wanted to drop out of her black gypsy-skirt.

Jarrod knew he had to face the situation, but he still needed to time to think. What that meant was he needed to speak to Keely whilst they were away. Quash the fantasies and maybe quit the pills. Maybe Rick had a plan that would be the answer to all his worries.

The next day was Thursday. Their last day in the office before impending doom of the team building fiasco the next day. Keely was all over the place cracking the whip and proving her tits were bigger than anyone's balls there in the office. Martin was in and out of her office and Jarrod had to wonder whether she was looking to move up the ladder. She was certainly acting odd.

At one point Jarrod caught himself watching her as she strode down the office with the powerful thighs he'd dreamed of, and wondered not for the first time whether she might very well be the devil reincarnated. It made such perfect sense. The devil had to be a woman with a mean sultry stare and a penchant for ridicule at every opportune moment. She was exactly the prototype you design.

"Don't get attached," Rick whispered. "You need a clear head. Those pills are not your friend." Jarrod felt his face go red. *Did he know?* he wondered, and then glanced around expecting everyone to be looking at him. He didn't know whether to feel embarrassed, or ashamed, but as he familiarised himself with the monotonous numbers on his spreadsheet once more, he felt a cumulation of the two.

Rick was acting odd at the end of the day. He removed a couple of pictures of anime characters from his desk and even slipped his *Star Wars* mug into his bag. He looked like he wasn't coming back. Jarrod glanced at his own desk, but it was devoid of anything personal. He never saw the point. He had no desire to make his workstation be anything more than as cold and unwelcoming as he knew it would always make him feel. No small trinkets would make him feel any better about the place that was for sure.

Keely walked out of her office as the day drew to a close, and clapped her hands to get the team's attention. She had a loud clap. Eloise squealed in fright as per usual and Iain stopped staring at the woman in the other team and dreaming of turning her skull into a fruit bowl.

"Meet in the car park at 10am," she said, and looked over at Rick. "Well done to Rick for setting this up. I spoke with them last night and they are looking forward to welcoming us tomorrow."

"What should I wear?" Eloise enquired. Jarrod had heard her discussing this with anyone who would listen. She was not prepared for anything that was to do with the great outdoors. Being adventurous to her was being fingered by her best friend after one too many glasses of Prosecco.

Jarrod had heard her whisper this triumphantly to a colleague once when she thought no one else was listening.

"You don't need heels or stripper clothes," Keely stated, completely seriously. "Also, and this is really important: do not wear anything red."

"Red?" Will asked, like she'd just told him he couldn't wear shoes.

"Yes, it's to do with their customs, so it's quite a serious matter. They told me that anyone who didn't conform would have to leave immediately." Many side-glances were shared at the odd request. Jarrod wondered what items of clothing he owned that were red. Unfortunately, he only had one T-shirt and that was a size too small for him.

"Are we not going out at night?" Eloise was still thinking about dressing up to be fucked by the locals, and appeared crestfallen.

"There will only be foxes and badgers roaming around," Keely huffed, sounding like she was fed up of babysitting Eloise already. "If you want to make out with them then be my guest." Humour didn't come naturally to her. Nobody laughed.

"It will be fun," Will grinned. "The fresh air…" He looked at Di who flipped him her middle finger. "The great company!"

"Bloody kids," Verity muttered.

Keely addressed everyone else. "Bring outdoor clothes. Waterproofs, walking shoes. There is nothing worse than being cold and wet in the middle of nowhere."

Jarrod tried not to look at her in anything other than a professional manner. She wore pin-striped black trousers with a blouse tucked in. Jarrod waited for her to call him into her office. He hoped she would even if just to check on him.

She glanced at him, and he struggled to look back. When he did, her gaze was elsewhere. Maybe she'd given up. Or perhaps she was laughing at him.

"It's about team-building. Relying on your fellow colleague. Getting to know each other more closely. Building trust, and bonds you can bring back to the office and help our team be the best!"

Heads turned, and smiles of anticipation beamed all around. Hysteria was building and they were like excited kids about to go on a school trip.

Soon they said their goodbyes and left the office.

Guilt grabbed Jarrod by the neck and refused to let him go anywhere but Paige's house.

She was there with her housemate, Mary. A rotund woman who lived in sweats and had the largest arse Jarrod had ever seen. In some cultures it was seen as sexy, but in Jarrod's it was just evidence of over-eating and under-exercising.

Paige was all smiles when she opened the door.

"Jarrod!" She grinned and flung her arms around him. "How are you feeling?"

Mary called from behind her, "If he's still puking and shitting then he can stay away!"

Paige turned and shot her a look. "Mary!"

"Just saying."

"I'm okay now, but I won't stay. I'm off on this work shit tomorrow for the weekend so wanted to see you before I went."

"I'm glad you did," she said, pulling back a second. She looked down at the ground and muttered. "Look, I'm sorry about things… you know… on Monday."

Her words made him feel worse. He'd all but forced her to do something and yet she was apologising to him. "Don't be silly," he said, slightly embarrassed, hoping it would breeze over.

"I've been thinking," she said, and leaned in. "If you want to do that again then there are other things we can do, too." She gave him a naughty smile he'd never been party to before. They'd well and truly left the friendzone behind. It was cowering behind the sofa hoping fat-arse didn't sit on it.

"Really?" He wondered what she had in mind.

She nodded. "Yeah. I was… you know… it was different for us… but I liked it. *Really* liked it, in fact. Why don't you pop in for a few minutes?"

Things were moving faster than he'd anticipated. He'd thought he'd just turn up, say hello, and be on his way. He hoped he might apologise for Monday and promise it would ever happen again and that would be that. Except now she'd admitted she liked it. And she wanted more. He really liked her. But he had to focus.

And she wasn't Keely.

She'd never be Keely.

"Sorry, but I really have to get going." She looked like he'd just slapped her hard.

"Not even for five minutes?" Desperation crept in and really made him feel like a prize dick.

"Sorry. Next week, when I'm back, let's make an evening of it, yeah?"

"A date?" She perked up slightly.

"Yeah. A date. Maybe get some food first."

She nodded, but he wasn't sure it was enough. She slipped her arms around his neck and they kissed deeply until Mary made puking sounds behind them.

"You want me to record you two?" she shouted. "I don't mind. Stick it on the internet and will split it three ways!"

"Bye Mary!" Jarrod called as they stopped. "See ya, Paige."

"Bye Jarrod."

He slipped away, just as confused as he was before. He wasn't looking forward to the weekend. He had a feeling it would change his life forever.

Chapter 4

The woman sat withdrawn from the others with eyes that could no longer spill tears. She was an empty vessel. Her heart had been ripped from her chest and she was in a complete fog. One that still allowed her to feel sick to the stomach and completely lost. A shadow cast over her from the building she now called home. In another life her name had been Claire, but now she went by Star. Not that any of that mattered now. In fact, the whole fantasy that she'd happily been living was now tainted. The hole in her chest where her heart once belonged was slowly dripping out her will to live.

Nothing really mattered to her anymore.

Her hair was matted into dreadlocks of different sizes, an expression of herself she'd not been allowed to show when she was Claire, and working in a large office. A tattoo of a flower and vines crept up her left-arm to bridge her love for the alternative with nature.

This haven was meant to be about peace and solace. A commune escaping the rigors of conformation she'd been forced to endure. A society within a society built with few rules but on foundations of strong values. It was everything, and yet now it was nothing at all. She'd thrown it all away just to have what she'd now lost.

Again, nothing really matters.

The man, her husband, stood concerned. "We have to be strong," he spoke robotically from behind her, torn between the expectation of the community and what a man should feel towards his wife. "It will do us no good." His name was Leo and he knew his words fell upon deaf ears. Star could no longer function and anything he said just made things worse. His face held too many memories of what they'd lost. And *who* they'd lost.

She began to rock. Gently at first, then gradually more vigorously. Sadness had smothered her ability to live. The snake of melancholy had slipped silently around her and constricted carefully around her chest until it was too late. She had given way to anger. How could she let that happen? How could *they* let it happen? She needed an outlet for her frustration. She wanted to be angry and needed someone else to suffer, even if it went against the principles of the settlement.

Their house was on the corner of the community. Away from others and open to the dangers of what lay in the woods. It had been a fear she'd harboured for a while but one she assumed to be born from being a mother. Ever doting, all she saw were dangers around her for her child, when previously it had been just the two of them and they lived for the moment; carefree thrill seekers. Living on a whim they did whatever brought them joy, but once the baby arrived that all changed.

"I'm trying to be strong," Star said flatly, barely more than a whisper and devoid of emotion. She had lost a few days, and nobody wanted to talk about it.

"We're not the first," he tried but knew he was just making the situation worse. He was helpless. It wasn't like he didn't feel the gut-wrenching pain, too, was it? He had suffered the same loss. You could argue that a mother feels deeper pain over losing a son than a father, but was that factual? He couldn't think his wife hurt more than he did, but judging by her near catatonic state perhaps she did. He was pragmatic and needed to be working towards a goal, whereas she was stuck in the emotional quicksand that not only held her tight, but threatened to pull her in deeper until she was no longer able to live. That's what worried him most. He couldn't lose his wife, too.

The elders had their well clipped responses. They'd dutifully visited them, and try as they might, the lectures of good intentions, very quickly felt old and worn. They were words and excuses written for another time and pulled out for any occasion. They lacked a personal touch, or of any consolation of hope, sympathy, or any real comfort. Leo wanted a rally call. Permission to go alone into the forbidden woods and take his chances, but this was not offered, and when he suggested it, he was looked upon like he was some inhumane beast and was quickly told those actions were strictly prohibited. Both Leo and Star had been relieved of their daily duties for a few days as if this would somehow magically heal their wounds and help them to forget. Here they were outside their home with only their devastating sadness to keep them company as elsewhere life went on.

A few days ago, their son had been running around like a perfectly happy and healthy ten-year-old. His infectious smile gave him a cheekiness that had made Star proud. He was always there. A human shadow at their side, ready and eager to learn. And then one night he disappeared.

Like the other children.

He wasn't the first.

One by one the children of Woden were being taken in the night.

"Why does no one confront her?" Star asked. "Why don't they let us go ourselves?" She turned her head, her face ruddy with despair.

"You know why," Leo said, carefully choosing his words. Tip-toeing through the minefield fully aware that one was more than likely to go off.

"I know what we've been told, but how do we know it's true?"

She held out pleading hands. Ones that once held tightly to her child and pulled him in for hugs. She could still feel his body clinging to her, yet he was no longer here.

"It's true," he said without conviction, but was he trying to convince her, or himself?

"That she's an evil witch?"

He nodded. "Anyone who has gone into those woods has never returned."

"But that doesn't mean…" she started with much gusto but quickly ran out of hope and words. "We have to try." She sobbed dry tears into her hands and wished the world was a kinder place.

"I know," he said, wrapping large muscular arms around her in pure desperation like it was all he had left to offer. "I know. We'll try… *I'll* try!"

She nodded eagerly. A mother willing to do whatever it took to get her son back.

"But we have to be ready for… you know… any eventuality." *His death,* he meant. He couldn't say it. In fact, he *wouldn't* say it. Not in front of his wife. Even though inside he thought it to be true.

Even paradise had its downsides.

He released his wife, stood up strong and looked out towards the woods. His eyes searched and searched to find something that might give them hope. He gritted his teeth and sucked back the fear that grabbed his insides with ice-cold fingers. He didn't want to go in there alone, but he also couldn't trust anyone. He didn't want to take his wife, but could he really turn his back on her? If he wasn't to return would she be able to continue without them both?

"Do you want to come, too?" he asked her, and looked down at the broken woman. She nodded enthusiastically, although still looking forlorn.

"I want our son back," she said, and at that point he was willing to do whatever it took to make that happen. "Please find Benny!"

But the forbidden woods looked dark. A cloud permanently hung above them and the place looked nothing but home for pure evil.

The Last Weekend

Chapter 5

There had been a huge argument about who should drive the minibus. Will and Dan had stated their cases calmly at first, but the testosterone levels had increased to the point they were ready to pull off T-shirts and fight it out to the death. Shouting and name calling had escalated quickly with each questioning the occupation and reputation of the other's mother. That took them to pushing and shoving each other until Keely got between them, reprimanded them in her disappointed tone, and pulled rank to drive herself. There was no way she'd hand over control to anyone else even if one of the angry men had stepped aside for the other. It once again proved their whole dick-swinging scene was futile. Keely's virtual balls would always be bigger.

Dan huffed, and in his full army regalia, fists still clenched and still breathing through his nose like a bull, jumped into the passenger seat shouting the words, "Shotgun!" so loud, Eloise ducked thinking there was a madman on the rampage somewhere – presumably in the car park of the large corporate business. The only thing missing from Dan's outfit was warpaint and a weapon. Will, on the other hand, was trying to act like he didn't care. He was plastered in branded clothing manufactured by school children in a poor country, and was about as suitable for the excursion as speedos in a snowstorm. His sweatshirt alone cost the same as a weekend away by the sea. Keely, on the other hand, had on a plain hoodie and cargo-trousers. She looked different in clothes that were practical rather than powerfully sexual. She was ready for any eventuality. Iain wore dark jeans that were square-cut and last popular in the 80s, a V-neck jumper over what appeared to be a work shirt now made casual with the top button undone, and devoid of a tie. This was obviously Iain's standard non-work attire. He sat looking blankly out of the window and cleaning his glasses with dribble.

"Sit back with me, Will," Eloise said. Her hair was perfect. Long, blonde, and with a few little curls that had deliberately been added so that they bounced with each movement. It would be interesting to see her visible decline in the coming days as she realised the accommodation was far from what she was used to. She'd wheeled out a bright-pink suitcase like they were off to the airport on a youngsters' 18-30 getaway to Shagalouf. No doubt she even had a monster-size pack of rubbers just in case the locals didn't fancy going bareback. She didn't care. *It's hardly the 80s,* she thought irresponsibly. She considered AIDS to be a retro issue that had long since died off.

Verity turned up in a shirt that looked like it might be more fitting on a cowboy. Looks were shared but nobody fancied saying anything to her. She had a face like thunder.

"He was being a prick again!" she said to anyone who was listening. "I might stay if it's half as good as home."

"Fuck men!" Di shouted. She was having a third final fag, blowing the last of the chemical plume up into the atmosphere to do damage elsewhere. She coughed hard and the sound rattled around her ribcage where her lungs once lived, hacked, and climbed back into the minibus bringing with her a thick smell of nicotine. Sharing is caring.

"That's the plan!" Eloise giggled.

Di responded between puffs with a "for fucksake!" by way of a reply.

Jarrod and Rick sat in the back doing their best to hide away from everyone else. Their comfort-zones were a long way from there. They both had separate visions of the minibus ending up in a crash with them both being the only remaining survivors. Jarrod popped a pill and noticed Rick throw him a glance.

"You have to stop those, mate," he muttered.

Jarrod swallowed it down and when he was ready looked at Rick. "Yeah, I know."

"How many are you taking?"

"I dunno." It wasn't a lie. He'd talked the doctor into prescribing a month's worth but every few days he had begun to double his dosage. How could he not? They numbed his anxiety and calmed him the fuck down.

"What about the others?" Rick was smirking, and tapping his feet. He leant against the glass and idly drew invisible shapes.

"The others?"

"You don't need to bullshit me. I've seen them. You been venturing on the dark web? Flying under the radar?" He was smiling more than Jarrod could ever remember. He also seemed more chilled than he had in a long time.

"I found some others online that work good, too. They, you know, complement each other."

"I'll bet. Look, do what you want but when you have no more, your body is going to fuck you up for a while."

"I know what I'm doing."

"Spoken like a true addict."

"Amen." They left it at that before flapping ears joined in and felt the need to lecture them on a subject they knew nothing about. Verity was sure to have an opinion she'd be unable to keep to herself.

With a loud show-off engine roar, an Aston Martin pulled up, and almost skidded into a space. The door swung open and out got Martin, one of the directors. He was dressed like Bear Grylls. The boot opened as if by magic, and he wrestled out a huge backpack with things hanging off of it. He wore waterproof trousers and a North Face jacket; he looked like he'd sleep hanging off a cliff if he needed to. And *still* sleep like a baby. Mr Adventure, born and raised in a city public school and holidayed in nothing less than five-star hotels with servants on hand, and yet here he was looking like he was a hands-on explorer.

Dan made a noise that suggested he was not happy with another alpha-male joining. "Fuck me. It's Corporate Action Man," he muttered under his breath. "I wonder if he has a fuckin' cord on his neck that makes him talk."

"If he has, we could cut it off!" Will laughed, holding up his hand for a high-five which Dan just stared at.

"Morning crew!" Martin called loudly, beeping the lock on his overly expensive vehicle and trotting over like he was ready for a hundred-mile jog. His chest was out and he looked like he might break into song. He'd probably watched the movie *Full Metal Jacket* the night before and now assumed himself to be a trained marine. He'd more than likely memorised how to deconstruct, and reconstruct an M16 rifle, not to mention some drill songs to sing for morale.

"Good morning, Martin," Keely said in a way that Jarrod had not heard before. The tone was now a little girly. Not quite flirtatious, but tickling around that area. Sucking up to the hierarchy. Given the chance, Jarrod assumed, she'd drop to her knees and swallow her way to a promotion. It sounded sexist but Emma in HR (ironically) had offered her boss a blowjob in return for a grade increase. He'd been a gentleman and settled on a handjob instead. Eloise was quick to slow dance with anyone on a higher pay grade than her, but when she showed them the backdoor to the club, they assumed she wanted to go home with them and declined.

Doors slid open, then banged shut. Bodies wriggled to gain comfort in seats that weren't made to do so, and the radio played some 70s pop in the background.

They were off. The large corporate eyesore got smaller behind them as they left the car park and headed out into the great unknown. White-collars slumming it in the wilds.

"What's the plan then, Ricky-boy?" Martin said in his loud confident voice like they were buddies. He'd been neglected to boarding-school and over-filled with self-importance, so fell into the role of leader like it was an expectation. What people didn't know was that he was bullied by a lad in boarding school. An ugly thug of a lad with curly red hair and the strength to hold him down for a long while.

Rick shrugged, and tried to lose himself in the rock-music being pumped directly into his ears by his own ear-buds. He wasn't interested in Kiki Dee and Elton John lyrically dualling about breaking hearts. No matter what anyone said, Kiki Dee would kick Elton's arse in a heartbeat.

"Expect the unexpected, is it?" Martin grinned like he was hoping they'd be left in the wilderness to fend for themselves. It was hard to tell whether it was an act, or not. He was also the sort of person who filled the silence just for the sheer hell of it. Yes, he was one of *them*. Alanis Morrissette had questioned people like him when she burst onto the 90s radio-rock scene.

Keely was quick to jump in and show she was in charge and not Rick. "They've a lot planned," she said. "I pressed them on details but they appear to be a mysterious bunch. I'm told it will be very educational for mind, body and soul. So, strap-on for the ride!" That caused a few giggles. Heightened hysteria often increased immaturity.

"It's probably nothing as bad as I've experienced on my tours," Dan said wistfully gazing out of the window. His mind back to a time where bombs and rapid machinegun-fire were the normal soundtrack to the day. "I saw some awful things."

"I dunno," Will chimed in, a hint of sarcasm pushing through. "Ireland rugby tour last year was pretty epic! Deano fucked a ladyboy; Tank took a shit on the hotel's pool table, and Rupert lost a bet and had some fat bird piss on his face! And that was on the first day!"

Eloise made a disgusted sound and screwed up her face whilst Martin laughed. "Oh no! You youngsters! Sounds like the daily banter from when I was at Uni!"

"Hardly the same as death, though," Dan muttered from the front of the minibus and gently shook his head. He wondered how they'd react if a sniper shot one of them now spraying blood and brains all over the interior.

"What about you boys?" Martin said, turning in his seat towards Rick and Jarrod. Rick looked scared, and Jarrod simply replied, "Well, I was in the 3rd Thornhill cub scout troop, and I can tell you, what happened at the 25th Anniversary Thornhill Jamboree can never be uttered out loud. We took an oath; a vow of silence if you will, for that weekend. Never shall I utter another word about it." He turned away not seeing how Martin had cracked up at that. The pills had well and truly kicked in now.

"You lot are a blast!" He raised his voice louder so that Keely could hear. "I never knew what a great team you had, Keely!" Jarrod silently thought it was because they were deemed insignificant and on too low a pay grade for him to give a shit. She was never going to sing their praises anytime soon.

"Oh, they are all special in their own way!" She glanced in her mirror at them. It was devoid of humour and sounded like more of a threat.

The roads of Wiltshire were less paved with gold, and more with cracks, potholes, and a sprinkling of roadworks – often with no sign of workmen but then Rome wasn't built in a day, and apparently roads weren't fixed that quickly either - though mostly you had a panoramic view of trees and rolling hills. The surrounding areas were filled with farms and RAF bases which meant there was a mix of natural beauty and sudden large, grey buildings hidden away behind huge fences and splattered with threatening notices.

"Who else is going to be there?" Eloise asked Rick, who was regretting being the main contact. He sat back in his bright-green hoodie and huffed again so she'd be in no doubt he didn't want to speak.

"Who knows." He didn't mask his exasperation and did his best to deflect the question. "It might just be us. The boss-lady spoke to them last."

"Oh," she replied, clearly disappointed. She was hoping for more young men who would follow her around sniffing her crotch, and vying for her to allow them to fuck her senseless. She wanted squaddies on release, or at the very least a stag-do or two. Shit, she wanted to be gang-banged by the Dreamboys, but that was never going to happen anytime soon.

"How did you hear about this place?" Martin joined in unaware of the intricacies of introversion. "I looked on the internet and couldn't find it at all? You get it off the dark web?" He winked like maybe it showed him to be cool in some way. Jarrod thought the dark web was mostly for murderers and paedophiles but he kept that to himself. It was also the source of his drug-habit.

"Yeah, it was there under a thread about human sacrifice."

Martin laughed again, and pointed at Rick. "I like this guy! His humour's so deadpan!"

Another thirty minutes later and Rick glanced out of the window, and then at his phone. He looked like he was about to press a button that might set off an explosion someplace.

"Another mile down the road and there is a turn off to the right," Rick called so Keely could hear.

"I know," she replied matter-of-factly, and then as an afterthought added, "Thanks."

Jarrod rolled his eyes at his mate, but Rick just ignored them. There was something inside him building up.

The minibus turned right into a lane barely big enough for two vehicles to pass. As it continued, the tarmac turned into gravel, and gradually more grass and weeds grew through the middle as it went through devolution from asphalt, to gravel then pure grass. Keely had to slow down so they didn't all start to bounce up on their seats and headbutt the roof.

"Whoa," Eloise said, grabbing onto the bottom of the seat. This road didn't look like it was going to end with a huge state-of-the-art hotel and leisure complex. She placed an arm on her chest to stop her bouncing boobs and looked around to hope someone else had noticed. She removed her arm when she found out everyone was looking out the windows and had no interest in her moving chest.

"Sorry!" Keely called back, then came to a stop at a crossroads. None of the three options appeared to be welcoming and a canopy of branches made it hard to see any distance. They were surrounded by trees like they'd stumbled into a forest. To the left, a well-worn wooden bridge could be made out, but the minibus would never get over it, straight on was a gate wrapped with barbed wire, and huge KEEP OUT signs written crudely in dark red paint.

"Go right!" Rick called, and slowly shook his head. "I thought she knew," he muttered. Jarrod noticed Rick had formed his fingers into a gun and was ready to shoot his finger pistol at any minute.

The minibus turned, and the wheels spun slightly on the grass as it struggled to find purchase. They passed a stream to the left, that another time might've seemed calming, but they were too excited to consider their tranquil surroundings. Keely carefully drove down a hill, the gradient of which looked like they'd struggle to make it back up again if there was a heavy downpour anytime soon.

Civilisation seemed far away. The next town was barely twenty miles south but nothing could be seen and they felt isolated from life.

The trees continued in front of them. As they turned and went around a huge stone, they found a handful of cars parked in what might've been a makeshift car park. A few looked old and weathered. Possibly abandoned. Green moss had begun to grow around the edges of the windows.

"This is it," Rick proclaimed. "Welcome to Blair Witch."

"Good one," someone said. It might've been Iain.

"Where are we staying?" Verity asked, as the vehicle jerked to a standstill.

"What did the guy say?" Rick pressed, enjoying the switch in power towards him.

Without enthusiasm, Keely said blankly, "He said, park in the car park and there's a short walk through the trees."

"A bit of local humour, I think," Rick grinned when everyone looked at him but no one asked him to elaborate.

They all spilled out, and soon they looked like a travelling yoga class as they stretched out their limbs. Either a few dips, or arms raised in the air and letting out noises that someone hidden away might be forgiven for thinking were sexual.

Di couldn't get a cigarette into her mouth quick enough and gave an orgasmic sigh as the nicotine kicked in and she puffed the first tainted breath into the air.

"Nice fresh country air," Iain frowned fanning away the smoke and loping ungainly away from her.

"Then move yourself, you fucking freak!"

“Hey, hey!” Keely was quick to shout and clapped her hands together loudly. “We are team building! So let’s all be positive, okay?”

Di snarled and took another deep drag whilst Iain’s face remained blank.

Verity was swearing at her phone as she stood with her arm raised high in the air. “No signal,” she moaned. “That bastard will have to get used to me not being around, won’t he?” Everyone there assumed that to be rhetorical.

“What does that mean, Rick?” Eloise said. “That local humour thing.” She was far removed from her world and it was only just dawning on her that this experience may be very different from how she first envisaged it.

“It means, follow me and I will get us there. Don’t worry, just a short walk!” He grinned, and everyone knew he was finding the situation amusing. The quiet lad was suddenly coming into his own.

Chapter 6

Whilst the heavy covering of trees kept the sun's rays off them, with only bright patches evident, there was a humidity in the air that suggested a storm may not be too far away. Jarrod had checked the weather, and the next day seemed to suggest a short downpour around midday, but these things had a habit of frequently changing.

Rick led the pack with Jarrod, Keely and Martin alongside. Dan was a few steps behind sulking that he was being shown up by the corporate twerp Martin, with his silver spoon up his arse and opportunities handed to him on a plate. The gobshite Will was more like some bumbling goon, conceding his position in the pack, and had turned his attention to his second main goal – slipping inside Eloise's knickers. Iain, Verity and Di were trudging alone at the back; together, but not together. Di was smoking another cigarette, and Iain was constantly fanning away the smoke;

happier to stand near and moan rather than to try and move away. Verity continued to clutch her phone like it was a weapon. She glanced at it every now and then as if some hidden mobile phone tower might appear and give her the signal she so desperately wanted.

Eloise played the role of the poor little female as she made noises at bugs that dared come anywhere near her. For the umpteenth time she waved her well-manicured fingers around her face, and made a strange blowing sound.

"Urgh! These bugs are all over the place!" She said, and squealed again.

"You're in the great outdoors now, princess!" Will grinned at her. "That's what happens!"

"Well, they shouldn't be allowed!" She had slipped into an immature voice. She had stripped down to wearing just a vest. She made a meal of the heat and was tugging at the top that her enhanced boobs were threatening to fall out of. The act was meant to allow some air flow to her boobs but all it did was give Will an eyeful – and hope. She continued to moan, "It's so hot! I hope there are nice showers."

Will smirked again. "Have you ever been camping? There might be a stream where you can strip off and jump in, but that's about it!"

"A stream? What like skinny-dipping?" She pulled a face like he'd just suggested something obscene.

He shrugged. "Or keep your undies on. Why are you suddenly acting all prudish? I thought you ran into the sea naked last summer? And you blew two blokes at the back of a bar in Spain, and let a seventeen-year-old finger you?"

"Shh!" She pulled an angry face and with her hands motioned him to lower his voice. The adventurers were out of earshot, but still. "I was drunk on all of those occasions, and the lad literally just brushed his fingers on my moo-moo and then ran off. I think my pussy scared him!"

"Your what?"

"My moo-moo. You know, pussy."

Will rolled his eyes and muttered, "I dunno why you did it though," Will had suddenly found his moral compass from up his arse.

"Says he, who had a threesome!"

"That's different. What man wouldn't, given the opportunity?"

Eloise turned to Iain who was a lagging a bit now. This was probably the most exercise he'd had in years. "Iain? Would you have a threesome?"

His face didn't change as he replied, "With you? Who else?"

"Not me! Just two other random women."

Iain frowned. "Do they read books?"

Will snorted and Eloise slapped her own forehead. "Who fucking cares?"

"It doesn't really matter, so probably, yeah."

Di looked shocked, and mid-drag-inhale still managed to say, "You don't even know what they look like?"

"Doesn't matter."

Will laughed and tried to high-five Iain who looked at his hand like it was infected.

"Bloody kids," Verity scoffed even though Iain was of similar age to her.

"Men are animals," Di said in total disgust, before coughing and hacking up phlegm. "That's why I kick them to the curb."

"Everyone alright back there?" Keely shouted, turning back to them with hands on her hips and keen to show she was boss and still fully in charge.

"We're fine," Will confirmed.

"How much further?" Eloise whined, and Keely looked to Rick. Will was now carrying her case as the wheels were pointless on any surface that wasn't flat and hard.

Without much enthusiasm he lifted up his arm and pointed in the general direction ahead. "Just a bit further, I think?" he said.

"You sure?" Dan jumped in. "You're not taking us on some pointless mission, I hope. I've been part of those, and I can tell you, that's when friendly fire happens!" Everyone ignored him. It was common practise not to encourage Dan to talk about his time in the army. If you did, hours would drift as he went into details filled with military jargon, co-ordinates and sad tales that made you wish you'd never asked. His steely-gaze would glaze over as he was back there. His fists would clench as he remembered. Someone had muttered a pop-diagnosis of PTSD, but who knew with Dan. Dan was a man, and men had no emotional weaknesses. That was beaten out of them either in their youth or within the first two weeks of basic training. But dressed in his camo, Dan looked like he could survive anything.

Martin jumped in. "You know where we're going, don't you, Rick-lad?"

"Yep," was all Rick responded with. He despised being called lad. The very tag suggested him to be young, naïve and of lower status.

The trees parted, and they were faced with a large meadow. The grass was knee-high and scattered with colour from wildflowers. Up ahead was a huge darkness where trees began again. In front was a large hedge that as they grew nearer a wall could be seen.

"What is that?" Martin asked. "It's like a secret place!"

There was a small clearing like a crude pathway that took them to the wooden fence that now dominated the foreground. As they got closer to the wall, they realised it was a lot taller than they first thought. A small door had been fashioned within it, and as Rick stepped closer, and his steps slowed down, a click could be heard. The door opened inward.

A guy dressed in jeans, a blue and white lumberjack shirt and sporting a large speckled-grey beard stood smiling as they pushed through the open door. He might've been there since the grunge period of the 90s. Maybe he left Seattle after Kurt Cobain's demise, took a wrong turn and ended up here.

"Welcome!" he said with a voluminous voice that seemed to echo off every hard surface around them, arms outstretched. They all said their polite hellos and glanced behind him at the trees trying to get a sneaky peek at what was to come.

"What is this place?" Verity was suddenly pushing forward, and asked as politely as Jarrod had ever known her. She had finally slipped her phone into her pocket resigned to it not getting a signal, but still hopeful enough not to put it in her bag.

"My name is Noah. And this, my new friends, is Woden! We are a small community who live off the grid and away from the distractions of your world. Here, in this beautifully idyllic place we eat what we grow and appreciate nature to its fullest. I must inform you our ways may take some getting used to, but fear not! When you leave, we hope you'll want to take some of our ways back with you!" It sounded straight out of a marketing PowerPoint presentation, or even from some failed drama-school pupil who'd given up on being in the movies and had ended up in some dingy tourist attraction performing to customers who'd rather not be there. He glanced around at everyone's clothing. "Good nobody is wearing red! Please can I ask that if anyone has anything red they leave the items here." He pointed to a large box. Jarrod was itching to open it up and see the red-clothing amnesty contents. *Probably Man Utd and Liverpool tops* he thought.

They looked around at each other, each willing the others to have some clothing contraband, but everyone remained tight-lipped. Everyone, that is, except Will.

"What's with red then? Is it a football team thing?" He grinned. Every group had the one person who wanted to be the joker, and there was a fine line between a joker and a fucking idiot. That was Will.

Noah tried to remain friendly, but he was now going off script so his flow falted with a noticeable stumble. "No, nothing like that… it has a tendency to anger.

"Like to bulls?" Will continued, taking the stance of a matador holding an invisible cape, and looked around expecting smiles. All he got was a few eyerolls. Not only was he an idiot, but now he was an embarrassing idiot. They were happy for him to dick around in the office, but now they were lumped in the same group he was; the embarrassing uncle who got pissed and groped the younger cousins, causing embarrassment to the family.

"Quite." Noah looked like he was about to say more but suddenly thought better of it. Perhaps he was thinking of ways to slit Will's throat and eat him.

Martin stepped forward to stake his alpha-male claim on the group. "I must say, I'm intrigued to see what you have hidden all the way out here!" His smooth-delivery was actor-perfect and if you didn't know him, he would fool the most cynical into thinking he meant every word. As a director, for every nice word that spilled from his false smile courting one person, behind him was another employee laid down under his arse being shat on. Standard socio-economics of cutthroat business.

"Then please," the guy said, taking a step to the side like a cross-between an old rocker and Willy Wonka. "Let's talk no further and continue into the heart of the community! The others will be pleased to welcome you!"

Noah, walking with a slight limp, beckoned them to follow him. He couldn't stop grinning as he looked over the new faces. "We do enjoy visitors," he confessed. "We're relatively small in numbers but outsiders continue to find us." He chuckled at some reverie. "And the odd ones never leave."

"Do you get many?" Verity asked, taking a step in front of Martin. "Outsiders, I mean." Keely had unusually dropped back; perhaps to reprimand Will and stop him from completely humiliating them all.

"A few. Like yourselves they come in groups. Some to understand how to live off the land, others to take a break from life. But one thing is certain, each leaves here changed. That is one thing I can guarantee you all."

Eloise had dropped back with Will. "It looks like it might be a cult."

"You think he might try and fuck you?" Will grinned, and used the joke to rub his hand down her back towards her bottom. "Mmmm, city girl. We only have inbred wenches here!"

"Cults aren't all about sex, silly!" She was enjoying the attention.

He cocked an eyebrow at her. "*Really?*"

Eloise giggled, and patted his hand playfully away. "But… if he has a big cock!" She licked her lips but it was closer to an impression of Scooby-Doo than anything remotely sexual.

"Behave!" Di scorned, not ever impressed with a man exhorting himself onto a woman. She had consumed a vegan protein bar in the hope that the mix of oats and pulses might counterbalance her continuous abuse of her heart and lungs.

"Kids," Verity muttered so regularly under her breath for the umpteenth time that it was already her catchphrase. She glanced at Noah and was happy to see him appear amused. Perhaps a weekend without her husband wouldn't be so bad after all.

At first, all that could be seen was the darkness of a forest, but through the trees, if you spied carefully, a large building could be seen. With each step it became more prominent; like a Magic-Eye picture it appeared to step out into plain view. It was an impressive structure, built of course, from wood, which more than likely was sourced from trees that once stood on the ground it was built on. The wood was dark and aged, weather-beaten from constant British downpours, and sporadic harmful rays from the sun, but it still looked defiantly robust. A large cross surrounded by a circle was proudly mounted on top. Odin's Cross (also known as the Sun cross) was a pagan symbol but as of late had been adopted by many white supremacist groups, and so looked daunting and slightly ominous. It was a truc and sad fact that a lot of the pagan symbols had been denounced by the various religious groups that reeked of propaganda.

Nevertheless, it was a church.

Next to it was a larger building that looked more like a barn, with the huge cross spraypainted on the side, and a large skull with lights above it hung over the door. The skull looked too big to be a cow or a bull, which gave it even more of an eerie feel. The impressive building appeared to be the centre-piece of the community.

"Wow! What animal is that from?" Will was first to enquire.

Noah stopped, and smoothed his beard as he said, "Nobody really knows. Some sort of mutant animal found here a long time ago. We cleaned it up and hung it there on the hall. It's a handsome thing, wouldn't you agree?" Approving noises were audible as they walked on.

The place opened up from there into a large flat and green square of grass. Near the hall was a large pole sporting a flag of yet more pagan symbols flapping gently in the gentle breeze. Surrounding the area was a mix of wooden cabins and larger buildings, a few of which were joined and looked like they'd been plucked straight out of the American Wild West.

"Wow! You live here?" Martin said, then instantly added, "Of course you live here, I apologise, it's… I guess we're not used to this. I was expecting… Well, I don't know actually!" He was babbling, and embarrassing at least half of them.

"Tents? Nude women? Human sacrifices?" Noah grinned through his beard, and waved off the comment as if he expected nothing less. "We're not trying to preach our ways, nor are we trying to make out we're superior in any way. So please, let me show you to your house and then we can all come together and go through the program. Is that alright with everyone?"

"Yes, of course," Martin said, still a little flustered. "We want to observe and fully understand your traditions, and of course respect them as best we…"

"Yes, please lead on," Keely jumped in before Martin got himself burnt at the flagpole.

The motley crew of colleagues who once in a strange turn of events epitomised normality were suddenly the outsiders. They were sore-thumbs stuck out for all to see. They nodded to Noah and drank in their new surroundings each with a different view and expectation. Some embracing it, and others realising this was worse than Hell itself.

"I still think you're missing a trick not having big-breasted nude women on show," Will chuckled.

"He never mentioned breasts! Pervert!" Di huffed.

"Kids," Verity had to add, once again. Everyone else ignored them. Their banal bickering was just transferred from their comfortable office to a new rural location almost seamlessly.

The house they headed towards sat slightly behind the others. It was like a huge cabin with two floors and a large roof. As with everything there, it looked well-built like it could've been built a hundred years ago.

They had just got to the door when the sound of running feet could be heard scampering from the side.

"Noah! Noah!" A boy shouted, waving his arms. He seemed extremely animated about something and only seemed to notice the influx of newbies at the last moment.

"Yes, Jacob, what is it, my dear boy?"

Jacob stopped, looked at the many new faces, was now slightly embarrassed, and beckoned Noah to bend down. The lad was about ten, but Noah still had to crouch towards him.

"She's been seen again," he said in a whispered voice, but with nothing but birdsong all around, each of the colleagues could hear him clear as day. His face now looked panicked and his lips quivered as if he might cry.

"Who?" Noah said, his voice at a normal level and walking the lad slightly farther away.

"The witch," he replied. "And this time she's taken Rosie."

Now with more urgency, Noah pushed the lad away from the group. "Okay, I'll be at the hall in a second. Gather the elders quickly, but let's not cause unnecessary panic. Okay?"

"Yes, Noah."

The boy set off like a sprinter, arms and legs pumping hard, and Noah called after him, "Stay with an adult!"

Noah straightened up, and adjusted the mask that he now wore to pretend that everything was okay. Just another day…

This only made Keely ask that very exact thing, "Is everything alright, Noah?"

"Oh, it's nothing," he tried to laugh it off but whilst his mouth twitched into a smile, his eyes wouldn't comply. "Make yourselves at home. In thirty minutes, come on over to the Main Hall." He turned and pointed to the building with the huge skull on it. "We'll continue from there."

"You don't have a watch?" Martin observed looking at Noah's wrists that only sported leather, and cotton friendship bracelets.

Noah appeared amused at the city folk still stuck in the ways of the old world. "When you've lived here as long as I have, time can be told by all that is around you." He winked, looked them all in the eyes, raise a hand and walked away. His limp now appeared to be gone. He was on a mission.

"Hippie-vague, they call that," Dan muttered. He didn't like hippies. He fought wars not pranced around talking to flowers and hugging other men. There was no evidence that

Noah ever did any of those things but Dan had his suspicions. If this place was a real place there would be a gun tower and better security. Any rambler could wander in.

"Thank God we don't have those same principles," Keely said, ignoring Dan and having a stab at humour instead. "Will would never make it in to work without a watch."

Will shrugged in a good-natured way and Verity shook her head. She was really trying to be polite but her face looked pained with the effort.

"Right, let's see what we have," Martin said, slapping his thighs like the beginning of a Morris dance, and Keely followed. They were almost the mum and dad of the group ready to tell the kids which rooms were theirs.

Eloise seemed to wake. It was as if she'd suddenly been rebooted. Her words pitter-pattering out like machinegun fire: "A witch? That kid said there was a witch, and someone missing? Am I the only one who heard that? What the fuck is this place? Are we going to die?" Her face got ugly when she refused to try and make it be otherwise. Concealer could only hide so much. The immaturity crept back in to leave a vulnerable girl who was unable to process the unknown.

"Chill out, Nancy Drew," Will joked. "He said it was kids playing." He was already coming up with ways to make her scared. If she rebuffed his advances he'd just kick into annoying brother routine.

Jarrod looked at Rick who was trying to supress a smile, but he was a little unsettled by talk of a witch, too. He'd seen enough horror films to know places like this harboured secrets and those were often surrounded by mass suicide, strict religious beliefs and men being burned alive in a large wicker effigy. He glanced over at the church innocently sitting slightly back from the hall. The sun cross appeared even more sinister than it had before. And the huge skull on the front of the Hall left him with chills running the length of his body.

Chapter 7

Noah ran up the stairs of the hall and burst through the double doors of the upstairs like some wild-west salon and him a bandit, with a determined, if not displeased look on his face. Ahead of him stood three elders made up of two men and a single woman. They were all aged between their late forties and early sixties and had lived within the community for as far back as any of them could remember. A lot of history flowed around the room and that wasn't always a good thing. They held on to a strong belief system, and were not welcoming of any change. Secrets also crept around the damp corners, staining the walls with not only regrets, but with actions that had to be taken. That was the way a place like this survived.

"What is going on?" Noah said, his face in a tight grimace. The pain suddenly more noticeable in his leg again. "You know we have guests!"

The tallest of the elders held up a hand, sensing Noah's discontent. "Calm down, Noah. That out there was unfortunate!" He pointed back the way Noah had entered. "But we do have a situation. Again."

Even standing still, Noah's leg began to ache, his need to get to the hall greater than the pain in his left knee. The humid weather of late had helped it, but every once in a while, the dull throbbing set in and he wanted to rip it off and chuck it at the nearest victim.

"In front of the guests!" Noah responded hissing out the words, unable to sweeten the bitter edge to them. "How stupid was that? They're probably whispering about it now; speculation and rumours building to make us look bad! How are we meant to keep this place a secret if these indiscretions are allowed to happen!"

The lady was called Herti and looked back at him with just as much anger. She'd not elevated to her position without standing up to angry diatribes from any man. She was in her fifties, with strong features and a jaw that locked defiantly more often than not. She was known for her stubbornness, and need to go by the book. Her world was simply black or white, and so things were either right or wrong.

Herti took a step forward and spoke clearly, "Noah. You'll do well to remember your position here and to whom you are speaking. Control yourself or we will be forced to control you our way…" She let that weight of words sink in. Many a man had been the victim of these people in front of him. The power and influence they held was immense. They were the judge and jury and besides a couple of unfortunate events, it had all worked out well.

He swallowed a little more than his pride as he said, "Forgive me, but I'm only trying to protect us. I have nothing but the good of the community at heart."

Herti dismissed his comments and continued. "Jacob is just a boy! We know what we are doing! We understand your position which is why you are still standing able-bodied in front of us… despite your outburst!" The threat was there hovering around and making itself known.

One of the men added, "Let's all think about this for a second, okay? We understand your worry Noah, really we do. That is why we're here, in this place to discuss it." They might be dressed like medieval lords, but they were still well-versed in the good-cop-bad-cop routine.

They sat at a large wooden table where many important decisions had been thrashed out before. Adjacent to them, was a head table where they'd sit to eat, situated in front of two lines of tables. Then tables that surrounded the room leaving a large space in the centre. The whole congregation helped to source, prepare, serve and clear away after the food consumed at meal-times each and every day. The community shared a harmony the outside world could well do with taking notice of. It was discussion of matters such as this that resulted in resolutions that suited them all. It had worked before, and it sure as hell would work again.

"The witch is back," the eldest of the men, Wilfred, said as if this was expected. His eyes narrowed as he waited for a response. "She has struck again."

"That is not my main concern," Noah batted back, and did his very best to calm his breathing. His temper got him into a lot of hot water, and his blood was still at boiling point. "I mean no disrespect, of course."

"The girl?" Edwin, the one with the longest beard asked as if her disappearance was of nobody's concern.

"Yes! The girl. We have to find her!"

The three elders looked at each other, sharing glances that suggested the matter had been discussed before he arrived. The vast experience and wise pragmatism stared back through three pairs of eyes.

"The witch is evil. She is what could bring this place down and you know it!" Edwin was defiant. An air of authority rose up and threatened to be followed with consequence.

"But the child is *missing… Rosie* is missing. We shouldn't be here talking about that but out there trying to find her! This is the danger."

"Calm down, Noah. It won't do you any good to get overly excited about this. We'll look for her, but as you are also aware, we cannot show the new guests something is wrong, can we? We must remain a calm and united front."

"I know, but—"

"No! Listen. Rosie is one girl. They are a gaggle of outsiders who are already looking at us like we're cannibals or something. Some preconceived ideology that we are the result of inbreeding: *strong in the arm and thick in the head.* The missing children are extremely unfortunate, but we need to find the witch. Kill the witch and we eradicate our problem."

Noah took a deep breath and stopped himself from banging his fists on the table. He took a deep breath, filling his lungs before exhaling, and when composed said through gritted teeth, "Then let me take a couple of people to sneak off and try to find her. We'll sweep the outer trail and work our way in. She can't be far; and she can't get out."

"The witch doesn't seem to have a problem with coming and going as she pleases," Wilfred muttered. It was meant to be under his breath, but then he looked at them all like he didn't care.

"What if there's a gap? A small one a child can squeeze through?"

More shared glances before Herti spoke slowly and carefully. "Fine. Go and have a look. If you find her, bring her to us. But DO NOT enter the woods!"

"Do we really think there is something to fear beyond them?" Noah argued and instantly regretted his challenging tone. "Look, I know what you believe… er, *we* believe, but what if we're wrong? Another child has been snatched away! How many is that now? Five, six? The witch is taunting us! Soon there will be no children left and then what?"

They all nodded, and shared concerned glances.

Herti nodded to the men as if they'd all decided, and said, "Then go and see what you can find but if you don't bring her back then you're the ones who will pay the price!"

Noah got up and nodded his head towards them. "As you wish," he replied, and relieved, turned from them and began to walk away.

"Noah? Just one more thing," Edwin, the large but calm man shouted.

Noah turned around. "Yes?"

The elder looked at the others individually, and with a nod of the head from each of them he continued. "We have reason to believe the woods are just a trap. A place to taunt us to step into danger."

"What do you mean?" Noah asked. Was he signing his own death warrant if he ventured into them? Did the elders know more than they were letting on?

"We don't think you'll find the witch there," Edwin said and turned to Herti.

"Noah," she began. "We think the witch is here. Living among us. All we have to do is find out who she is."

Noah had so many questions but he didn't know where to start, and more to the point he felt the answers would not be forthcoming.

He should've walked in calmly and asked what the boy was talking about, said nothing about going out on a mission and then left under the cover of darkness.

The elders had lost their bite. They'd turned into a bunch of old women fussing over what might happen and not showing the witch that the community of Woden would not roll over for her but fight back. They were just pointing fingers at each other. What did that mean? Were they going to start drowning people? They didn't need an investigation, they needed action!

They must do anything and everything they could think of until they knew in their heart of hearts that one thing was for certain.

The witch is dead!

Chapter 8

As Jarrod followed everyone into the house, the smell of wood was overpowering. It was a lot bigger than it appeared from the outside, with the interior finished off well by a skilled craftsman. There was a lounge area which consisted of two sofas and a few mismatched chairs, arranged in a square and with a huge plain rug in the middle. A goat's skull was proudly mounted above the fireplace and above it was a flag with the same familiar pagan cross on it. Adjacent was a kitchen area that had homemade, but well-crafted cupboards on the walls. There was a large preparation table, and a sink with pipes that were most likely connected to a tank full of collected rain water.

On the other side were a couple of ground floor bedrooms. The first was a small one that Rick was quick to claim, and next to it was a slightly larger one Martin promptly declared would be his. He was grinning like a kid away from home for the first time. Nobody would be surprised if he ran and jumped belly-first onto the bed, or initiated a pillow-fight.

"This'll do me!" he said swinging his bag off his back and entering his new room. "Looks like we're the first line of defence!" He grinned at Rick, but Rick was ignoring him and instead closed the door to his room with a bang.

Everyone else was already spreading out through the house. There were no more rooms on that level, so with Keely firmly in the lead, hauling their bags, they followed single file up the stairs at the end of the hall. There was a loud clump-clump of feet upon the hard wooden stairs. Decorating the walls was the odd photograph showing smiling faces of strangers they might never meet. The corners were dog-eared, and may have once been well thumbed as the owner reminisced on old memories. *We always smile for the camera,* Jarrod mused and wondered if they were all as happy as they were trying to portray.

On the next level were two large rooms filled with a line of three beds in each. The furnishings were sparse as if the occupiers were only ever staying for a night. It was a potential wet-dream for an interior designer or an IKEA enthusiast. The place could be set alive with plants and soft-furnishings, but that sort of décor was foreign and futuristic to these parts. Tainted with chemicals and manmade fibres.

"Right then," Dan said chucking his army backpack onto the bed. "Looks like this is the men's room!" He was almost beating his chest as the testosterone oozed from his every pore. Perhaps he pictured a dartboard and a calendar with ample-bosomed babes grinning at the camera with false come-to-bed eyes.

“Yep,” Will agreed, and walked in with him. The two frat-brothers-in-arms had buried the hatchet in the quick way men do. Jarrod looked at Iain, as Di and Verity followed Eloise into the other room, assuming it to be theirs.

“Urgh!” Eloise said loudly. “It smells all musty!”

“Suck it up, Princess,” Di rasped back at her. “You’re not in Kansas anymore!”

“Huh?”

“Forget it.”

“*The Wizard of Oz*,” Verity muttered walking to the far end and looking around to see what needed to be cleaned. “It was a movie.” She pulled out her phone once more and checked the signal. She might pretend to be cross at her husband but she was sure making a fuss about letting him know she was there.

Jarrod looked down the hallway between them and saw another staircase. He was more than willing to give it a go rather than endure the butt-slapping of the alphas. He didn’t fancy waking up in the morning being tea-bagged by Will, or having a cock drawn on his forehead in marker-pen by Dan.

“In you go, Iain,” he said. “I’ll look up above.” Iain didn’t seem to even acknowledge him and turned into the room anyway. Whether he was happy or disappointed about the situation he wasn’t giving anything away. Iain didn’t prescribe to emotions. He floated through life in a non-committal fashion never seemingly bothered by any outcome. Everything just appeared to be okay. Eloise once said she thought when he ejaculated, he’d barely sigh or change expression, just wipe his cock and carry on with his day. His shirt was never crumpled and that said a lot about a man.

Jarrod left them to it as he heard the excited calls of, "Roomy!" from Will towards an unfazed Iain. Give him an hour and they'd all be wearing matching shirts, singing drinking songs and trying out their new nicknames.

The second staircase was smaller. At the top was a single large step before being presented with two doors. They were small rooms like the two on the ground floor. More of an afterthought really, or perhaps more to do with engineering. A bed was against the far wall, with light cutting through the bedroom from a window in desperate need of cleaning. He placed his cheap but practical rucksack on the bed and stood at the window. It drew him towards it.

Across the large square was the hall. The church was to the right of where they had come in. Ahead were more buildings, and behind them other houses could be seen almost cowering; understanding they were of less importance the further away from the square they were.

It was hard to imagine how life could be in a place that had no technology. He wondered whether there was a single room with a computer, and electricity, but that raised too many questions. They didn't appear to be hiding anything, they were just a community that wanted to escape the rat-race of society in the twenty-first century, and who could blame them? Life had peaked and mankind was being punished as it witnessed its own demise.

When he did see figures they were adults. The place had a definite lack of children around, which statistically struck him as odd, although from a practical point of view could suggest it was single people, or adventurous couples who escaped to here, rather than families. It's harder to talk a kid who's in love with their electricals to give it up for a primitive lifestyle.

Behind him, he heard footsteps come up the stairs, and turned to see Keely poke her head around his door.

"Looks like this floor is ours," she said flatly.

"It looks that way." As she turned away, he added, "You didn't fancy bunking in the girl's room, then?" He wanted to keep her talking. It was stupid. He was acting like a teenager.

"What do *you* think? Those are people I wish to sleep near? Besides, a boss should have her privacy, right?"

He chuckled; in a way, his friendly response might loosely be seen as flirtation, and as she turned away, he followed. She placed her bag on the floor and was also drawn towards the window. She knew he was there looking at her from behind.

"Imagine what fun we can have up here," she said almost in a whisper, never pulling her gaze away from the square outside. It was a loaded statement, deliberate in how it could be taken in a number of ways. Very calculating. He expected nothing less.

Unless he'd imagined it.

He looked at her. His boss. A woman who scared him on many levels, and yet intrigued and excited him, too. He thought her being up here was less to do with him and more to do with distancing herself from the workers. In an ideal world she probably would've swapped him for Martin. Mr Action Man. He'd probably roll out a pack of aromatic oils and relay some bullshit about meditation retreats in Tibet before coaxing her in to lie on her front naked whilst he oiled her up on the premise of relieving the knots and stresses from her body.

After a couple of beats, she muttered, "You just going to stand there staring at me?"

"I wasn't… I mean…" Jarrod stammered.

"Relax, Jarrod."

"We should probably go back downstairs," he managed.

"As you wish." He didn't but the lines between what was and what wasn't appropriate were blurring, and besides, he felt like he was being caught up in these stupid fantasies that would do nothing but fuck up his self-esteem. It wasn't the first time.

His hands we twitching and instantly he wanted a pill to swallow away his anxiety.

When they returned to the lower level, Dan and Will were shouting and laughing like drunken sailors. Jarrod was glad he wasn't sharing the room with them. It was a car crash waiting to happen and one of them would no doubt end up in tears.

Eloise had a face on her like she'd just sucked somebody off and was still contemplating whether to swallow or not, and Di was rolling her eyes and waving an unlit cigarette around like it was a weapon. Verity finally appeared having wanted to unpack fully before continuing.

"How many nights we got 'ere?" Di's deep voice boomed rhetorically. She coughed and tried to make out it was because she'd not had a fag for a long time.

"Too many!" Eloise answered, waving her hands like she'd stuck them where she shouldn't have. Reality bites and it had taken a huge chunk out of Eloise, who'd realised she would be getting hot and sweaty, her make up would melt after an hour, and her hair would fall out of place.

"Come on," Keely said, confidently. "What doesn't kill you will only make you stronger!"

"It won't matter when I'm dead!" Eloise grinned at her own joke, and Di looked at her fag like she was trying to light it with her mind, then gave up and dropped her hand to her side.

They all walked down to the ground floor where Martin was in deep conversation with Rick. It was, of course one-sided, as Rick was sat down in a chair not even looking at him, and Martin was in the middle of some story where he was the hero and more than likely had saved the world.

"...We got back home after three days much to the relief of all our parents!" He heard the rest of them and tried to act surprised. "Ah, here you are. I was just telling Ricky here about the time I found some lads lost in Wales. It's a bit embarrassing really... I mean, it could've ended so tragically had I not gone looking for them. It's not about me, though, nor the injuries I sustained, but more about—"

"We should probably make a move," Keely said cutting him off before he dropped his trousers and started masturbating at his own story. Some people had trouble talking about themselves; Martin was not one of them. Any few seconds of silence could be filled with a story he felt compelled to tell, and each and every one of them was designed to make him look like a superhero.

What the others didn't know was that Martin's teenage years were hell. Older boys used him for anything and everything, and being smaller and younger, he had no choice but to go along with them.

"Er, yes, of course." Jarrod tried to supress a giggle when he saw Rick grinning from across the room.

They filed out of the door, were hit instantly by the bright sunshine, and headed towards the large hall. The huge skull may have been eyeless, but the empty sockets still looked like they were watching them.

Keely was in front, showing once again she was in charge.

Up ahead Noah appeared. He was distracted and his face was a picture of frustration before he realised they were there, and he did his best to paint a smile back on.

"How is the accommodation?" he asked, throwing up his arms like he was about to embrace them all. He was met by nodding heads and grinning faces, and even Eloise was doing her best to be polite.

"Very nice," Keely said, speaking for them all - something they'd all become accustomed to.

"Then let's go over here," Noah said turning to his right and pointing out behind the buildings in front of them. "We have a couple of new houses we're currently constructing." At first it felt like they were being corralled away from the main buildings. The expected tour of the hall, the church and some of the other buildings was not forthcoming. Jarrod found that a little odd. Noah clearly was on a mission to get them onto a task immediately.

As they began to walk, Jarrod noticed people slipping out of the hall and walking together with authority. There was something mysterious about them, and it was one of the first times he felt uneasy there. One of the older gentlemen with an impressive beard looked over at him almost sizing him up. However, just as quickly, he turned away and spoke to the man and woman with him, and they disappeared around the back and out of sight.

The humidity was strong and made them sweat. Verity's sudden, quick succession of sneezes blasted out loudly, as dust particles from the house finally began to tickle her nose. Her loud outbursts made Noah jump at first.

"Blimey, Verity!" Will said loudly, as she expelled another shouted sneeze. He leaned into Eloise and said, "You can tell by the way a woman sneezes, how she reacts to an orgasm!"

"Rubbish!" she said, but was clearly thinking about it.

"Well," he said under his breath. "You sneeze like someone's stood on a cat's tail!"

She looked embarrassed, and Jarrod was suddenly picturing holding her ample naked hips and looking around the alleyway as a similar sound came from her mouth. At first it had made him feel triumphant, but it soon became annoying. He thought it best not to share that with the group.

"Well, you've only heard that when I sneeze so…" Her retort fell flat.

As they continued along a path that snaked around behind the current crop of houses, they could see others being constructed.

"We always seem to attract a few extras every few months," Noah said proudly. He stopped walking and spread out an arm to show the construction work, and continued, "The community has grown quite substantially in recent years." He narrated like he was the guide on a paid tour. "We are extremely lucky to have a couple of people now with expert knowledge in house building, and as such this has allowed us to plan and build with the future in mind."

Keely was standing next to him like the control-freak she was lapping up the details and no doubt looking for ways to use it against him. Perhaps that was unkind, but she had previous form.

"What was your initial expectation for the community… if you don't mind me asking?" Keely asked. It wasn't like her to be so polite in asking an intrusive question.

"Are you, or were you, a religious group?" Martin interjected not wanting to be left out. He wanted - at any chance he had - to show he was higher up the hierarchical tree.

Noah found this amusing. "We're a Pagan community with loose Scandinavian links, but a lot of the ways have been diluted with time…" He stopped for a second and turned to them. "Paganism has a tendency to scare people. We are not in the business of scaring, but embracing people here. That being said, we still have our rituals which outsiders do consider to be a little odd." He flashed a small smile and continued to walk. "A lot of us worked in cities, with gruelling schedules, and mind-numbing commutes, and eventually we had enough of the daily stresses. We were working all hours of the day for money, status, and power, but no matter what we achieved, and what we splashed our cash on it never seemed to be enough until… I got ill. The evil of capitalism is rife, and yet we never stop and think about that. We've evolved from defined social classes into a melting pot of pure greed.

"You see, when you are no longer satisfied depression is quick to find a home in your soul. I got ill. I ended up in a retreat and found like-minded people…" A structure came into view, and a shirtless muscular guy stood up, wiping sweat off his brow. He looked like he'd fallen off the cover of *Men's Health* magazine. The rugged-guy-look the publication tried to fool the average dad-bod man into thinking could be achieved. Ninety-nine percent of readers gave up after a week, with the other one percent continuing diligently for twelve months, achieving their goals and leaving their wives for younger, trimmer versions only to be cheated on themselves. A further year later, their bodies had welcomed back the belly and man-boobs with open arms, but now they were all alone with baggage and memories in a damp bedsit and wondering where it had all gone wrong.

"Troy!" Noah shouted, raising a hand. The guy dutifully flashed a smile but he didn't seem overly pleased at being stopped halfway through his work. From somewhere else some rhythmic banging could be heard, but that stopped when they began to talk.

"Ryan!" Troy called, turning behind him. From a dark corner peeked a teen who eyed them suspiciously. They'd turned their back on strangers from another life and didn't welcome seeing any now.

"I've brought you some help," Noah said in a tone that appeared overly polished and something that Troy should be ecstatic about. Instead, Troy nodded to him, and again with a forced smiled replied, "So I see." This clearly wasn't good news for him, and by the blank look on his face suggested he saw it as babysitting; the notion of it being helpful was a stretch.

Eloise muttered a "Wow!" as she eyed up his ropey-muscles that glistened with sweat. A tribal tattoo covered one shoulder and upper-arm, and he swept his fringe back, before swinging down to meet them. He was reluctant and reticent to socialise. A workman who didn't want to be interrupted.

"Show off," Will said to Eloise, but his grin was quashed by her open mouth, and sudden swallowing of breath.

"You know that sound of a cat's tail being stood on… you might be hearing it soon!" she said under her breath.

"Control yourself. I bet his fingers are grubby."

"Thank you, Noah. Welcome, guys," Troy said addressing them in a business tone. "It's always great to have help. Has anyone built a house before?" It was said in the same way someone might ask if anyone had ever had a headline gig at Wembley Stadium. He clearly wanted to move things on so he could grab his tools again.

There were a few shakes of heads before the alphas puffed out their chests and metaphorically stood up to be counted.

"I helped my dad build a wall in the garden," Will said proudly. "A builder friend saw it and said it was one of the best he'd seen. He couldn't believe I'd hardly had any training."

Rick rolled his eyes and said, "I wonder if it's still standing?"

Martin actually did take a step forward before offering, "I built a wooden structure in Kampala, a small village in Uganda when I took a gap-year out from Uni." He shrugged. "It was incredibly rewarding. The head of the village was really pleased with the workmanship of it… To be honest, I was just happy to help…" He looked away slightly and waved off any silent comments. "It wasn't just me though. I had a great team who listened to my instructions well. I think that's the key. You can have a great leader, but every leader requires workers who respect them."

Rick once again commented to Jarrod. "Did he just call himself a great leader?" Jarrod tried hard to suppress a smile. The alphas were in full dick-swinging mode.

Dan was having none of it, and with gritted teeth took his turn. "I built structures out of sandbags when killing the enemy in Afghanistan. Hot, extreme conditions and whilst bullets and bombs were going off around us. Just something we did. It was about strength and speed. I can't say whether or not they were great to look at but they kept me alive and that was the main thing."

Will took his life into his own hands by responding with, "I think our guy here is looking for a bit more skill than laying a few sandbags around!"

Dan looked like he was about to give a free demonstration of his hand-to-hand combat skills when Iain raised his hand. The very act of it seemed an odd thing to do for a middle-aged guy. He was still wearing his jumper and was looking quite red now. Perhaps he had hidden gang tattoos nobody knew about, or possibly considered that Eloise would squeal at the flash of his bare arms.

"Yes," Troy said slightly irritated. "Jumper-guy?"

"I've built over six-hundred houses on Minecraft and The Sims. I mean, I know it's not totally hands on, but I understand the construction of homes rather well. It's all about foundations."

Troy just stared at him like he wanted to walk over and rip the guy's head off and dropkick it as hard as he could into the forbidden woods. Instead, he just replied, "Sorry? *What?*"

Unmoved, and completely misunderstanding the sarcastic tone in the question, he almost smirked when Iain responded with, "They are computer games, but they require a certain knowledge and understanding of structures□"

"If you're a ten-year-old!" Will laughed. "Even Sandbags over there knows better."

"Oi, Wall-Boy! I can kill you with one finger, should I wish to!"

"Guys!" Keely hissed at them.

Troy shook his head in disbelief and then proved that sarcasm was a hidden trait of his by responding with, "Okay, we have a spectrum of experience here, so whilst you might find this boring, we'll be starting with the *basics*." He emphasised the last word like it was a slur, and he was dismissing every last one of their boasts "We've got a lot of work to do!"

Noah bid them farewell, but reminded them dinner would be in the hall later that afternoon. He turned, and with a waving hand, set off back towards the other buildings.

"I hope you're all feeling strong!" Troy grinned. "We've got a lot of work to do!"

The Last Weekend

Chapter 9

The emaciated faces glanced out hopefully through the breaks of the trees deep within the wood. Hands with broken nails and anaemic skin clutched to posts, or trees for balance. Hungry eyes surveyed the produce of fresh new offerings. Cracked lips were licked with dehydrated tongues, and hands shook in anticipation of a feed.

Smiles of relief spread over scarred faces, as hope had answered their prayers. Open sores glistened in the sunlight whilst others were crusted over with scabs, neither of which bothered them anymore. The smell of infection was thick in the air. It lingered and clung on to their dirty clothing, but they'd all grown immune to the gut-wrenching stench and it was considered normal.

Stick legs had lost muscle tone months ago, and clothes hung off them like they were playing dress-up. Even in weak moments when they'd questioned everything they'd been told, this proved all they needed was prayer. The strength of belief would outlive anything. The body may appear to be failing, but the soul would remain strong and eventually would make them powerful on the outside, too.

But to assume they were weak was naïve. Desperation, and survival had seen them regress into primal creatures, experienced at fighting to the death, and doing whatever they needed to do to live. Each of them had blood on their hands from previous victims, and thought nothing of doing it again.

And again.

They shared glances, but nobody wanted to speak. What if the illusion was shattered and this was just a dream? Then what? Fever had taken the lives of their own, and the first signs were usually hallucinations.

The warm breeze was welcomed like fresh water, and it danced the accepted fragrance of sweat and bile around them. So used, were they to the smell that it was almost comforting.

Each fought internally to supress the urge to run out of their hiding place and grab one of the outsiders. To use the element of surprise to jump on their backs and lean around to the exposed neck and bite as hard as they could. The very act was effective and they'd seen it bear fruit many times before, but then the others had got involved.

The bad people.

And that was when the trouble really happened.

They lost people to such foolhardy actions.

Friends had been slain. Limbs liberated from their bodies in ear-piercing screams that had them closing their eyes whilst one of their own writhed in pain and spurts of blood.

There was time. When the moon came out so did their opportunity.

The strong, and healthy outsiders flaunted themselves without the knowledge they were being watched.

Picked out.

Chosen.

Behind the people were the small and innocent faces of the young. The future. The ones stolen and reprogrammed to be evil.

But the real evil was the woman they dared not speak of. The one they considered to be immortal. She was older than time itself.

She was the witch and she'd killed people without so much as a single touch. That was what was so scary about her.

The magic. Nobody understood it and therefore she was to be feared.

Chapter 10

There was a reason why the group of misfits worked in an office. Manual labour for the majority of them was not something they enjoyed. They'd been working for about an hour when Eloise sat back and huffed. Physical exertion wasn't something she subscribed to unless she was inebriated, and bouncing naked in a reverse-cowgirl position. Even then, she'd be quick to roll back over and make the man do all the humping. Although of late she'd found herself bent over in an alleyway, and gripping empty beer barrels whilst someone thrust behind her. She'd also found herself screeching in pleasure and grabbing the attention of those innocent passers-by, so it wasn't all bad.

The sun had peaked in the baby-blue sky, and only tiny whisps of cloud were evident up above in a haphazard fashion. Whilst the sun had begun its slow descent, not even the trees nearby had been able to stop the heat. The open field left them exposed to the elements and was all the more reason for the careful construction on the houses.

"How much longer do we 'ave to do this for?" Eloise questioned and flapped the front of her vest, doing her best to generate a breeze down her sweaty cleavage. She made a face to depict her feelings of forced labour, but everyone was used to her histrionics. The Instagram girl wouldn't be taking selfies anytime soon. Her face was ruddy, and shone a little with perspiration, even after she wiped it. Her appearance embarrassed her. She was a long shower and a huge makeover away from allowing any cameras to come near her.

Troy stared at her for a second, and whilst other men might've had lustful thoughts, his mind was far from that and bordered between disappointment and anger. "We'll stop when we're done," he snapped. He was a man who believed in pushing through to get a job done. His biggest frustration with the community was having to babysit the city-slickers who wanted to experience the country life *without* experiencing the country life. They wanted the shiny brochure, the whistlestop tour, and a few photographs to pretend they rolled their sleeves up and got stuck in, and yet he was meant to pander to their every need and work twice as hard to cover them. He wasn't having it. He'd escaped a life of that and yet here he was a constant repetition with only the landscape to make things different.

Di was smoking again, something that also annoyed Troy, and so she'd been sent to stand next to the first clump of trees, far enough away so her poison couldn't affect his health. Banished like a naughty schoolgirl – not that she seemed to mind at all. Instead, she defiantly had her back to them all and appeared to take as much time as a person possibly could. It was a silent protest, and one that kept her out of the sun, and away from hard work.

Verity constantly frowned in a way she found quite natural. She was a human contradiction. Happy to spout about equal opportunities and glass-ceilings when she failed to get a promotion, but now was questioning why she, as a woman, was having to do manual labour.

"Should we be doing this?" she said loudly, but not to anyone in particular. "I mean we've not had health and safety or anything. This is a man's job. They want to do this and yet suddenly here we are being told what to do by a man!"

Troy stopped for a second. "Hey, Mona?"

"Mona?" Verity replied.

"He's calling you that in relation to your moaning. Jesus!" Rick commented.

Troy grinned for the first time. "Exactly. A bit of humorous banter. Anyway, you see that saw there?" He pointed to the sharp bladed tool sat on a makeshift bench.

Verity nodded. "Yeah."

"Don't touch the blade. You'll cut yourself… Oh, and the rope there." He pointed up to some rope dangling from the second level over the side. "Don't go up, make a noose, sling your head through it and jump off. You could hurt yourself." His mouth twitched, and Dan and Will laughed like they were desperate for Troy to like them.

"If it's sharp it will cut you. If it's electric you might get a shock. If it's hot it will burn. If you see water be careful not to drown. There you go. Consider yourself fully versed in health and safety."

"Health and safety isn't really a laughing matter," Verity scowled. She wasn't a fan of humour at the best of times let alone from a sexist stranger.

"If you've got common sense then you don't need me to treat you like a baby, right?"

"Right," she said, but she was building up to one of her moods. In fact, he'd need to understand health and safety to keep her from throwing tools at him when she had one of her stress attacks.

To their credit, Dan and Will were working together well, and had been bearing the brunt of the hard labour as they took the large half-logs, and pulled them up and into position. Their competitive nature wouldn't allow either to slack, and whilst both were tired, they refused to admit that fact to the other. Jarrod and Rick were cutting wedges into the logs, and Martin was cutting the aforementioned trunks in half. Nobody questioned where the fuel came from that powered the machine being used, it was just another question that seemed a little odd. Troy didn't look like he'd take any sort of prying well. In fact, he was spoiling for a fight, no doubt happy to throw down work gloves like some gauntlet, and settle any misunderstanding with his bare fists.

The other lad, Ryan always managed to find a job away from everyone else. At some point he'd disappeared and never returned. Troy didn't seem to care.

"Good work, team!" Keely said at one point in a brief rally cry that was meant to motivate. Troy didn't share her feelings and grunted in disapproval. She was getting stuck in; moving like a machine grabbing materials and hammering in nails wherever required. She looked hot and tired, but also refused to admit defeat. Managers were of a different breed.

"How long have you been here?" Keely enquired of Troy. This was why she was a boss. Cool under pressure, and still acting like it was nothing.

"A few years," he muttered. Then he stopped and turned to her. "The buildings were about to fall down. They are the heart of the community and if you don't get that right, then you have no foundations. I keep telling them that… *not that they listen*." For a brief second it almost appeared like Troy would open up his feelings more; Keely was clever at that. He glanced around at everyone and then like an invisible bolt of lightning had hit him, he jolted to attention.

"We should take a break," he proclaimed. "I'm not very hospitable, I'm afraid." There was a flash of an apologetic smile that was foreign to his face, and mostly aimed at Keely. "We'll head back up to the hall."

Keely nodded, and turned to her team. "Guys! We're going to take a break."

Dan and Will nodded respectfully to each other in a mutual appreciation of their hard work, and Eloise muttered some profanity under her breath but it wasn't easy to make out the words, nor who it was aimed at, but she clearly felt the need to express her displeasure at the whole experience so far. Verity was with her, shaking her head like she felt they were one binding short of a chain-gang, forced to work in high temperatures just for food and shelter.

Jarrod nodded to Rick as they placed the log on the floor and wiped their hands on their jeans, before standing back to look proudly at what they'd achieved.

Rick smiled in a way Jarrod hadn't seen before. As usual he'd not spoken much, but Rick had taken to the work outside with a whole load more enthusiasm than in his crumpled shirt and skew-whiff tie back in the corporate office. He had to wonder why Rick turned up there each day. In fact, he was beginning to get a second-wind of enthusiasm at leaving the hellhole himself.

"This has been alright," Jarrod said, in a way that was positive without giving too much away. "The expectations are laid out here in roles of things to be done. Not some vague misunderstandings that set you up to fail."

"Makes you stop and re-evaluate your life, doesn't it?" Rick agreed. The two of them working hard outside in the elements was something Jarrod could not have envisioned a few weeks back. That being said, crossing the line with his best friend and losing control of his boss-fantasies wasn't exactly there in the tea-leaves of fortune-telling either.

Di was lighting up another fag, and taking a huge drag like she'd not had a smoke for hours. She closed her eyes with pleasure like the very act was somehow sexual, tilted her head back and gently blew out the evils.

"Jesus, Di? How many fags d'you bring?" Will asked with mixture of humour and concern.

She exhaled another huge plume of smoke that quickly danced up above and disappeared, and shrugged. "A case I brought back from Majorca. I didn't think there'd be any shops around here."

"You ever think about giving up?" he pressed as they walked forward falling into lines of three.

"You ever think about not asking personal questions?" Her response was snapped back. Bitter and with bite. Smoking appeared to be the only thing that made her happy. That and arguing and being grumpy.

"Just making conversation," Will was quick to add and glanced at Eloise with an eyeroll.

"For future reference, don't bother."

More people were milling around the buildings as they got closer to the huge square. A huge banner had appeared and despite the lack of money and shops to frequent, someone had gone to town with flags and colourful pots of flowers. There, in the middle of the green a stage was being erected. There was a hype of activity that was a snapshot of how a community could be successful. Nobody hung around idly. Not one person sat with eyes glued to a small handheld device, scrolling with boredom and desperately needing to be entertained. Short attention spans reducing day by day.

"This place appears to be a well-oiled machine," Martin commented loudly. He was showing he was observant whilst subtly praising the commune, too. Jarrod saw through his bullshit. Successful management was built on narcissistic foundations, and glued together with gas-lighting and a corporate version of Stockholm-Syndrome – essentially making underpaid, and over-worked employees feel needed whilst appreciating those above them and remaining unaware of the careful manipulation going on. Keely was slightly more subtle, even if she did coerce him with her womanly charms behind the locked doors of her office. He hoped Martin would never expect to do that too.

Troy was too long in the tooth to be lubricated up, and retorted, "We're good at what we do. You have to be or we'd either die or disband."

"Very true," Martin agreed like Troy needed any sort of affirmation from a guy who thought he knew everything.

"What's all this then? Is it for us city folk?" Martin had just stopped short of saying it in an accent.

"Tomorrow is our celebration day to mark the anniversary of when this place opened."

"That's wonderful! We're pleased that we can be part of it, too!"

"Nobody said you were invited," Troy was quick to hurl back. "But knowing how hospitable we are, I'd be surprised if you weren't." He grunted, which might've been a reaction to his attempted humour, or else a slight disdain at the possibility of being so. It wasn't easy to tell. In fact, it probably suggested his true feelings towards them. He was a guy who cared not for fleeting relationships. A hard shell that could be your loyal best friend if you showed commitment. If not, he had no time for small-talk bullshit.

"What's the plan?" Keely muscled in with, grasping back all the leadership she could, nudging past Martin in the process. The move, if nothing else, appeared to amuse Troy. She was all about power and control whether it was subtle or not.

"Back to it for a few hours until the bell goes. We stop for a meal, then later there are various recreational activities you'll be able to choose from."

"Really?" Keely said in a way that was a little flirtatious.

"I won't go into the details. I'm not a salesman, as you may have gathered by now." He tried to smile, but again it looked slightly painful and came off as creepy. He had the rugged good looks that made him appear smouldering instead.

"Exciting!"

"That's subjective." A corner of his mouth twitched.

Keely laughed. "A joke! Wonderful. Another hidden talent."

The hall was in front of them and the skull of the unknown beast still looked ominous. They filed in through the doors, and noticed a staircase off to the side, as they walked through into the large open space of the hall. It was set out with tables going round the outside in a square, but a raised table at the far end that was clearly for the important people.

Noah stood grinning at them and looking a lot less stressed than he had earlier.

"Welcome to the hall!" He smiled clapping his hands together. "My, you all look like you could do with some water! How's it been?"

"Wonderful!" said Martin before Noah had finished.

"Yes, very good," Keely confirmed.

"Bloody hot!" Verity hissed. "Bit obvious, I'd have thought."

"Troy? They been a help?"

He took a deep breath and composed himself. "I couldn't have done it without them."

Noah laughed loudly at that. "You're a card!"

"What?" Eloise muttered but she was ignored, although a couple of locals had noticed her flapping her top and flashing glimpses of her boobs. It appeared that even in these communes, boobs could stop traffic.

"Anyway, I have things to get ready for the celebration tomorrow. Ten years! Can you believe it! I'll see you all at supper!" They held up hands but in truth they were all too tired to engage in conversation.

They were swallowed up by others as people gathered together with random mis-matched mugs of water. A small gaggle of teenagers was laughing together and it was hard to think there could be any negativity towards living this life. It suited every single one of them.

Except there was a lack of smaller children. That did appear odd.

They were shown to a line that handed out plain white ceramic mugs to them all, and after accepting them they walked to the spaces on a large table and sat down. Muscles were already aching, and skin felt exposed and tight from too much sun. Blisters began to appear and energy-levels were low.

"I could do this for a life," Dan said, nodding in general to them and holding aloft his mug. "Beats sitting in an office doing accounts." The truth was, whilst he was a hard worker when he wanted to be, he now relished his cushy job sat in a large comfortable chair and embraced by either air-con in the summer or a warmth from the heating in the winter. He didn't mind the elements of the outdoors for weekend adventures but he no longer wished to forcibly live with them seven days a week. He'd grown to love his creature comforts.

Iain scoffed at that. "I wonder how much accounts you do," he remarked, unaware of how Dan wanted to smash his nose flat with his fist. "I thought you just filled out spreadsheets; drag equations to the bottom of the page!" Iain was a qualified accountant and resented anyone who insinuated they had the expertise and certification to hold a candle to the daily complexities that he endured. Even if he was no longer in a role that warranted it… and dragged equations, updated the results into another spreadsheet, and pissed about making fancy graphs for the rest of the time to show results.

"Whatever, boffin!" And just like that he resorted to name-calling and failed in the assumption this had won the fight.

"You're a valued member of the team," Keely was quick to inject into the conversation. A large invisible band-aid she assumed would cover his wound. She turned and looked at everyone, and added, "You're all valued members." Her words were cut straight out of a managerial training program where some stranger from an outside corporation had charged two-hundred pounds an hour to tell them how to motivate their own team. Jarrod always thought that for an extrovert it was an easy gig, and couldn't understand why more charlatans didn't do it.

Verity looked royally pissed off. "This is slave-labour!" She lifted up her arms, which had sweat rings under the armpits of her shapeless T-shirt. "I smell fucking awful. My boobs are wet and I'm knackered!"

"You're doing well, Verity," Martin encouraged. "This is what getting stuck in is all about. You should be proud of how hard you've worked."

Keely once again felt the need to interject. "You've all been a credit to our team, and to the company in general. Whatever happens from now on, you should all remember that."

Eloise gulped down her water and sat as far back on the bench as she could before losing balance. She wanted the break to last forever and was desperate for a shower and a change of clothes. She considered excusing herself and heading back to the cabin to wipe herself over with wet wipes.

Martin was scanning around like he was searching for the next victim to approach with his intrusive questions, all in the guise of friendly inquisitiveness, and a chance to boast. It was then that he thought he saw him.

A flash of the ginger curls that still haunted his nightmares.

Big Trevor Nettles. The bully from his boarding school.

There he was looking back and sneering at him.

Martin looked away, shocked at who he'd seen. He grabbed his water and gulped down a couple of mouthfuls before braving another look.

The guy was gone. Maybe he was just dehydrated. Maybe.

Jarrod looked down at the water that had quickly warmed up as he noticed Rick nod subtly to someone in the distance. If you weren't looking at him, you wouldn't have seen it, but Jarrod knew Rick was up to something, and it only brought a smile to his face.

"What you smiling at, Mathews?" Will said without malice. "You got wind?"

The question went unanswered as a teenage girl approached them shyly, and said, "Would anyone prefer to help prepare food for supper? We'd love to have some volunteers?"

"I will!" Eloise was so quick to volunteer that her boobs almost escaped from her vest. She looked around at the others. Her eyes pleaded with her colleagues to join her when Di shrugged her interest, Verity gave a half-hearted nod and Iain also looked up as if he was for it – he'd used muscles he'd not felt since school when made to climb up and swing on the monkey bars. He'd agreed for fear of ridicule by old schoolteachers and bullies alike if he didn't comply. Which was ironic, as he got stuck halfway up, pissed his pants and then cried, only to be ridiculed by the teachers and bullies.

"Okay, please follow me," the girl said, looking at each of them, and then with her arm, she summoned them forward. Iain folded the sleeve of his jumper back with careful precision so each fold matched perfectly.

Another ten minutes and the rest of them were trudging slowly back out to the field with the village a little way behind them. The sun felt just as hot as before and their aches were growing greater with each step.

Jarrod was sure he saw movement in the trees. A flash of something unnatural. He also wondered whether it was just his eyes. A mixture of sun and tiredness, and he hated to admit he wasn't used to the physicality of the task. It had been years since he'd last felt so many muscles in his body ache with overuse. Nowadays, if he felt tired, he stopped what he was doing, it was as simple as that. The need to grit your teeth and summon inner strength to push through pain wasn't an attribute he was aware he possessed.

But the woods were so dark. Almost unnaturally so, and when he looked up into the sky there appeared a mass of fat, pregnant clouds.

Starting back up when muscles had cooled down was painful for people used to slouching back in ergonomically designed chairs with the room temperature monitored and regular breaks insisted – this wasn't through the caring nature of the business but to embrace the threat of being sued should a barrister feel the said company was in any way negligent in Health and Safety.

Motivation wasn't as high as before and within minutes Jarrod felt exactly as he had before they'd stopped for their break. It was like being back at school doing some sponsored sport event where the novelty had worn off and he wanted to rest. His mind wandered back to Thornhill and his mundane life and he found himself soul searching and asking himself honestly, did he really want to go back there? He didn't know. Maybe this was the roll of dice he needed. Or was it just that this was so different?

Where earlier there had been a rumble of chatter amongst them, now their low energy levels dictated the lack of talk and they focused purely on the task at hand. Each glance up saw a colleague hard at work albeit at half pace. They'd lost half the workforce, so it was even more obvious that the construction had taken a hammering.

Troy wasn't pleased with it either, and had no problems in expressing his thoughts on it.

"What's the point?" he said to his captive audience of Martin and Keely. "The house construction is one of the most important jobs. The community cannot grow without sufficient housing. We have enough people to do the cooking. They'll be sat around and getting in the way."

"But they weren't the best at manual work, so perhaps you've not lost too much?" Keely was trying her hand at diplomacy. "I agree this housing is important."

Of course, Martin couldn't remain tight-lipped. "A roof over the heads of the community, especially in the months of harsh conditions is of the utmost importance for the survival of any community. It's basic logic."

"Exactly." Though Troy was quick to see the smoke being blown up his arse.

Jarrod thought they could be anywhere; they could be thirty years in the past or thirty years into the future. The simplicity of what could be seen was refreshing, uncomplicated and organic. Di was off working elsewhere, the smell of nicotine had disappeared and was replaced instead by nature and the odd whiff of body odour. In the office, Jarrod was used to the smell of coffee, Di's stale residual cigarette waft, and Eloise's sickly-sweet perfume.

Jarrod had no clue what might come later, and at that point he didn't care. He was happy to embrace the new experiences, and he was experiencing a second wind to get the walls completed on the ground-floor plan of the house.

A large bird shrieked from above, and perhaps that was the very first sign of danger. Of course, they wouldn't realise that for a while now. The sun and peaceful surroundings led them into a false sense of security that this was a corporate event and no matter your feelings, you always had the safety blanket of rules and regulations. Except here they didn't.

Not that they knew that of course.

They had stumbled into the lion's den and unbeknownst to them were surrounded. And some of them wouldn't get out alive.

Chapter 11

The bell was loud enough to be heard way out in the field, and above the banging and sawing where they were working. Troy mechanically downed tools immediately, and clapped his hands a couple of times.

"That's supper," he called, and was suddenly moving them all quickly to gather up everything and place them into a large container inside the new house, desperate for them to walk back with real urgency. "We cannot keep the elders waiting." There was a vague tone of fear that had uncharacteristically crept in. Not a lot had been said about the elders. They were an unknown quantity and the way the fearless Troy was acting swirled up a little anxiety as to who they were and what they represented.

Rick looked completely happy. He was still as silent as normal, but now he looked comfortable – despite the tiredness and pain from working so hard. He walked beside Jarrod and whispered, "What d'you think of it here?"

"Mate, I'm not sure I want to go back to my old life. Being outdoors feels so natural and… I don't know." He scrambled for the right words but his smile couldn't hide his happiness. It was like being a child again but with more meaningful chores.

"I knew you would. These fakers are pretending. They are making the right noises, but when the going gets tough – *and it will* – you watch them run."

"Like Billy Ocean?"

Rick looked confused. "The song?" The musical penny dropped and he smiled so broadly Jarrod wondered whether he'd ever seen so many of his teeth before.

"Yeah," he said. "Just like Billy *fuckin'* Ocean!"

"What's going to happen?" Jarrod muttered, when they'd moved on a few more steps, but it was almost rhetorical. He knew Rick would only say if he really wanted to. He'd always had a mix of naivety and mystery about him that kept people from hanging around too long. Apart from Jarrod, that was. He knew the internal struggles of trying to fit in. They'd both ignored the bandwagons stopping by and lived their lives by their own feelings and not the perceptions of others.

Troy ushered them along so they were walking at quite a pace, and considering the work they'd put in it was a real feat, but nobody complained. They knew they would rest when they got to the hall and rumbling stomachs negated any thoughts of complaints. Rick was wrestling a smile on his face the whole time, enjoying how Troy was showing vulnerability. He wasn't in control and he hated it.

The square in the centre of the community was empty of people, but the stage was fully up. It would've represented a ghost town had the excitable chatter not spilled out of the doors and windows of the hall.

Everyone was sat down at the tables when they finally entered, and Troy almost man-handled them onto the bench seats before a gong sounded and the place fell quiet. A look of relief washed over him as he took his own place.

Dressed in matching black shirts, the elders stood staring slightly ominously over their people. A slight wave of tension flowed around as if something untoward would happen should they not be satisfied. The community may be free-loving and open to outsiders, but it was clear it still ran its own rules and regulations.

Jarrod's eyes darted towards the backs of heads and took in this place that could potentially be his new home. He was still anxious of all the unknowns and made a deal with himself to ask more questions before making any further decision. He glanced around every darkened corner of the place, taking in the subdued faces he could see, and the various goats' skulls mounted on the walls. Earlier they'd looked fitting, and in keeping with the village, but now they appeared slightly more sinister. His eyes soon found the others in the group that had gone off to help elsewhere. Eloise looked like she might burst in to tears, whereas Di wore a blank expression but her hands fidgeted as if needing the feel of a cigarette to make her happy. Verity looked like she might murder someone if she didn't eat soon and stared at the empty plate in front of her, and Iain was wide-eyed drinking in the new culture like it was something he'd share with his role-playing buddies when they next dressed up to fight fictional dragons.

"I'd like to formally welcome to Woden our newest arrivals," the man with a beard said with a booming voice that echoed against the walls. Smiles appeared on faces with relief that everything was in order, and then a slow, and loud clap rang out in unison.

Clap, clap, clap, clap.

Not the pitter-patter of happy hands coming together at sporadic speeds, but in an eerie and sinister unison that was nothing short of cultish. Eloise moved her hands to clap with the beat but fear looked to grab her tightly. It was like that moment of looking over the edge of a high building. The feeling of being completely safe, then suddenly fear pounces on all your nerve-endings and completely changes the perception of the situation.

The man was called Edwin, and he raised a hand that signalled at once for everyone to stop. Will, not paying attention, clapped again albeit with less enthusiasm, but still enough to turn heads, and see faces of disapproval and contempt.

Edwin did his best to smile over the blasphemous act, and Troy looked slightly pale like he might be held responsible for the slip. Nevertheless, the man took a second to glare before addressing the situation head on, and said, "We have our customs and ways, which to you might seem a little odd and peculiar, but whilst here we ask you obey them." His smile then fell instantly as he added, "We don't tolerate mocking, nor a total disregard to what we consider to be important rules. Enforcing our laws and punishing guests is not something we enjoy doing, but will if the need arises…"

Martin pulled a mock shocked face assuming it was their idea of humour, but as he looked around, he realised not one single person was smiling. In fact, they all once again looked serious. Very serious.

"…Right. Well, let's eat." With that there was the sudden cacophony of chatter as friend and neighbour talked like they'd not seen each other in weeks. The humdrum of voices with a splatter of different pitches.

The table furthest away from them got up, and in single file they took their bowls and disappeared through a doorway. The wave of people continued down the long first table, and only when the last person stood, did the first person of the next line begin the Mexican wave again.

"This is very organised," Jarrod noted quietly to Rick, who nodded in agreement.

"You need firm rules or a place like this wouldn't last. It's all well and good having those hippy-commune types of places but being free-spirited only goes so far. If you could do what you wanted to then people have a habit of turning mean."

They stood up as the line got down to them. The sea of talking now had the added sound of cutlery clanging and the odd laughter, so they no longer needed to lower their voices to a whisper. This was the happy hour.

"This isn't a hippy commune, then?"

Rick shook his head. "Far from it. This is what the country will eventually be. Money, wealth and greed will only go so far. We're already seeing the ugly nature of industrialisation, and how the planet is dying from it. There are small communes like this all over the country; and they are growing. Fast. But under the radar."

"Really?" They shuffled forward in the line. "I thought this was the only one?"

"Oh, no. The media stays away from them. They're scared to report it as they assume these places to be run by crazy militants harbouring weapons and building underground bunkers. Anything you do read will be propaganda, painting them as tinfoil-hat conspiracists hiding from little green men and such." He stopped to read Jarrod's face, and when satisfied, continued. "They have it backwards. These communes are not taking over the country. People, of their own accord and volition, are choosing to leave their lives and move here. The normality of towns and cities are therefore shrinking, and that's what they don't want to report for fear of speeding up the process."

"Why not let people do what they want?" But even as he said the words he knew, and Rick confirmed his thoughts out loud.

"Money and power. Popular society can only survive with money and power, neither are mutually exclusive. It's not just within this country, but the government is scared of how we'll look to the rest of the world. These radical changes are not something the Americans would tolerate; we'd be mocked and would become the handicapped cousin nobody will talk about."

Jarrod grinned. He couldn't help it. "*Really?*" It really seemed to be a huge revelation to him. How had it not slipped out yet? Surely the media could only supress so much, right?

Rick nodded. "Of course. How can we help them take over the world with no power? No money? No defence?"

The words sank in, and Jarrod wondered what the movement thought about defence. How would they counter being taken over?

The doorway swallowed them up as they saw a line of large pots, and were greeted by the smiles of those serving.

"Welcome!" A guy said smiling widely. "Great to have you here!" He ladled something soup-like into the bowl, the smell instantly told Jarrod how hungry he was, and talk of the failing world of industrialisation was lost momentarily.

"Thank you," Jarrod replied, as Rick just nodded.

Next a women handed them bread. She smiled, and looked a little unsure of them both. The bread looked great and was a welcomed accompaniment to the soup.

"Hi," she managed, holding Jarrod's gaze for a second, before turning to the next person.

"Is this a big shock to you?" Rick said suddenly as they headed back out the other door, and into the large hall again.

"Yes, and no… I mean. It's different from what I'm used to but it's structured. There's something comforting about that."

Rick grinned, unable to hold back his happiness, then leaned in as he admitted, "I'm not going back. I'm staying here."

"*Really?*" The repeated words he'd uttered half a dozen times since they spoke hung in the air. He was shocked at the words, although not completely surprised. It made perfect sense. "How?"

"You can, too, you know?" Rick dismissed the question of how he planned to do it. Jarrod had entertained the idea all afternoon but was he now seriously considering it, too?

He realised he was. Very much so.

They walked back to where they sat, a glass of something had been placed for each of them on the table.

"I'll think about it."

Rick winked, and nudged him playfully. "I thought you might. We're alike, mate. We don't have anything to keep us out there." Jarrod found he was chewing his lip, thinking about his life. A sad, and rather depressing montage flashed in his mind's eye. The only thing of remote interest was Paige. Her life was ultimately as sad as his and he fleetingly thought about going back to get her, too. To save her. But a wave of selfishness washed over him as he felt if he did they would be stuck with each other. They were friends, but now he'd opened Pandora's Box for more. He didn't want that, at least he didn't think he did, and knew it sounded bad. Really bad; but that was how he felt. They would be Sid & Nancy minus the drugs and fame. Or the Kurt & Courtney. Either way he could only see a relationship based upon a depressive downward spiral that would ultimately see one, or both of them, dead. For everything they thought they needed in each other they could be their own worst enemy. Dwelling in depression only served to keep them under - unable to look up and know happiness was there if you were only encouraged.

"What's up?" Rick pressed as the last of the others sat down and they began to eat.

"Nothing really. It's a big step… but you're right, there is nothing for me. Just Paige, I guess."

"You're not dating though, right?"

"No, but…" He didn't know what to say, and without realising it he pulled his phone out. He knew he had no service, but there was an unread WhatsApp message from earlier that morning.

"But what?"

It was from Paige.

"Nothing."

He clicked it open and saw it was a picture. Paige topless with a slightly embarrassed lopsided smile.

Because you never got to see them… xxx

It didn't change anything, a fact that, given the situation, made it even more sad. He wanted to thank her politely, which was never the correct response. He knew her. She wanted more. She was after an Emo-song romance. She wanted Gerald Way or Patrick Stamp to sing out through dark lyrics the pleasure and pain that entangled itself around her heart, kick the arse of a Hollywood shine, and instead building to a romantic tragedy penned by Shakespeare, and fuelled by Ritalin. A self-harm romance that dragged him by the neck down with her.

He kept the picture to himself, quickly clicked out of the app, and slipped his phone away. It was something he'd soon learn to live without. Perhaps one of the few guilty pleasures he'd struggle to adjust giving up.

He'd completely lost his train of thought, and as he looked back at Rick, he realised Rick was expecting more, so flashed a smile that still weighed him down with apprehension, and said, "I'm all in, mate."

"You won't regret it," Rick said, and looked pleased to have him on board, then set about dunking the bread into his soup.

Jarrod still had an endless string of questions but didn't want to come across as needy.

"And the elders? What are they like?" Jarrod knew Rick was hiding a lot. He knew more about these people than he was letting on to everyone else. It was complete bullshit that he'd stumbled upon this place. He'd planned it carefully and Jarrod's only concern was whether or not he'd be an accessory to actions that would be deemed illegal anywhere else but there.

"There's no David Koresh character here. Nobody thinks they're God, and certainly there is no one person having sex with everyone else, brainwashing them into thinking it's setting them free…"

"That's good. I don't much fancy having sex with any of them… I do have a question?"

"Shoot."

"How do you know so much about this place?"

At first Rick tried to hide the amusement, but half of his face was unable to contain his true feelings. "That's a conversation for another time, mate."

"I guess so," Jarrod agreed, and whilst he was desperate to know, he knew he had to let Rick tell him when he was comfortable.

"By the time I am ready to tell you, you'll already know and the answer will be irrelevant." Vague words twisted around to mean nothing.

Jarrod grabbed his spoon ready to dip into his soup but looked around at all of the strangers he'd just agreed to become part of, and as he took a bite of the meat that tasted like nothing he'd ever had before he wondered exactly how Rick fit into this picture.

He had so many questions. Like why were there not many children around? Would they keep recruiting to maintain numbers? Were people really so quick to give up their lives in order to join?

His eyes fell onto a couple who were playing with their food, and looking slightly out of place. The woman got up and disappeared, and the man placed down his cutlery in slight frustration, and was quick to excuse himself apologetically and go after her. The complexities of human beings meant that drama was more than capable of finding a home anywhere and there was nothing you could do about it. But this was the first crack Jarrod had seen in a place where everyone claimed it was paradise.

Apart from talk of a witch.

The Last Weekend

Chapter 12

Pale and scratched hands gripped onto trees, and faceless creatures hid among the shadows. Hearts beat with anticipation and they could hardly contain their excitement.

New blood had drifted into town and that spelt a feast of treats for every one of them.

Diligently, they waited a few minutes until after the bell had stopped ringing. The little village sheep all filed into the great hall – even the visitors. Nobody wanted to feel the wrath of the elders. The ones with stern faces and hidden evil for those that dared not to live by their rules.

It was a well-oiled plan that gave them at least thirty minutes to roam around freely with only the slim chance of being caught. The rewards were worth so much more than the risks. Forced to live by their own means, this was the only treat they had. Creature comforts became a distant memory as they lived day-to-day with only thoughts of survival at the forefront of their minds.

Last year a child had run out looking for something he'd left behind. His little legs pounded on the ground as he burst into the house and disrupted them. He barely screamed before they scooped him up and whisked him off into the woods. Pleading tears were useless to them. He was no more than an animal they'd caught. Empathy was never taught to them and the fight for survival was so much stronger.

They gave him to Her.

She was so happy with them.

So, so very happy.

He'd not been what they'd been searching for but still he brought them so much joy. That night they lived like kings!

However, that was a while back and they wanted to feel like that again. They swarmed into the building excited to see what the visitors had unknowingly brought them. They quickly, silently, and efficiently, split up into each room. Hungry hands rummaged through bags and pulled out anything that might be of benefit to them. Snack bars, books, medicines and condoms were all pocketed. The luxuries of modern day they didn't want to be without. Despite what *She* said, they needed these things.

One of them shrieked. An uncontrollable outburst that had them all running to him.

He stood over a bag and pointed to the clothes.

Mouths gasped and without thinking they stepped back.

"Put it all back," the rasping voice said. "We need to leave now!"

They'd never experienced this before. It worried them. They had to go back and tell her.

Prepare her.

Everything was about to change. It was a sign.

The second coming. Clothes, lots and lots of clothes, and they were all red.

Chapter 13

The drink sat waiting for them on the table was definitely alcoholic. It had a kick to it. No one had asked whether or not they wanted it, and luckily not one of them openly had a drinking problem, or objected to the fact. It was some type of moonshine, no doubt homebrewed in one of the larger buildings adjacent to the hall; a strange type of wine, but every now and again a woman would walk by and top up their glasses until they didn't know how much they'd consumed. She'd smile knowingly, happy to appear hospitable.

Jarrod's head was getting fuzzy. It was the drunken feeling he'd known before, and Rick hadn't stopped grinning throughout. Eloise now looked a lot better about things and was talking loudly, and shamelessly flirting with anyone who'd listen or pay her attention. She'd been embarrassed about her sweaty and dishevelled look when they first arrived at the hall, but the alcohol had her embracing it. Like most people, she'd freshened up in the toilets - a block situated at the back of the hall that was well-plumbed containing cubicles, sinks and even half a dozen showers – now without a care she spread love to anyone around her. She even glanced towards Jarrod half-expecting him to grab her by the hand and explore the darkness with her, but he looked away. He was overwhelmed with everything not too mention his unhealthy obsession with Keely. He'd never go off with Eloise when Keely was around.

Soon the plates were cleared, and the tables were moved back towards the walls, and some people disappeared to clean up. A motley crew of musicians appeared, made up mostly of acoustic guitarists, a drummer and a guy with an impressive long beard that made him appear wizard-like, swinging a fiddle before setting about it like a man possessed. Whether this was for their benefit, or something that happened daily, cheers still rang out and there was a general feeling of jubilation.

Without any encouragement – nor fear of indigestion – the locals were up and whooping, clapping hands and grabbing each other to dance. It proved that after the daily chores had been achieved the chains were cut and everyone was free to let their hair down and enjoy themselves. Evening entertainment was limited and it was clear the locals were incredibly social possibly blurring the lines between kinship and friendship.

Jarrod sat back with a smile that played upon his lips. He liked to see everyone having so much fun, it felt more of a community of people who had common goals and interests, rather than a few strong-minded and hugely influential people with powers of suggestion and persuasion. Trends and fashions appeared non-existent and people were just allowed to be people.

But the elders were noticeable in their absence. They clearly had other things that needed to be done.

Martin was walking around inviting himself into smaller circles, but Jarrod could see that people were wary of him. He was intrusive by nature whether or not he meant anything by it and these people, despite their basic appearance, were no fools. Eloise was talking to Noah, whilst twisting her hair flirtatiously, and periodically tugging the front of her vest down. Iain was in deep conversation with a man and woman about something that seemed very serious – Jarrod wondered whether he was boring them with equations or the hidden secrets behind statistical analysis. Dan was dancing like an embarrassing uncle at a wedding – his mind and body were miles apart in ambition and execution, and Will wasn't too many steps behind, grinning at a woman of a questionable age, possibly in her late teens. Di had just left with another unlit cigarette in her hand, Verity was nodding her head and talking to a woman with dirty-blonde hair, which just left Rick. He had slipped away a few minutes ago. He could be planting a bomb, or just as likely taking a shit, but he'd been careful to go without being seen.

"You're almost smiling," Keely said to Jarrod over the music. She got up and moved closer. Her hair was pulled back in a scruffy bun that suited her. She looked tired, the physicality of the day worn like a badge of honour, something they both shared.

He made a non-committal face, and nodded towards the centre of the room. "How can you not feel what they feel? It's like a wedding reception every night."

She agreed. "It's infectious, I grant you." She picked up her glass. "This stuff is great, by the way… but strong!"

He grinned. He was more than buzzing now. "And free!" He took a swig and glanced over to the corner of the room where he saw a woman staring at him. She was deep in the shadows and looked to be wearing a cloak. She pulled up the hood which completely hid her face, and vanished.

"What are you looking at?" Keely asked, not that she was interested. More to the point she was wondering why he wasn't paying her attention.

"What aren't I looking at?" he replied and turned back to her.

"I would say that is obvious. It's a shame you have no backbone. If you were more of a man then we could have a lot of fun." She winked but it was a beat too late. He assumed she was talking about her, but actually she could just as easily be talking about the other women around. There were a few but he wasn't here to grab one like he was a traveller looking for a wife; he was happy to take his time.

"The early bird catches the worm, but it's the second mouse that catches the cheese." He wasn't sure how much it fit what he was trying to say, but then he didn't truly know himself either.

"You seem more at home here…" She turned away glancing at one of the mounted skulls, then looked back at him knowingly. "I always thought you might."

"Maybe you do know what I want." Out of the office he felt ballsy. Deep in the heart of the countryside she couldn't do anything to him, and if he decided to stay then she was no longer his boss.

"You'd be surprised at what I know."

"Leave your door open," he said, and got up.

She went to say something. Maybe it was going to be suggestive, or perhaps words of vulnerability would escape from her mouth before she could stop them. Her bottom lip moved but she quickly clamped her mouth together, forced a smile, and walked towards the dancers determined to put on a show.

Jarrod's eyes followed her; he glanced back at everyone, turned and left the hall. He needed some fresh air, and his body was aching.

The silence outside engulfed him like an avalanche. A gentle breeze danced in the moonlight as the sun had finally disappeared. In the distance the odd person could be seen heading back to their house but most of the community were behind him, drinking and being merry.

He smelt the smoke first. He turned and saw Di shrug as if she knew he was going to scold her. He had no intention. Who was he to question another person's vices? He knew he was fucked up, and the mere thought had him feeling for the bottle of pills in his pocket.

"I know," she said, taking another drag that made the end of the cigarette glow, before tilting her head back and blowing the smoke away into the darkness. "I should give up, right?"

"Di, you do what you want. If you enjoy it, then continue. I'm not a preacher."

She half smiled, and looked down. "You could be. You've got a gentle way about you."

"You mean I get walked over?" Jarrod muttered, but she was already shaking her head.

"No, no. Honestly. You have kind eyes and you listen. Those are great traits. Don't lose them."

"I…" he went to argue, but was lost for words. He had no idea how to respond to compliments that were quick to say, but often soon forgotten.

She appeared amused by his stumbling tongue, took a final drag and flicked the butt as far away as she could, before glancing at him.

"Be careful, Jarrod," she said in a sage-like manner before glancing all around and making her way back inside. Before she fully disappeared, she stopped and said, "You're her bitch." Then the hall sucked her inside and he was suddenly alone.

Jarrod turned around again and looked as far as he could. Normally, for him, he could see the glow of a nearby town on the horizon but here it was dark. There was the odd flicker that might or might not have been from a candle in a window. Was that why everyone stayed together? The hall was filled with lights, a generator hummed far off and again made him question how the community could pay for the fuel to power it.

That's when he heard it.

A screeching howl. He dismissed it as best he could as a vixen, or some other animal. Except, he'd heard vixens in Thornhill, and the pitch was higher, and quicker. This was slightly deeper in its tone - and followed by what sounded like a low rumbling growl.

Jarrod looked around to see if anyone else was about, then suddenly felt alone. He thought about turning round and slipping back inside, but a voice broke the silence.

"Is everything alright?" Noah stood smiling at him. An old weathered man portraying wisdom and age. Skinny build, but ropey-muscles hidden under his shirt. The sleeves were rolled up and tattoos of an indeterminate design teased out.

"Er, yes. Yes. I was just… getting some fresh air…" He felt like a kid caught peeking through a changing room curtain, but soon calmed down. "It's a little overwhelming. In a good way, I might add."

Noah nodded and place a paternal hand on his shoulder. It squeezed him in what might've been a flex of power. "Yes, for a couple of nights people embrace it, but those that want to stay longer are often overwhelmed, *as you say*. They understand the transition and know the sacrifices." The words hung in the air knowingly, and Jarrod wondered whether Rick had mentioned their plans to anyone else. Noah acted like he was conducting part of an interview process.

"Transition? You're happy to take in new people?"

"Our minds are strange things. Yours knows of your intentions and you're wrestling with what you will miss if you stay. We're always happy to have new people! It's what we want. To continue to grow and expand the community. You'd be more than welcomed."

Jarrod quickly felt the need to add, "I've not made up my mind yet, but…"

Noah held up his hands with his palms showing. Strong and authoritarian. "There is no rush for a decision. This isn't a cult. You don't have to stay and you're free to go at any stage. Often when I look at a stranger, I can tell whether or not they will stay. I don't need to speak to them."

"What do you think with me?" He felt embarrassed to ask.

"We both know." He sighed. "This community sticks together. It's a really great place to live. If, of course, you can let go of your old life."

Jarrod chewed his lip slightly. He looked at the woods beyond the houses. They were dark. So very, very dark.

“And your land ends behind the woods?” he questioned.

There was a slight slip of Noah’s friendly mask as he replied. “Never go beyond the woods, Jarrod. It’s not safe. In fact, don’t even enter the woods.”

“What d’you mean? What’s there?”

Noah turned towards the track they’d followed when coming into the village. “Out there is fine. It leads back to your vehicles and then into civilisation□” He turned the other way and pointed. “But out there it’s different. Look, Jarrod, it’s not just us who are different around here. Beyond those trees… well, everyone here knows to stay away. It’s beyond dangerous.”

“And the colour red? Why is that so important?”

Noah held his gaze for a few beats looking deep into his eyes. It was like he wanted to tell him everything, but he also wanted to remain vague. “If you remain here, everything will become clear.” Rick had pretty much said the same.

“Fair enough.”

“Anyway, I’ll see you later, Jarrod. Or tomorrow if you’re turning in for the night.”

“I don’t know what I’m doing,” Jarrod said. He held up his hand and walked away, heading towards their house.

As he got closer he felt eyes on him. He whipped his head around but nobody was there. His eyes were more used to the darkness but all around were pockets he could not see, but he could feel something.

Eyes on him. It could’ve been his mind. The lack of pills or his anxiety of the future, but at that point in time he thought something out there was sizing him up. Wondering whether or not he’d live.

He opened the door to their house and slowly made his way down the hallway. It was quiet as he made his way up the first set of stairs. From there he turned and walked down towards the other staircase, all the while looking into the rooms.

He was alone. That surprised him. He didn't expect to be the first person to come back to the house. He felt disappointed in himself.

As he reached the top of the second staircase, his legs felt heavy with the physical work he'd performed, and he slipped into his room. His bag was on the bed but the zip only half closed. His head whipped around as he expected to see some poor soul stood there holding his pants or a can of shaving gel like some sort of consolation prize.

He was alone – but felt like he was being watched.

He walked to the window and caught a glimpse of a figure entering a building.

Rick.

The man with a plan. A fish out of water in the corporate hellhole, but who now unbeknownst to the others had slowly slipped into complete control. Here he was no longer the quiet guy that people took the mick out of. He knew a lot more than he was letting on. Did he trust him? He pondered, but the truth of the matter was: did he trust anyone?

He pulled out his phone, slipped his finger over the front and brought up the picture of Paige. He sat back on his bed looking at her.

Really looking at her.

The best friend with whom he'd fallen over the line of friendship. Impaling her with his penis before she finished him off. He wasn't sure he regretted it. He couldn't take his eyes off of her tits, and wondered whether he was a pervert or just a man. He'd never seen them, and he was resigned to never touching them with his hands. Life was all about sacrifices. The battery life was draining from his phone and soon it would be dead. He placed it down on the bedside table. With no signal it was now just a masturbatory tool.

It had been a long day. He stripped off his T-shirt and shorts, balled up his socks and slipped under the covers. He needed a shower but he'd wait until the morning for that experience.

Sleep grabbed him before he could even relax, and his dreams were fitful. He didn't hear the others slowly slipping back in one by one. Drunken stumbles and suppressed giggling.

He also didn't know what else was going on in and around the little village.

Or the breath from the witch that sniffed him as he slept.

Chapter 14

Eloise had danced and drunk the pain in her muscles away. At least that's how she saw it. She'd rebuffed the drunken advances of Will as he had slid up to her on the dancefloor. He thought he was so cool that she'd be up for anything. The feeling of an erection against her had put her off. It was about time she raised her expectations on a night out.

"Shall we go somewhere a little quieter?" he'd said and allowed his hand to rest uninvited upon her hips. She wasn't feeling it. She wasn't feeling him. He wanted nothing more from her than a vessel to ejaculate into. She knew him. He was always quick to spout out his weekend conquests like it might be impressive, and now he was all puppy-dog-eyed and panting at her like she'd so easily succumb to his charms, whisk him back to her room and open her vagina to welcome him in.

"Nah, I'm okay here," she said and brushed his hand away. He'd taken it badly. She'd looked around and there were only a couple of nubile females and chances were, they'd be all hairy and smelly down below. It only reinforced her decision to keep him at arm's length.

"You sure?" he frowned, like perhaps she'd made a mistake and hadn't realised he was offering her quick, and unfulfilling sex.

She nodded and moved closer to a local guy who looked worried and excused himself immediately from the situation. She felt gutted and when she looked back, Will was disappearing back to the table in a strop. She looked for Jarrod. She was a little wary of them getting together in front of everyone, but for all his weirdness, they had a brief sexual chemistry, even if neither of them wanted to admit it. He thought she was an airhead, and she thought he was a depressive prick but after a few drinks… but it wasn't going to happen.

Soon, everyone else had dispersed. Di was probably out chain-smoking, and she'd not seen Rick or Jarrod for a while now. Verity had muttered something about her phone before slipping away. The last time she'd seen Iain he was almost falling asleep and she assumed he'd managed to take himself back to the house. Keely was sat with her resting bitch-face on and nursing the remaining drops of her drink, Dan was chatting to someone but clearly making his way out with Martin close behind.

Things were slowing down. Even the music's tempo suggested it was almost time to call it a night. A couple of the band had gone and the ones remaining looked more like a group of friends having a jam rather than a well-oiled musical machine entertaining the masses as they had been earlier.

A few women in their twenties could be seen walking around and clearing away, and had this been back in Thornhill the lights would all be on full, singletons would be making a last-ditch effort to find a shag like a desperate game of musical chairs, a fight would be spilling out into the street which amounted to a few poorly executed roundhouse punches that missed their intended target, and then some wrestling on the floor whilst girlfriends screamed and worriedly called the fools names, and taxis would be queued up in an effort to transport the drunk back to their places of residence without receiving abuse or the contents of their passengers' stomachs, or other bodily fluids, left behind.

Eloise's eyes were sore and she rubbed them a couple of times before realising she would be lonely tonight. She sighed and looked all around for possible suiters, but there seemed little to no interest. It was another reason she wasn't taking to this place. The only offer she'd had was from a male-slut she already knew.

With disappointment she walked towards the doors, and out into the moonlight. At first the lack of light slowed her down. Voices could be heard from various pockets of the village, and she could make out the flicker of candles. The houses did have electricity, but it seemed they still preferred the dim, and more subtle light from candles.

She looked over to her own temporary residence and saw there was the slight glow of light from the second floor. With some resignation, she walked towards it.

She stumbled through the door and past the lounge and kitchen area. She walked further down the hall, past a door, ajar and with light from a small lamp seeping out.

It was Martin's room.

She stopped and looked in. He stood without a shirt on and was slowly stepping out of his trousers. He was in better shape than she expected, with a tattoo of an eagle on his shoulder.

She took a deep breath. Something she couldn't explain came over her. She pulled off her vest and slipped into the room.

"You started without me," she whispered, startling Martin, who turned and grabbed his chest.

"Eloise," he said in relief. "I wasn't expecting..." His eyes dropped down to her bra, as Eloise swiftly unclipped it and whipped it off, her enhanced breasts dropped slightly with gravity.

"I know," she said and walked towards him. For the first time Martin was lost for words. He had no idea what to say. He stood paralysed in nothing but his boxer shorts as she glided towards him. Her shorts now undone and sliding down her generous thighs. There was a twinkle from the diamond in her pierced belly-button.

"Look, Eloise," he began but his words were lost as their mouths came together. Her hand grabbed gently at his crotch, and she was pleased to feel his hand on her bare arse.

They remained locked as one for a few glorious seconds.

He pulled away. "I can't," he said, the disappointment evident on his face as shadows danced all around.

"No one will know," she said determined, her hand slipping inside his waistband and grabbing him. Half-heartedly he stepped back, his defensive hands touched breasts and he tried hard not to cup them.

"*I will*," he managed, as she stepped forward eating up whatever ground he made. "*I*□"

"You want to, and I want to," she said, looking at him through hooded eyes. She took a step closer again.

"But it doesn't mean we should," he said, and this time there was more determination in his voice. He cleared his throat and then pointed towards the door. "Come on. You have to leave. We'll pretend this never happened, okay?"

She stopped still and looked at him like he'd just struck her hard across the face. "Martin?" she said, her fight now seeping out. "You can't do this? I'm offering this to you."

"Eloise, I'm going to have to insist you put your clothes back on and leave."

"But□"

"Now!" he hissed, and in the candlelight he suddenly looked evil. He was overwhelmed with morals and frustration. What his body wanted, his head and heart didn't.

Eloise's face twisted in anger as she stomped into her shorts and roughly pulled on her vest. "I can't believe this," she fumed and left his room. She was mortified at being pushed away, and wandered left towards the staircase, her thoughts confused, and tears welled up in her eyes. Why was she so stupid? She knew she was needy, and alcohol only exacerbated the feeling. It wasn't like she had ever really had a crush on Martin. He was a fit guy for his age but nothing special especially in comparison to all of the guys in the office. So why did she just throw herself at him?

She ran as quickly and carefully up the stairs as she could. She wiped a tear away as she slipped into the room. There was a mound in the bed and a smell of stale cigarettes where Di had already turned in for the night. Glancing over, Verity was also asleep and gently snoring away. Nobody moved as Eloise grabbed her large pink suitcase, stuffed her bra inside, zipped it up and left the room. She didn't have a plan, she just wanted to get back to Thornhill as quickly as possible.

There was no way she could face Martin in the morning. He would be only too pleased to tell everyone what she'd done. He'd leave out the part of him fondling her arse and kissing her back though.

She looked around the room one last time and left. She walked as quietly as she could back down the stairs and along the corridor. She didn't even steal a peak into Martin's room, but quickened her pace and found herself out of the house and headed off purposefully to nowhere. As she walked round the houses, the darkness swallowing her up and with only the drive of embarrassment she wandered towards the woods.

Except her bearings were all wrong. She missed the path leading to the woods near the church, and instead had somehow wandered in a circle back in the direction she'd started as her mind replayed the mortifying scene again. She was now stepping into the forbidden woods.

There was movement to her right but at first she dismissed it. A dark shape that floated; hovering around and causing a breeze to suddenly spring up.

A thick fog materialised from nowhere, and as she went further into the woods the path became harder to follow, nothing was familiar and before she knew it, had disappeared completely.

Branches snapped and away in the distance there was a howl. She glanced up at movement. Something red darted between the trees.

Don't wear red, they had been warned.

She stopped dead in her tracks and turned full circle. She felt stupid. She was the woman in movies she despised. Blonde hair, jiggling boobs, helpless and running from safety into danger. She gritted her teeth, and whilst her heart was now beating harder and faster, she gulped and clenched her fists. She refused to give up.

And pulling a large cumbersome suitcase was really beginning to annoy her!

She thought for a fleeting moment about going back. She thought she remembered the way, but everything suddenly looked the same and she started to second guess herself. The fog reduced her visibility, and she had no idea whether she was heading back to the commune, or deeper into the woods.

A loud crack of a branch from behind spun her around. Another whoosh of red almost bright in the darkness.

A sudden rustling to the side whipped her head towards the sound. She wanted to run but felt rooted to the spot. She moved one foot in front of the other inch by careful inch. Her suitcase caught on branches, and she tried to heft it up just as she heard something that sounded like a growl.

She spun round once more, in time to see the grinning face of an old woman, clad completely in red.

"*A gift*," she cackled. Eloise went to scream but was struck over the back of the head.

Everything went black. Her body folded as it hit the ground hard. The night snatched away the sound of the old woman laughing in delight.

The Last Weekend

Chapter 15

Star looked around the room of her home, the place she'd been so happy with up until her son had been stolen from her. Now, everywhere she turned she was faced not with what she had, but what she'd lost. She couldn't carry on. She loved Leo with all her heart but she had to have her son back.

"Are you sure about this?" he said walking in with a backpack on – the very one he'd turned up with all those many years ago. "I can go on my own."

She shook her head. She didn't want to hear it. "We've spoken about it," she snapped, her voice dripping with malice. "I've been waiting for news of my son, and I refuse to do the same for you, too. We need to do something about it. We have to try." *My son.* Like the child wasn't his, too. He hated how she isolated herself with grief and failed to understand how much he was hurting too.

He held his hands up in defence, then pulled her into his arms. "I know. It's just… I don't know, maybe on my own I can sneak around…"

She cut him off. "You don't know what's out there any more than I do! Let's face this together – the way we always have done." She was right of course. They were a team; always had been. Ten years ago, when she'd been Claire working as an Admin Clerk, they'd made the decision to leave friends and family behind to escape normality and come out here. Her mum had been angry. Crockery-throwing angry. Red-eyed-evil-spitting-when-she-talked angry. All it had done was push them farther away, and more quickly. Her dad just ignored them and to Star that had been worse. She'd been a daddy's girl. She idolised him. She'd explained to her parents this wasn't forever. They weren't leaving the planet. Behind those words she'd believed it. She assumed they'd settle in and each season would leave and stay with her parents.

But her mum thought she was running off to a cult with Benny in tow, and Leo was the instigator. She warned her how he would shack up with a harem of women and pimp her out to every cock available. They both struck with words they could never take back. The damage of these was such that when they left, they had no intention of dropping breadcrumbs, nor ever retracing their steps.

The village had welcomed them with open arms. They were fully accepted by strangers who needed very little in return. At first, Star admitted to feeling like the bubble would burst at any moment. They'd be pulled in, accepted and imbedded into the daily life before being told their fate. Except that never happened. It was like going away with friends, until the friends became family.

But now their feelings had changed. Not that they blamed the elders, but it wasn't *their* sons who were being taken in the night. Did they not see the threat towards their community? How could they build when the youngsters were being taken? They were the future.

Within her distraught feelings of loss, she couldn't understand the elders' hippy mentality. There was a time to hug and keep the peace but there was also a time when you had to fight. Your children are the single thing you should always fight for, no matter what.

Leo slid his arms around her waist and kissed her neck. It was a surprising show of affection from him. He'd never been one to kiss and cuddle, not after the initial honeymoon-period of their relationship. They'd tried a few things – no she'd tried a few things - to spice up their alone times, and he'd dismissed most of them. Then their son came along and that was all Leo had ever wanted. Since then, they'd held hands and cuddled, but since arriving at the village the sex had been a bi-annual duty void of passion.

"Let's get going," he whispered in her ear which seemed more intimate than it should. She nodded, and they broke free from their embrace.

"I love you," he said, to her as he grabbed her hand. "I know I don't say it enough." He brushed her cheek and gave her a quick kiss on the lips.

She was an emotional wreck and that only sent her over the edge. "I know you do," she replied. "I love you, too."

They kissed. Hard and passionate, the way they tried bi-annually before each carefully orchestrated sexual encounter. This time, they pulled away and walked from their house hand in hand breaking all the rules as they headed out to the forbidden woods.

Behind them, in the distance Noah stood and sighed. He hated rule breakers, and whilst he understood the yearning in their hearts, he couldn't overlook the danger they were bringing towards the village. If they found their boy – *and that was a big if* – all they would bring back would be evil.

He turned and walked away shaking his head.

Star squeezed Leo's hand, squeezing so tight it hurt, as the darkness swallowed them up. The trees bent down towards them and ahead the paths changed before their very eyes. The atmosphere changed and a thick fog coalesced along the foliage in front of them. With each step it got thicker and they struggled to see in front of them.

"Mum-my!" a voice called out. It was Benny. They'd recognise it anywhere.

"Benny?" Star stopped still and they both turned around.

"Mum-my!" The sound echoed in another direction. Whipped up by the breeze like it was a single note dancing just out of reach. Teasing them and wrenching their hearts all at once.

"Benny!" Star called and set off running as fast as the lack of visibility would allow. Leo followed calling to her with a little more trepidation.

"Star, wait!" He knew of the rumours about the witch. She fucked with your mind and distorted reality.

"Mum-my!" The sound danced, echoing off the trunks of the trees, disorientating them and making it hard to follow.

"Benny!" she called again, as Leo reached out to her.

"Star, don't be fooled."

She looked at him like he'd called her a bitch. She wanted to smash him in the face. He didn't know, did he? A man can never know what it's like to lose their child!

"Mum-my! Help me!" The sound seemed to move. The pitch of it drawn out in a creepy way. But she had to believe in it, didn't she? Without hope what else was there?

"You heard that!" she spat out with contempt in a tone she'd not used with her husband in a long time. She was desperate and swinging out at anything that would keep her from her son.

He held up his hands defensively. He knew she'd never listen to him whilst she could hear the voice. He had to admit, he'd heard it too, but a child would remain still, wouldn't they? Or come towards its mother's voice. Not move away each time they felt closer?

"Where are you!" she shouted into the night and took off once again. She was zig-zagging but ultimately heading deeper into the unknown. Leo looked back and could no longer see the safety of the break in the trees. They were in deep - far, far too deep.

"Help me, Mummy…" the voice sounded desperate but there was something slightly autotune about it. Star whipped her head around. Leo didn't like it. He turned to his wife struggling with words that would not anger her.

"Mum-my!" The voice finished with a sob and Star took off like a sprinter hearing the start-gun. She pumped her legs and Leo had to do his best just to keep her in sight.

"Star, wait!" he called. "Claire!" In desperation he called the name he first knew her to be. Trees now blurred to the sides of him. It was getting harder to see.

The fog was now so thick they could no longer run. They were confused, their sense of direction all but gone.

Star had slowed down to walking pace, and he pushed on to catch up with her.

Then they saw something more than trees and bushes. It was a small shed. As they got closer more sheds appeared all in a circle. The fog had lifted to show a break in the trees beyond the small structures. They could clearly see flat ground devoid of trees. In the distance was a large and elaborate house. Fantastical, it appeared like the portal to another world. Domineering and dripping with gothic architecture and well-maintained grounds running from it. For a moment they forgot why they were there.

"Help me!" the voice came from inside the shed nearest them. Leo rushed to the door but a huge padlock taunted him. He reached into his backpack and removed the metal bar – his only weapon. He wedged it between the lock and the metal bolted to the shed and with a huge throat-racking war-cry he slammed the bar. There was a crack and he fell to the floor.

But the lock was broken.

Leo got up as Star pulled open the door.

Benny sat shivering on the floor hugging his knees. When he saw his parents, he got up and ran to them.

"Benny!" Star scooped him up and covered him with kisses. Leo was soon there too, embracing the two most important people in the world to him.

Then there was movement.

A small figure appeared.

The little girl called Rosie who'd been taken the night before.

"Will you take me home, too?" she pleaded as if this would ever be in doubt.

"Of course, we will, sweety," Star said, holding out an arm for her come too.

"Can we find our way out?" Leo worried in a whisper to his wife.

"We have to."

"Don't worry, Mummy," Benny said. "I know the way."

They were dubious, but walked away from the shed and refused to look back at the house. Benny and Rosie held hands and skipped ahead whilst Star and Leo followed. The kids showed their bravery as they hummed and giggled together like it was one big game.

The fog reappeared but this time it seemed to part, guiding them back.

At one stage Leo thought he heard the chitter-chatter of whispers behind him and when he looked he thought he could see two large, red eyes. He kept it to himself and quickened his pace, hoping never to return to the woods again.

They couldn't explain the relief as the break in the trees appeared and spat them out into the field that eventually led them back to the village. Outside the woods the night was clear and they broke into a jog to get back to the safety of their home.

Through all of his feelings Leo felt anger. Had he listened to them then his son would still be locked in the shed. Tomorrow he'd ask questions of them, but now he had a little girl to return to her parents.

Tomorrow was another day.

Tomorrow things would get worse.

Chapter 16

Jarrod felt her over him even though the night was black. Movement in the room and the outline of a woman floating. He closed his eyes again not quite conscious and assumed he was dreaming. Fear paralysed him.

"Jar-rod! Jar-rod!" the elderly voice sung out to him. Her sour breath tickled his face. A strange moaning sound could be heard. Leather fingers with sharp nails scratched him. Cloth tickled him. More movement swirled around his head. He opened his eyes and saw an old woman. He screamed and bolted up right.

Then a scream from outside whipped Jarrod's head towards the window. Maybe it was more like a shriek. He was up and out of bed before he remembered where he was. Flashes of an old woman had him looking around the room before he eventually looked out at the village. Quiet and still.

A sting on his chest had his fingers exploring a raised line. A long claw-like scratch he couldn't explain.

Standing at the window in just his underwear a breeze flowed refreshingly around him from a night that remained warm. Everything was still but there was an eeriness about it. He wasn't used to it being so quiet. He thought he saw something red darting in the distance, but he couldn't be sure. He wondered whether he dreamt it. Exhaustion could well force the brain to places it wasn't used to. His mind of late was no longer his own. His pill intake had become erratic as he overdosed then went extended periods without any. Who knew how it was affecting him psychologically.

"You heard it, too?" a voice said from behind him, making him jump. He felt like a dick and wanted to punch himself in the head for having such pathetic reactions.

He looked back and saw the silhouette of Keely. He thought she was naked, but as she stepped into the room, he saw she was wearing only a vest and knickers. An incredibly sexy look on a forty-something-year-old. A tight top, and small knickers that exposed her hips. Both red. Very red. He couldn't take his eyes off her.

"Stare much?" she grinned enjoying the power she had over him. She knew what she looked like. She'd been deliberate in choosing the outfit, not to mention the gym was her second home.

"Sorry," he said, looking first at his feet and then turning around towards the window. He was a pathetic specimen of a man. No, scratch that. He was acting like an adolescent boy staring at a woman for the first time.

"I'm joking," she said, and slowly walked towards him. He tried to remain dismissive towards her advances, acting as if whatever was outside the window was more interesting. Keely was a woman who had to control every situation. One of her arms slid uninvited around his body, as she whispered, "Have you been in my room?" He thought about the old woman.

"Your room? No. Why?" he said, swallowing and trying to remain calm.

"Something of mine is missing." Her feather-like touch was arousing. No matter what he tried to think of, his nether regions were side-tracked. Hypnotised by the tickle of her nails.

"Missing?" He was struggling to keep it together. She did it to him, and he hated the way he felt. Most people just hated their boss and that was that. He did, too, to a point. Other times he wanted to fuck hard in every which way imaginable. He couldn't explain it.

She nodded, "Something intimate." Her words were formed and hit his ears but his brain couldn't function properly. She wanted him to know but didn't want to outright tell him.

"I've not been in your room." He took a deep breath - determined to finally be a man about this situation. One that could slip from his grasp and end up being replayed over and over in his mind whilst he rhythmically pounded his hand and fantasised about what might've been.

His eyes took her in. He'd never seen this much of her before. God had given him balls and it was about time he used them.

"*You're not supposed to wear red,*" he said in a shouty-whispered voice. He was now Clint Eastwood, and she some barmaid wench from a cowboy film saloon. Sometimes you had to be someone else to be brave.

"You're not supposed to look at your boss in her underwear, and yet here you are." Her voice matched his minus the nerves.

He gulped. "And you're not supposed to slip into your employee's room wearing next to nothing in forbidden colours."

She grinned. "Touché. But to answer your original question: D'you really think they'll be looking at my underwear?"

He shrugged. "It's just that□"

"Look, if you want to take them from me then do it." He went to say something, a mix of agreement and apology when she cut him off before he made a fool of himself.

"I spoke to someone tonight who warned me away… told me there was a witch who walks around at night and has a particular taste for outsiders." He felt an icy chill and tried to convince himself he'd been dreaming. Her hand slipped from his shoulder and a finger traced the scratch she had found.

"Really? They were probably trying to scare you," he managed, but this time gritted his teeth. He really wanted her to stop leading him around by his penis.

"And missing children. That child earlier that spoke about the kid gone missing? That's not the first; in fact many have been taken from their beds at night. You hear that?"

"No," he said, feeling vulnerable that her hand was still on his chest and fingering the scratch. He was more thinking about the situation they found themselves in, rather than the hearsay.

"I'm sorry," she whispered, stepping round. "It's all lies, right? They're feeding our fears and expectations. Maybe it's all part of the experience. Keep us on the edge. Add a bit of excitement…" She let the last part hang in the air.

His mind began to spin and he felt light-headed.

She removed her vest and looked at him seductively. He swallowed hard, moving his hands together. Unsure where to put them.

"Jarrod!" Her voice was stern.

He blinked. Her vest was back on again but she grinned at him. "Focus, Jarrod."

"Sorry," he bowed his head, hating how all he ever did was apologise.

"Don't," she said. "Maybe tomorrow…" she teased but didn't elaborate. Instead, she winked, turned around and walked slowly out of the room, giving him a wonderful view of her arse that for the most part hid her thong.

He was left open-mouthed and fuelled with fantasies, and completely unsure why she was doing what she was doing. She was doing enough to keep him hopeful, but was he cynical to wonder why?

He turned back to his bed, and took a couple of steps ready to get back under the sheets when he heard a sound from behind him. Footsteps were retreating quickly down the stairs. A voyeur watching the scene unfold from the darkness? He had to wonder who had snuck up and what it was they wanted.

Chapter 17

Verity was only half conscious that she was turning over and over in bed. She was used to her king-size bed and woe-betide her long-suffering husband should he dare to move anywhere near her side of the bed. She favoured stretching out in a star-shape manner and acted like she'd been molested should he accidentally touch her.

The bed here was a single, and it made her feel huge. Each time she turned over she pulled the covers half off, really annoying her. Sleep, and being in a familiar place at night, was hugely important to her. She'd hated sleepovers as a child for the exact same reason and she couldn't even consider camping. The thought of lying on the ground to sleep was almost barbaric.

A dream had woken her. She was breathing hard and sweating. She'd imagined a figure in the room leaning over and whispering over and over, "Get out! Get out! Get out!"

She remembered it pawing at her. An old lady dressed in a red robe like she was *Little Red Riding Hood*, all grown up and heavily influenced by the wolf. Her faced was twisted, wrinkled and frightening.

She was facing Di whose eyes were still shut, her covers down showing her baggy T-shirt with a cigarette brand on the front. It made Verity chuckle if nothing else.

That's when she realised there was movement the other side of her. The side with the window and nothing else.

She turned over in a painfully slow roll and screamed.

Iain stood there dressed in plain pyjamas, facing the corner and it appeared he was masturbating.

"Iain!" she shouted, but he continued.

Di stirred, and perched up on an elbow before realising what was happening.

"Iain!" Verity said again.

"Oh, Jesus H Christ!" Di said but continued to watch.

There was a thud and then heavy footsteps could be heard. Dan walked through the already open door.

"What's w□" he saw immediately. "Iain! Wake up, mate." Iain appeared to be sleep-wanking.

"Look away, ladies," Dan hissed, but neither were complying.

"If he wants to come in here and play with his thingy, he deserves all the humiliation he gets!" Di said, grinning.

"He's a pervert!" she said, not realising the hypocrisy of her words as she watched Dan turn Iain round.

"Iain! Wake up!" Dan said louder this time.

Iain's eyes shot open. He looked at Dan and then at the women. "What are you doing to me?" He was alarmed, assuming it was some sort of hazing.

"I found you like this!" Dan said, carefully covering Iain's cock with the loose trousers.

"Kids!" Verity said, except this time there was actual humour there.

"Night ladies," Dan said, ushering an embarrassed Iain out of the room. Then Dan stopped. "Where's Eloise?"

"She's probably fucking some hippy," Di said in an uncaring manner.

"Probably," Verity agreed, although neither of them could remember whether or not she'd been there when they'd gone to bed the night before.

"Night, lads!" Di was acting like she'd enjoyed herself. In fact, for her, it had been the highlight of her stay so far.

"I need a fag," she said as she grabbed her lighter and another pack.

"Really?"

"It helps relax me," she said, as Verity lay back down and turned her back to her.

Di slipped on her shoes, and carefully walked out and down the stairs. The place was silent as she left the house and sat on a wooden bench.

As she lit her fag and took a drag she thought it had been a nice change to come there, but she was already missing home. You never knew what you had until it was gone. Someone had said something like that. Or was it a Joni Mitchell lyric, she couldn't be sure.

It was quite peaceful sat there looking out towards the large stage, and she wondered what the community had in store for them that day.

In the distance she saw figures walking from the forbidden woods. She couldn't tell how many there were but it looked like at least one of them could've been a child. It was odd that having been told to stay away from there she should see people clearly breaking the rules.

She saw more movement a bit closer. It was Noah, lurking in the shadows, his limp was familiar as the darkness swallowed him up.

That confirms it, she thought. *This place is fucking strange.* She couldn't wait to get back to her flat and relax of an evening with Love Island.

When she heard the howl, she flicked her fag-end away and scooted back into the house, suddenly wanting to be around others.

Chapter 18

The shower had been lukewarm at best. That being said, Jarrod thought it was going to be cold, so any type of warmth was welcomed. His chest stung from the cuts that had appeared, and it did prompt a few of questions. There was so much Jarrod didn't know about Woden and how it was run - their energy sources and plumbing for a start. He assumed they liked to preach about sustainability and off-grid living whilst sneaking creature-comforts wherever possible in a clandestine manner. Maybe it would spoil the illusion and stop new joiners buying into their ideology.

On his way back to the house, he was aware of a commotion. Lots of shouting and whooping. He wondered whether it was some daily hippie reaction to the sun and mother-nature. He pictured naked, wobbly bodies, raising aloft happy-hands to the gods. However, that wasn't the case.

Ahead of him he saw Rick standing at the door, a mug in his hand.

"Coffee?" Rick asked, nodding towards his drink.

"That would be great." Rick waited for him to come close. He stood in a plain T-shirt that fit his skinny frame perfectly. It was probably for a teenager.

"Good night?" Rick said, flashing a smile that said a lot more, then turned away as Jarrod followed him into the house.

"Not bad." Had it been Rick watching from outside his room? They were both being vague.

"Uh-huh," Rick muttered grabbing a mug and putting it next to a large tin. "Keely wasn't sleep walking then?" Another loaded question.

"No," he replied, and went to say something mildly amusing but gave up. He was caught between spilling the beans and joking around, then suddenly the moment had passed.

A noise from outside the door interrupted them. Martin walked in, a fake smile plastered over his face. He looked tired but was doing his best to hide it.

"Here they are!" His words were overly enthusiastic, and they both knew some type of boastful story was about to tumble out of his mouth. "The two young bucks!"

"Hi," Jarrod replied politely. Rick was never going to answer him and Jarrod couldn't allow them both of them to appear rude.

"You know," Martin said, his eyes drifting off to a land of make-believe. "I don't know about you boys, but I feel good from all that work yesterday. It really makes you feel alive, doesn't it? It takes me back to my time in Africa. Of course, back then the heat was much more unforgiving, and we were surrounded by death and disease. But you work through it. Making a difference gives you the perspective required to push on. You go to bed sweating, unable to move, and often being eaten alive by insects, and you wake up aching like you have the flu… but you push on…" he paused for effect but left his words trailing as if emotion was taking over. "You have to. Some of the nicest locals I met back then never made it."

Rick stole a glance at Jarrod with a subtle raise of an eyebrow as Martin looked far off through the window and into another continent buried deep in his mind. One that he probably saw on some documentary and injected himself into. Then he snapped back to reality.

"I guess that's why I'm an early riser now. If you wake up an hour earlier each day then you can offer an hour of good to someone else, right?" Jarrod thought *the hour was better spent staying away from people with your bullshit*, and Rick shrugged, then looked at Jarrod. "He just washed his balls, so I guess that helps someone?" Martin looked lost for words his mouth dropped open slightly before he forced out an awkward chuckle.

"Haha! You two are funny!"

There was a shuffling sound and Di appeared, looking more dishevelled than any one of them had ever seen before. Her hair wasn't playing nicely with her, though it looked like she'd tried to force a brush through it, instead of it being carefully straightened to perfection. The lack of electrical sockets had forced her to pull it into a fierce ponytail. That might've helped iron out her skin a bit, but mostly it just emphasised that her life was an Oasis song of 'Cigarettes & Alcohol', and it would only get worse.

"Di! How d'you sleep," Martin asked, although it was easy to see. She now had the eyes of a twelve-round boxer with weak defence, and skin so dehydrated she now resembled the living dead. She wore a baggy, shapeless blue T-shirt. Darkened teeth flashed out from the gape-mouthed yawn.

"Not well," she managed. Then suddenly added, "Dunno where princess is. She either expertly made her bed or she never slept in it."

"Eloise?" Martin said, and guilt slipped his happy mask. "What makes you say that?"

She shrugged. "Her stuff's gone. I've not seen her since last night."

"When she came to bed?" Martin pressed, but Di shook her head.

"No, the last time I saw her she was trying to grope some local in the hall. Typical Eloise."

Martin looked at the lads, then at Di. "No one's seen her since? Rick? Jarrod?"

The lads shook their heads, too. Jarrod wasn't sure when he'd seen her last, probably about the same time as Di, he figured. They'd all been caught up in their own worlds.

There was a commotion in the hallway as Will and Dan bumbled in with Iain in tow. They were the picture of a *stag-do the-morning-after-the-night-before*. Hyped up with hysteria and testosterone. Not Iain. He looked like the weird cousin who they'd been forced to invite.

"Aye-aye!" Will said loudly, as everyone turned to look at them.

"Have any of you seen, Eloise?" Martin immediately asked them.

"Nope," Dan said. "She looked like she was trying to give some local lad a handjob. That was last night."

"Was she?" Di said, and despite what she normally said sounded shocked.

Dan shrugged. "Well, not quite but as good as."

"What does that even mean?" Di muttered and looked around at the other faces hoping someone would enlighten her. In her day, you knew whether or not you were holding a guy's cock, there was no question about it. Nowadays, it appeared all body parts, and objects easily slipped into any number of body cavities, leading to no end of unexpected outcomes from the open minds of the sexually adventurous.

Then Di began to grin. "The only handjob I saw was Iain, giving it to himself!"

"What?!" Rick and Jarrod both said but at slightly different times.

Dan was still being over-protective of him. "It was a misunderstanding. He was asleep."

Martin slapped his own forehead. "Really?"

Di was as animated as when it had happened. "Yeah, he was facing the corner in our room like it was Blair Witch, but beating his todger for all he was worth!"

"What's happening?" Keely asked walking in, and a few steps behind ambled Verity. She'd come from outside rather than from her room. She glanced around but gave nothing away. Jarrod felt generally awkward.

"Eloise," Martin said. "No one has seen her since last night. Apparently, she never slept in her bed."

"There's no *apparently*," Di jumped in. "She didn't. It's as simple as that. Where's Iain?"

Keely shook her head. "That girl is a liability." She looked around at everyone as she strapped her authoritative face on. "Anyone know where she might be? She mention anything to anyone?" Just like that, Iain's incident was dropped.

Guilty faces looked back at her, but nobody admitted to anything.

"Anyone?" Keely pressed, and this time she looked at Jarrod, as if she was aware he'd been known to have sex with her.

"She probably tried it on with someone and they told her to piss off," Will said rolling his eyes, and not admitting he'd done his very best to get into her knickers before being rebuffed.

"Okay, I'll mention it to Noah when we eat…" She paused, ready to change the subject.

Iain chose the wrong moment to walk in and looked suitably sorry for himself.

"Iain, me old cocker!" Will laughed. "Alright?"

"Fine," he said ready to move on. There was a lot of uncomfortable smirks, but when Keely spoke up it brought the focus back to her.

"I've been out and about this morning and I heard something incredible."

"Go on," Martin encouraged, happy to change the subject from Eloise, or Iain for that matter.

"Remember the child who went missing?" She paused. "Well, it seems that somehow, she came home last night, along with another missing child. Now, I don't want to get involved in local gossip but it's a very strange occurrence indeed."

"Where were they?" Di asked, and the others looked from her back to Keely, keen to hear the answer. Di thought back to when she was outside smoking.

She shook her head and pulled a face. "I dunno. I didn't hang around but it all sounded a little strange." She looked at her watch and said, "Right, let's go for breakfast. We might find out more then."

"You must always look after your children," Verity said to no one but herself. It was delivered in a sinister fashion, and nobody fancied asking her what she was on about.

They all spilled out of the house and began to walk across the short grass of the square towards the hall. The stage was set up fully with steps, seats, and microphones, whereas before it had just been a shell, and considering the underlined sustainability message, there appeared to be a lot of unsustainable materials used, but perhaps they were only using what might otherwise end up in landfill.

Up ahead they could already hear laughter from within and it was clear the whole community loved to get up and get on, or perhaps the celebrations of the day had already begun.

Noah appeared at the doorway full of smiles and beaming like a loon.

"Good morning!" he exclaimed almost hysterically. "It's a wonderful day!" He bounced up and down with no issue of his knee giving him any problems. He glanced behind, still grinning, and spoke like it was a secret.

"I probably shouldn't tell you this," he began, "but some children went missing and now they have returned! I'd rather be completely upfront with you all."

"That's wonderful!" Keely said, nodding and encouraging everyone else to do so. "Thank you for telling us."

"Anything I can do for you all, just ask!" Noah said.

"Well," Keely began. "And this is a little bit embarrassing. One of our party appears to have gone AWOL." She tried to make light of it, like it was her phone she'd misplaced and not a human being.

"Missing?" Noah's face dropped. He was all serious now. "When?"

The group was a show of shrugs, shaking heads and downturned smiles.

"Last night, we think," Martin said, desperate to grab some authority back.

"Oh," Noah commented, albeit to himself. "That is troubling."

"Unless she got lucky with a local?" Dan winked. "It wouldn't be the first time, and she does have a, er…"

"Reputation," Will replied. The hypocrisy of what he was saying wasn't lost on anyone. The sad truth of society was that a bed-jumping man would be high-fived and congratulated by their peers whereas a woman would be shunned and treated like a pariah.

"I'm sure she'll turn up!" Noah said with a false smile. "Come, come. Breakfast awaits!" He turned and was moving away at great speed.to

They followed on in the main room of the hall and wondered what awaited them for the day.

The Last Weekend

Chapter 19

That morning Marsha's eyes shot open and there in front of her, not more than a few feet away, was the face of her child staring back. Emotionless and blank.

Marsha actually pinched herself. Her thumb and forefinger grabbing some loose skin and using her nails sent pain rushing in milliseconds throughout her nervous system.

It hurt, and the child remained. She thought about the night before when Star and Leo had appeared with her daughter in tow. It was possibly one of the best feelings she'd had since first holding the child in her arms after her birth. The feeling of deep and true love that can only be experienced by a parent longing for a child of their own.

At first, she thought she was seeing things! Some offering from Woden, with Star and Leo like returning warriors from Valhalla.

"There you are, Rosie," she clucked, clicking back to reality. "Are you okay?"

The child nodded slowly but in her eyes she seemed vacant. That panicked Marsha. She wondered now as she had done the night before: *what has happened to my daughter?* She'd been missing twenty-four hours, which was a lot less than other missing children of Woden but still, each hour away from her ripped her heart out over and over. The night before she'd, cuddled her child like she was the most precious thing in the world – which, of course she was – but the child seemed rigid the whole time. The love was only one way. The trauma had grown a shell around Rosie and Marsha already worried whether she'd be able to break through it.

"Let's go and get some breakfast, love," she said getting up and out of bed. "Where's Daddy?"

The child remained silent, and her face still blank. She turned and left the room almost defiantly ignoring her mother's words. The other side of the bed was empty, not unusual, and she yawned as she got out of bed. She just wanted the three of them to laugh and joke, and be the little family unit once again.

The sun shone through the curtains, emulating the euphoric feeling she struggled to maintain. She felt so happy knowing her child was home and she couldn't wait to tell the world. She was realistic in her understanding that it could take time for Rosie to return to being the lovely little girl she once was, but Marsha was sure they'd be happy again soon, and then truly at peace.

The excitement of the night before had got to her. She didn't want to go to sleep for fear of her child being taken again, but her husband Heath had insisted. She'd got up a couple of times to check on Rosie before realising that she had to let it go. The child was back and the next day she would speak to the elders about how they could ensure no child was ever taken again. She'd raise awareness, and if the children had to sleep in the same rooms as the adults, then so be it. That would have to do. She would hate for any other parent to go through what she had.

She changed her underwear, and stepped into some shorts, pulled on her T-shirt and slipped on her flip-flops, all the while humming a non-existent tune. She walked out of the bedroom and watched her daughter at the bottom of the stairs stepping carefully over the still body of Heath, her father, and Marsha's husband.

Marsha screamed.

He was laid out in a classic crime-scene pose except his neck was twisted back the wrong way, and blood was pooled around, and underneath it. The child didn't even look back as she continued into the room below like it was the most normal sight imaginable.

"Oh my God!" the woman gasped, both hands at her face and unsure of what to do. "Heath!! Heath! Are you okay?"

Holding the banister as her legs buckled, she made it down the stairs. It was obvious Heath had fallen and broken his neck. He was far from okay. In fact, he'd never be okay again.

Had it been an accident? she wondered, but as she got closer, she realised that wasn't the case. It couldn't be the case.

It was no accident. His throat had been slit.

She was sobbing as she looked up and called her daughter. “Rosie!! Rosie!”

There was movement in the other room and Rosie appeared. Her face still blank and completely devoid of emotion.

She held a bloody knife in her hands as she said sweetly, “Yes, mummy? I think daddy had an accident.”

“Rosie? What happened?”

“He fell,” she replied like she was answering a question about her favourite food. All the time she smiled, although her eyes remained dead.

“W-when?” Marsha stood up at a measured pace, and held out her hands. “Please put the knife down, love.”

“This morning. I ran to see if he was still alive. I checked his pulse!” She was excited and looking for praise.

“Well done, Rosie. Well done.”

“He was,” she looked down at the knife. “So I had to slice his neck!”

She lost balance with the shock. Her shaky arm raised as she pointed and said through sobs, “What?! You did that?”

She nodded. “Of course. He can’t live, *can he?*”

Marsha took a step closer to her daughter. She’d never once been fearful of her until this day. What had the witch done to her?

“Look out!” the girl screamed pointing behind her mother.

Marsha whipped her head around, and looked up the stairs. No one was there. *What had she seen?*

White pain erupted in her abdomen, and as she looked back her own child was plunging the same knife rhythmically in and out of her. With all her strength she pushed, and kicked the child from her, but it was no use. Her daughter was persistent, and Marsha was rapidly losing strength. Her arms were heavy and her head light as she struggled to breath and stay conscious.

The last thing she thought about was the overwhelming smell of blood.

Her blood.

And then she died. At the hands of the daughter she thought had been saved.

The Last Weekend

Chapter 20

Noah felt like he was some sort of messenger boy running errands between the elders and the others within the community. He was getting too old for this shit and if he wasn't going to be promoted fully to elder status, then he would pass on the baton of this thankless task and live out his life with ease. He often thought his role was the most challenging. The elders had each other to make the decisions with, however he was just one man and often what the community told him was not appropriate to pass on without a little censorship, or tact – and that was all down to him. He knew he was having an off day but still. Sometimes utopia seemed a little far away.

He had pleaded with the elders to allow someone to go to the forbidden woods, and they'd not relented. However, unbeknownst to him, and of course the elders, Leo and Star ignored the warnings and set out on a suicide mission. He'd been as surprised as anyone that not only had they made it back alive, but had returned with their missing son, and the missing daughter of Marsha and Heath. Noah had been only too pleased to tell the elders of the successful mission. They'd nodded and accepted the news, unable to show the happy emotion one would expect from the glorious news that two children had been found and brought back safely.

And then the child, Rosie was sat cross-legged in the square covered in blood, and humming happily to herself. A knife sat in the dirt, and crimson breadcrumbs led back to her house where the grisly scene of her dead parents awaited him.

"Oh, Jesus," he'd muttered to himself though they were not Christians. He turned back to the square but the child was gone. She'd disappeared again. They were in an even worse state than they had been the day before, and Noah had to break the news to the elders.

"Edwin," Noah said, quietly sidling up towards the older gentleman with the wizard-like beard. "There's been an accident."

Edwin nodded like this was a normal occurrence, looked up and caught the eye of the other elders. "We'll delay breakfast for five minutes whilst we discuss this matter," he said.

They all slipped out of the main hall, and in single file, ascended the stairs to their meeting room. Nobody said a word until they were they were all sitting. The importance of the situation was not lost on anybody there and all looked very serious.

"This looks important if you are interrupting our meal, Noah. I'll assume this to be the case, correct?"

"What is it, Noah?" Herti said concerned, and playing the role of the matriarch. At one time she'd bordered on being handsome, but time scarred her face and the elements had prematurely aged her.

"It's about Rosie," he began.

"The missing child who returned?"

Noah nodded. "It looks like she's… erm… How can I put this?"

"Succinctly would be advised," Wilfred chipped in.

Noah nodded. "Right. She murdered her parents."

"Marsha and Heath? Dead…? That small child?"

Noah ran his left hand through his thinning hair. "Yes. As unbelievable as it sounds. Heath was crumpled at the bottom of the stairs. It looks like he either fell or…"

"She pushed him? That *small* girl?" Wilfred said almost mockingly. The elders shared a glance between them and Noah had the familiar feeling he would never be seen as anything but a foot soldier.

"Yes, but his throat was cut, too."

"I see," Edwin muttered and looked at the others. "And Marsha?"

"It looks like she was stabbed. I saw Rosie sat out there on the grass singing to herself. The knife was in front of her on the grass like a toy she'd grown bored with."

"Where is she now?" Herti asked.

Noah paused, he didn't want to say.

"Noah? Answer the question."

Noah looked at them individually weighing up which of them had the kindest eyes. It was draw, none of them did, in fact they all looked like they wanted to hang him up and skin him alive.

"She's gone."

"Gone?"

"She was last seen entering the forbidden woods again."

"Oh dear. That's really not a good sign."

Edwin barked out, "Have you checked on Benny? Star and Leo?"

"They seemed fine earlier," Noah was quick to say. "I saw them all out laughing and joking."

The elders shared another conspiring look and not for the first time Noah wondered whether they were telepathic and could hold silent conversations together. *That* would explain his tardy invitation to join them.

"Right, arrange for the bodies to be moved to the church whilst everyone is at breakfast. For now, if anyone asks, the family are spending time together, got that?"

"Of course," Noah respectfully responded. He waited a beat and before the elders were about to stand up he added, "Look, if I may say, we either stay put and have the witch come and take us one by one, or we go and fight her." He held up his hands. "It's just a suggestion. These people here love the community. They are Woden through and through. Ask any of them and they will say they'd rather die fighting than to be plucked out of their beds at night and murdered." Edwin went to speak, but Noah jumped back into his speech. "Leo and Star found those children easily – *too easily*. She knows what she's doing. She's turning the children against us. She's changing her habits. She started by sneaking around, then she started stealing animals, and then the children. Now this! What's next!" His voice raised and again just before the elders scolded him, he softened it to a more respectful level. "I apologise for the tone. I'm as passionate as anyone. Hear me out. We continue with our celebrations this afternoon, but then we fight fire with fire and send a group out into the woods. Not a recon mission but to kill the witch!"

Herti nodded, but spoke carefully. "We cannot condone such a witch hunt. That is not who we are as people of

Woden… however…” She looked firstly at Wilfred, and then Edwin. “Noah, if you were to put together a band of brave folk to go on that mission, then we cannot stop you. We admire your passion - your guts and glory approach – but we cannot condone it. If something happens then on your head be it – I’m afraid we’d have no choice but to make it known you went against our wishes… on your hands would be the blood of those who came to harm... but if you prevail, then we will celebrate and you will become an elder.”

The others nodded with each word. “Agreed!” They hailed together like some great law had just been passed.

“Meeting adjourned.” They got up and the elders disappeared. Noah was left standing there on his own, collecting his thoughts, thinking about who would join him and wondering whether he’d just signed his own death warrant. The fine line between success and failure in this village was often along an invisible precipice.

They would no longer be passive. They would fight her and everything she had.

But would it be enough?

Chapter 21

There was a murmur of hysteria as the ragtag band of work colleagues entered the hall. Noah showed them to their table and tried to forget about the meeting he'd had.

Jarrod noticed something behind Noah's eyes that was slightly vacant. He seemed distracted and heavily burdened with something unknown. Were they that much of a responsibility? Or was there something else going on? Was he to be held accountable of word getting to the outside world that Eloise had gone missing? Perhaps that was it. The unwanted exposure to their unorthodox practises could have the whole lifestyle shut down.

"What's for breakfast?" Keely asked Noah as she took her seat. Everyone else fell in line and Jarrod was quick to make sure he was nowhere near her. He struggled ridding himself of the picture of her in her underwear.

"Coffees will come around soon, and then there is an option of porridge, toast and fried breakfast."

"Wow! That's impressive!" She grinned and glanced over quickly to Jarrod, before turning away. Had the power shifted between them? He wasn't sure. In fact, he wasn't sure about anything anymore. His hand slipped to his pocket unnoticed, but after a couple of pats of his pockets, he panicked.

His pills were missing.

"Well, yes, and no," Noah admitted. "These options are available but as you can imagine it's not exactly all-you-can-eat. We make the most of it, but we also rely heavily on groups like yourselves to donate money that we can buy staples like bread, milk, and meat. We do produce those, but think about how much we need to feed all of these people."

"Oh, I see."

"Yes, we'd love to be able to say we were fully sustainable, and believe me we are so much more now than we were a few years back, but still, we have a way to go."

"You have livestock?" she asked though she'd not seen any; however, there were a number of buildings they'd not been shown, and fields hidden by the houses.

"Yes, yes," he said rapidly, although he was suddenly vague in his response, and for the first time acting a little shady. "They are looked after by dedicated farmers with greater knowledge of animals than I!" He laughed, and changed the subject. "Today is a good day!"

Martin jumped in, clearly feeling like he was being silenced and needing to chip in. "You've done a sterling job here, and can I say so far, I see no reason why we can't support you in the future. We could almost look to partner in order to make you fully sustainable. Can I also say, I love everything you do here, and we'd love to be more involved."

"Really?" Noah said, a smile breaking through and making him look suddenly hopeful. "Well, I do have a rather pressing matter that I need some volunteers for." He instantly regretted saying that though, especially as they were going to support the community in the future.

"Really?" Martin said, sitting bolt upright. "I'm sure we'd love to help you in whatever it is!"

Noah pictured the bent spine of the cloaked woman in the red cape. The witch who looked so weak, and yet had proved just how strong she was. "Well, enjoy your breakfast and perhaps after we can discuss who would like to stay here and help out, or who would like to join me on a rather delicate matter."

Heads turned to each other as mystery and unspoken fascination filled their faces.

As the coffee was poured Jarrod sat back and scanned the hall. He wasn't the most intuitive of people but there was a darkness working its way around. He couldn't put his finger on it but there was a change in atmosphere. At first, he noticed a small pocket of people. Whispers whipped around them leaving concerned faces. Glances to the wider audience trying to mask clenched jaws and fists armed and ready for action. Some secret news was floating between the people and it was causing a reaction. The day was meant to be a celebration too which only made it all the more obvious.

"Sleep well?" Rick said, looking out towards the mild commotion. The words weighed heavy with something else. Was Rick chucking out an invisible rod hoping to catch lies, or genuinely asking as a friend?

"Not bad," Jarrod replied, his mind flashing between the memories of tiny red thongs, and his fantasy-induced carnal desires… and the realisation of being watched. "You?"

Rick nodded slowly, in no rush to respond. He stifled a yawn, and stretched his arms to the gods above before saying calmly, "Be careful, mate."

Jarrod's stomach dropped. He turned to his friend who met his gaze. "What d'you mean?"

"You've done this before." But before they could continue, Dan was loudly suggesting his theory on Eloise's disappearance.

"She'll be home now snuggled up in bed. She's not cut out for this lifestyle, not like us outdoorsy types. We have staying power."

Di had been unusually quiet, probably wondering how long her oat bars would last, and when she could fill her lungs with poison again, but managed to add, "I'm worried about her. She's a lot of things but I don't see her just running off in the middle of the night!"

Verity appeared to agree. "Yes, as independent as she likes to make out, she also likes to be looked after."

"She liked to make out, all right!" Will smirked but quickly realised that everyone else was looking serious. "She'll be fine," he quickly added, but when he stopped to think about her, he wasn't so sure.

Jarrod was distracted as the wave of whispers got closer. Each time somebody leant into the person next to them they looked shocked, glanced around and then proceeded to tell the person sat to the other side of them too. Until it came to Verity, then they abruptly stopped. The newcomers were not part of the gossip. When Jarrod looked up at the table of elders, they appeared to be troubled, as well. Frowns and concerned faces were the make-up of the day. Maybelline would struggle to hide those blemishes.

Jarrod reacted to Rick's words, their hidden intentions finally penny-dropping.

"Sorry, what?"

Rick sat back in his chair with a newfound confidence. Here his awkward weirdo routine was replaced with an unfazed blasé. It was like being invited to tea with the quiet kid in class. When you got there he was no longer quiet and within his own environment suddenly found himself.

Except this wasn't home to Rick, was it?

"Your imagination has a habit of running wild with you, Jarrod. I'm not having a go. I'm merely pointing out what you already know. There's a reason you're prescribed drugs."

Jarrod chewed the inside of his lip. His knee-jerk reaction was to deny any such accusations but he knew it was true. It was like he grabbed a thread of something and the thread turned into a rope that pulled him into a fantasy. He went to respond but couldn't find the words. His foggy mind was habitually struggling to know what was going on let alone formulate a response.

"Look, I know you're different… Fuck, mate, we're *both* different but you have to reel it in a little, yeah?"

Jarrod found himself nodding. He was a little embarrassed and not for the first time wondered exactly what he'd done.

Before he could catch the words, he blurted, "I've lost my pills."

"Fuck the pills, Jarrod. You don't need them here." He took a moment, glanced around to make sure that no flappy ears were picking up his frequency, and said, "There are other things that will take your mind off those mind-numbing sweets. Trust me." The words seemed to stop abruptly, like he wanted to offer further assurances but thought it best not to.

But of course, that might've been his badly wired brain metaphorically handing him the shit-end of a stick.

Like the night before, they'd followed suit in queuing up and joining the line to get food. Once again, the people serving smiled politely to them and did their best to make them feel welcome. Jarrod had to wonder how long that would last and whether one of them was actually muttering the word, "Cunt" at them.

"Nice to see you again," the woman from the night before said, but just as Jarrod felt special, she'd moved on to Rick, and he was left to move on. They were polite to everyone. He wasn't special.

"I could get used to this," Martin stated, as they sat down at their table again. He glanced at Keely who let slip a small smile.

"I bet you could," she said. A pang of jealousy reared its invisible head and pounded Jarrod in the kidneys. He couldn't help it. What the fuck was wrong with him?

His hands searched for his pills again. The resigned, and disappointed feeling of another Groundhog Day.

"Eloise is missing out," Will said, before taking a bite of toast so large half the slice was gone when he pulled it away. It wasn't clear whether he'd just remembered or wanted the fact to be raised again.

"You're going to get indigestion," Verity said with a tone like she hoped he would. "My husband eats like a pig, too."

"Sorry, Mum!" The words slightly muffled by a mouthful, and his jaws grinding away machine-like as he chewed.

Verity pursed her lips, immediately taking offence and assuming the words of motherhood only served to suggest that she was past it, and no longer attractive, not able to contribute to society. Her inner feminist was seething and searching for a soapbox. She wanted to jump up on the table and rip her clothes off and shout, "Look at me! A gorgeous woman with large pendulous breasts, a flabby stretch-marked belly and a wonderfully wild bush of nether-region-hair! I'm natural! I'm me! I'm a woman!" But she didn't. She muttered about him going and fucking himself, before chugging down some coffee that was as bitter as she felt.

"He needs more than a mother," Di said, drinking water instead of coffee, citing it to being a harmful stimulant – all whilst fiddling with the unlit cigarette she was getting wet over. The thought of it polluting her air-intake, and not understanding the hypocrisy of it was lost on her argumentative streak to be forever right.

"Neutering," Verity said, which made Di laugh and Keely smile.

Iain was sat back in silence, his plate pushed aside, and was looking all around as if he might be given free rein to go and speak to somebody of his choice. His Dahmer gaze was slow and analysing. In his mind he separated people by gender, and then attraction. To Iain, his tastes were unique as he favoured plain women of a more rotund build and with long, naturally coloured hair. He was over being caught masturbating in the women's dorm. Sure, it was embarrassing, but it was hardly in the top ten things he'd been caught doing with his dick on show.

"You okay, Iain?" Dan asked him. Not because he cared, but to set himself up for a joke.

Without breaking his gaze toward a woman who was sturdy and in need of a make-over, he replied, "I'm comfortable, thank you."

"That right?" Dan said but his well of jokes were dry to that. Instead, he made do with commenting, "At least you're not whacking off, so for that we're all blessed."

Noah walked over to them, and this time he was smiling. He must've found his happiness somewhere between the bacon and the pancakes.

"How was breakfast? All good, I trust?" This time his eyes weren't lying, and the caring host-Noah was back with them.

"Wonderful thanks," Keely said, at the same time as Martin who simply said, "Wonderful!"

"Right then," Noah began. "This morning we are going to split up into two groups. One for those of you who like a bit of adventure, and those of you who'd prefer something a little easier. No pressure. This is about what you want to gain from your experience. Have a think about it and meet me outside in ten minutes, okay?"

There was a lot of nodding, and flashes of teeth. The anticipation and hysteria were still evident even a day later. The truth of the matter was this broke up the monotony of their boring little lives. They were all too focused on either work targets, social standings, or popularity on social media platforms, whereas here, there was none of that. The stresses that suppressed their normal freedom were gone, and here they were liberated.

Slowly they all filtered out, either to go for a toilet break, a cigarette or just to stretch their legs. Each hoped to hang around long enough that any manual labour tasks were distributed elsewhere.

The sun was bright and already feeling warm as the crisp morning air disappeared. The day before somebody had mentioned rain but that looked to be wrong. The sky couldn't be any clearer.

"Can I have a word?" Keely said to Jarrod, and for a second his heart skipped. The juvenile response embarrassed him. Next, he'd be thinking about love-letters, poems and scratching their names in hearts on trees.

"Sure," he said. The others pretended not to care, though ears were half-cocked, and sideways glances told that they were dying to hang back.

She beckoned him over to the side away from everyone.

"Look, Jarrod. About last night." Her tone was not one that suggested she was proud of her flaunting, and he was all too familiar with the lines of being let down. "You need to understand our relationship." His eyes widened a touch. Hope springs eternal. He was moving his head in affirmation before she'd even finished. Or was he getting this completely out of proportion?

"But…" she began, and it was unusual to see her struggling with how to phrase something. Mostly she opened her mouth and a tirade of words stormed out firing shots at anyone within earshot. "You have to understand privacy. Our boundaries."

He now felt confused. What was she going on about.

"I know I walked in wearing… well… not a lot." She glanced around to confirm no one had crept up behind her, or a microphone boom arm would be arching from above to catch the clandestine confession.

"But I forgot where I was. I heard a shout and came to check on you."

"In your underwear?" Jarrod said, and he felt suddenly exposed, and stupid. "But□"

"I saw you, Jarrod. Later on, stood there in the shadows… touching yourself."

"I wasn't. I…" But now he was confused. She'd been there almost naked holding him. But now she was making out that it was all him. Like *he* was the pervert and *she* the innocent bystander.

She held up her hands. "Remember in my office last week?"

He did. Of course he did. How could he forget.

He nodded. "When you pulled□"

She waggled a finger at him. "No, when we spoke about your conduct. I cannot keep you out of HR for much longer. I've done my best to turn a blind eye to your fantasies."

He thought about her wriggling her skirt up as she perched on her desk. Except this time, the picture jumped, and moved like static on an old TV. It jumped around until she was stood up behind her desk telling him to quit daydreaming.

"I don't understand," he said, and it was like the morning after a huge drinking session. One where bits and pieces were appearing in a different order about the night before. Each piece made the picture clearer, but also reminded him of something embarrassing.

"You have that meeting with the mental health worker, don't you? Next week, right?"

He was nodding very slowly and now remembering discussions in a room he'd never been in before. Custard-coloured walls with mismatched furnishings and a fat woman with dimples and flaky skin. He'd talked to her about his ex-girl-fiend, and she'd stopped him when he'd begun to talk intimately about her. She'd raised her finger the way Keely was doing now and told him that those intimate details were something he should keep to himself, and yet to Jarrod, they were important. He was there to talk freely, and in private, and yet when he talked about the problems in his last relationship, she baulked at him explaining he grew bored of having to insert his fingers into her anus. He felt *that* was where things went downhill, but this woman insisted on talking about feelings, and empathy, when his response was in regard to keeping his fingernails trim, and licking them before insertion.

And of course, it didn't stop there. He'd talked about Eloise. He mentioned how her perfume annoyed him, and the way she constantly flirted and yet, when they were out, two drinks in and he was penis-deep inside her in the alleyway they both considered to be a familiar place. But the woman waved this off, too. She struggled to keep the disdain from her eyes, and her lips battled not to turn in contempt. She was judging him, like they all did.

"Maybe you should change rooms with Martin, or Rick…"

"No!" Jarrod almost spat out. "I'm sorry," he said, but he wasn't. He'd not expected to see his boss stripped down to such a lack of clothing, and he'd hoped there would be more. He'd lost it. He now remembered standing there with his hand down his underwear as she returned to her room. She'd seen him, and he knew it. She'd looked right at him and said nothing. She'd removed the rest of her clothing and put on a solo show, but now, in the light of the day she was twisting it around.

"I said, I'd help you through this, didn't I?" she said, stepping closer and placing a hand on his shoulder. It was not the touch of a lover, no matter what his brain conjured up, but purely maternal.

He nodded. "I just thought□"

She placed a finger gently on his lips. “I know,” she said soothingly. “I know.”

Keely walked off and Jarrod was left to realise that his fantasies had been just that. Did she do what he remembered in her room? In a panic, Jarrod grabbed his phone from his pocket. Still no signal, and now the battery was low.

He flipped it on with his fingerprint and was pleased to see the bare breasts of his best friend. At least that happened. He felt guilty again. The chemical imbalance in his brain felt almost physical.

Where the fuck were his pills! His fists were balled up and he felt like he wanted to hit something. He looked around the commune. The contrast of happiness and something else rumbling underneath.

He took it all in. The stage, the people, the forbidden woods in the background, and wondered just what else was in store for him that day.

If only he’d known. If only.

The Last Weekend

Chapter 22

Star closed her eyes and hugged her son once more with everything she had. She couldn't help it. He was back and she didn't want to stop the feeling of him being in her arms.

"Give the boy a break!" Leo grinned, unable to stop smiling. He was just as bad and they both knew it. If Star wasn't smothering him, he was lifting him up and swinging him around like a prize.

Despite all this elation, Benny wasn't talking, and they had to admit they were a little concerned. And now they'd heard rumours.

Rosie was missing again. Worse, her parents were both dead. There was talk that Rosie herself had committed it, though Leo struggled to believe that the small child could do that to her parents. The family loved each other. They were a picture of perfection and what he hoped people saw when they looked at him and his family. Heath was a big broad guy, so how a little girl had murdered him was truly unbelievable. Fucking Chinese whispers!

"Hey Benny? Shall we go and kick your ball around?" Leo asked, knowing his son loved to go out in front of the house and kick the football back and forth. "Hey champ?" He tried again when he got no response.

Benny looked at him and shook his head.

"He's had a traumatic time, haven't you, sweetie?" Star said, not ready to let him out of her sight just yet.

"I know… I just… Maybe he wanted to do something a bit more normal."

"It's okay, Leo. He'll do things when he wants to do them, won't you, Benny?" But Benny didn't respond either way. He continued to look past them, his gaze directly out towards the forbidden woods.

Leo tried to remain positive but there was a deep sinking feeling in his gut that he couldn't shake. He was scared about the stories of Rosie and what had happened. He looked over once more at Benny. The lad looked for all the world to be the same child he'd brought home from the hospital. The one he'd sat up at night feeding six ounces of milk to, then burping him. The blues eyes and the cheeky smile; except he'd yet to see the latter since returning.

He was so glad to see his son back with them. Or at least he would be if this was him. It was stupid, and he knew it…

He couldn't quite put his finger on it, but this was not his son.

As soon as the thought left his brain the child's head turned round on a slow swivel like the devil-child, Damian in *The Omen*, and then he saw the smile. Except this wasn't the one he remembered, this one was knowing and down-right evil…

The Last Weekend

Chapter 23

Jarrod could see it now, or at least he thought he could. There were small glances between Martin and Keely. How had he not noticed it before. The subtleties of adultery when you took the time to glance.

"It's been going on a while. Why d'you think he's here with us?" Rick was talking quietly with his back to them. "You'll have to obsess on someone else now."

Jarrod didn't know how Rick knew. "I wasn't…"

"You were. Shit, on some level they all have. Even Eloise would buckle up a strap-on and slip it to her. I don't get it."

"You're not attracted to her?"

Rick laughed like the notion was so absurd it was amusing. "No. No. Not in the slightest." When he noticed

Jarrod wasn't laughing, he slapped him playfully. "Look, I get it. I've seen it before. She has this way about her. She prances around spellbinding all you lot and that's when you get into the trouble you do."

"She's not your type of woman, then?"

Rick scanned around the area. "You like her because of what your mind has conjured up. Those pills you're addicted to only make things worse, but you know that right? You're seeing a shrink, too."

Jarrod was about to say something but Rick waved it away.

"That doesn't matter. And for what it's worth, it's probably a good idea, but those pills are the real issue. And look, mate. I'm a nobody. I don't know shit, but I observe."

Verity came wandering over wearing a plain black hoodie that swamped her. Her huge boobs were barely kept in line by her bra and wobbled considerably as she walked. With her thick waist and plentiful thighs, the look made her look like a human bauble.

"I ache," she declared, as she got closer. "I'll do something a little less strenuous if given the chance."

"Noah did say there were other options available," Rick said, although Jarrod wanted her to be made to work hard again. Everything about her annoyed him. All she did was fucking moan. Not for the first time, he pitied her husband. The woman probably even moaned when his cock was in her mouth.

"Didn't he also mention something else he wanted?" Jarrod said, when Verity had grown tired of them and turned away. Rick raised his eyebrows and looked like he knew more than he was letting on.

"What is it?" Jarrod pressed.

Rick looked out towards the woods that still had large looming clouds over them like some meteorological phenomenon. "Are you superstitious, Jarrod?"

"Not really. It's bullshit, right? Doing things to ward off bad luck…" He stopped, conscious not to continue just for the sake of speaking. Rick never jumped over someone in a conversation, so happily allowed them to blabber on.

Rick looked at him with eyes that searched deep inside before saying, "He wants to put a team together to find the witch."

"What?"

"You heard me. The witch is real and somewhat problematic to the commune. They want her dead."

"And that's easy? To kill a witch, I mean?"

Rick was amused by that as much as Jarrod was intrigued by this revelation.

"I wouldn't think so. Maybe Noah knows of some witchy-Kryptonite that we have, to go attack."

"It feels a little farfetched…" Jarrod looked over at Martin who was deep in some conversation of heroism, and whilst Keely wasn't exactly hanging onto every word, all he could see was her laid back on the bed as she had been the night before, but it was Martin stood ready to comply. Dan and Will were like teenage boys jostling with each other. Di was surrounded by tobacco smoke and Verity looked like invisible daggers were shooting from her eyes. That was the extent of the motley crew that Noah was looking at to fight against evil. A bossy cougar, a know-it-all, a retired veteran, an overgrown kid, a toxic-smoke-breather, and a total bitch. With the slut of the group missing. The witch must be scared shitless in her cavern.

"Then who's abducting children?" It was a fair question.

Noah appeared from the church behind them, the limp now slightly more prominent in his walk. He raised a hand when they locked eyes.

"Are we ready then?" he asked, full of enthusiasm. All the small conversations ceased as they came together as one.

"Okay, as quick as you like, split into two groups. One that wants an easy task and the other who is up for a challenge?" Jarrod expected most of the group to head over for the easy challenge. At first there was hesitation as sheep looked to be guided by the actions of others. Heads looked around before Martin was first to say, "Challenge over here!" Keely nodded and remained next to him. Dan pushed Will off balance, but both sidled up to Martin and Keely as Rick and Jarrod walked up close to them too.

Iain looked genuinely perplexed as Di and Verity made it very clear that they were stood together away from the others.

"Come on, Homie!" Dan called to Iain which sounded odd. Two Gen X's talking like they were millennials. Weirdly, it worked, as Iain ambled over.

"Wonderful! I wasn't expecting so many adventurous people! Especially after all your hard work yesterday!" Noah looked genuinely pleased and clapped his hands together once loudly.

From out of one of the other buildings adjacent to the hall, a woman with long, fiery-red hair and a blue band that kept the wildly flowing hair out of her face could be seen. She was wiry, and wearing a long-sleeve T-shirt, covered by baggy dungarees. Her face was friendly and Jarrod wondered once again what the difference would be in the locals' demeaner if this was a cult? Really, they would act the same. Everyone was friendly and welcoming, and whilst it was nice, you couldn't help but wonder. It wasn't natural to be happy constantly. Life wasn't like that. He knew they were all at one with nature, they practised yoga daily, meditation and probably Sting-influenced tantric sex. Their food was homegrown, natural, low on sugar, high in fibre and not processed muck, and of course there was no social media or television to guilt trip them into feeling a certain way, but hormone levels were variable, and mood swings, and life-experiences made us act in certain way - these were perfectly natural.

"Julia," Noah beamed as the redhead glided in. "These two are yours."

"Oh, you two are going to have so much fun," she said, skipping a touch and beckoning them both towards her with hands covered in silver rings.

"The rest of you, come with me," Noah said. "We'll meet back in an hour or so when the festivities begin!" He stopped walking even though they'd only just begun, and said, "I'm really pleased you're here to join in with it!"

"What's planned?" Martin enquired ever Mr Engagement. His corporate successes showing by the way he was always able to appear interested.

"Oh, wait and see!" Noah chuckled and began to walk on but everyone could see that the hysteria of it was too much, and who could blame him. The place was great for him, but perhaps these moments of celebration were what separated the days from the norm of every other.

"There are songs played. Food and drink and then a huge fire is lit with an effigy of the witch burnt!"

"The witch is real?" Keely decided to chip in with.

There was a beat where Noah appeared to almost stutter, but he was careful in his response. "Every ritual is based upon truth. We see burning the witch as a sign to ward off any evil spirits around."

"From the woods?" Keely pressed, nodding out towards the trees. The clouds above the treetops remained static and threatened rain like they were armed guards warding off trespassers.

"Of course," Noah said, but left it at that.

"But do you believe she's real?" It was shaky ground. Her polite conversation was at the mark where she was bordering on being rude, but when Keely smelt something she wanted more information; she became a professional interrogator. If Noah wasn't careful she'd try underhanded tactics of waterboarding, fashioned by her crouching over him and pissing in his face until he spilled the truth. Jarrod smiled at that thought.

Noah appeared to smile to himself as the village was left behind them, and they followed a path around to the part of the woods they were allowed in.

"The world is full of things we cannot explain. There are powers beyond our comprehension…" He looked up at them all, watching how they were listening intently. Maybe they wanted tales of magic and sorcery. They expected broomsticks, cauldrons and black cats except that was far from reality.

"Okay," he began, as if he'd given up trying to keep things to himself. "Gather around."

They came together. A silence fell upon them as they expected to hear tales of folklore and legends. They really longed for a campfire, marshmallows, and moonshine, but this would have to do.

"I have a serious question for you all about something I want to do later. There is no pressure, and really nobody is expected to join in… but, I must stress, if you do agree to join me in this activity then it must be kept here in Woden. You cannot tell anyone when you go back to your life away from here."

"Sounds dangerous!" Will said, nudging Dan. "You might want to opt out, Dan."

Dan shook him off. "Boy, you wouldn't know danger if it crept up on you and bit your pecker off!"

Keely raised her hands for calm. "Boys, please. Let's hear Noah out." The two men looked scorned.

Noah nodded a thanks, then took a step back to give himself some room. He looked back at the woods, but soon he turned, and his gaze was clearly on the forbidden woods.

"Legend has it that the woods hold evil. Deep within them is a large house owned by a witch. We believe…" he looked back at them all. "That she wants this commune. And by that, I mean she wants us all dead. Anybody who sets foot in those woods disappears. Any who did make it back have died in suspicious circumstances." He stopped for dramatic affect. His mind taken away as he thought about Rosie and part of him worried for Leo and Star. *Would they be okay?*

"You want us to venture into those woods?" Martin guessed, and this time all of his usual gusto was missing. The paint from his mask had paled, showing his true colours. He struggled to hide his anxiety.

Noah had a blank face but let out a sigh, and then said, "It's a big ask… Like I say, there's no obligation. It's something we've decided to do and now we need to do it. Pull up our britches and go in there to take the witch on."

"Prove that the woods aren't evil?" Will asked, not fully understanding the extent of the mission.

Noah, again wasn't sure how to respond, so Rick jumped in. "Kill the witch. Noah wants us to go in and take on the witch, right?"

Uncharacteristically, Iain suddenly piped up. "Is this like role-play? You plant some villagers, or whatever to jump out and scare us and we have the mission to go and kill something dressed as a witch?"

"Something like that," Rick answered and locked eyes with Noah. Jarrod saw the look - a silent agreement.

Noah's mouth twitched a touch before grinning. "That's it," he said. "A test of bravery for you all. A final act of team building!"

"Piece of piss," said Dan. "I've walked blindfolded through minefields with enemy snipers taking pot-shots at my head. A little wander in some woods with a few locals is hardly going to have me shitting my pants." The claim seemed unlikely, unless both the landmines were spaced out and few in numbers, and the snipers were children not strong enough to pull the trigger.

Will thumped his chest and proclaimed, "Yeah, and I'm not sure about witches but I've fucked over enough bitches!"

Martin rolled his eyes, and tried not to laugh, colour returning to his face.

"I'm in," Keely agreed.

"Me too," Jarrod, and then Rick confirmed.

"Iain?"

"Guess so. I've nothing better to do."

Noah felt guilty not completely telling them the truth, *but how could he?* It was a hard sell to get strangers to put their lives on the line for a cause they knew nothing about.

"Right, we need to cut down these bushes here," Noah said, taking a large sack off his shoulder, and pointing to a vast area of vines and small clumps of plantation. "In here you will find some loppers. If some of you can cut, the other half can collect. These will be taken back and used on the fire."

They split into two groups. One of which pulled open a large gravel bag which they would fill up with what they cut down, whilst the others held the loppers like weapons as they traipsed off into the undergrowth.

"That was bullshit, wasn't it?" Jarrod mentioned to Rick as they went deeper into the brambles.

"Which bit?"

"The bit about later. The act that it was a role-playing exercise."

"What do you think?"

Jarrod picked up the large, pair of ratchet loppers. "I think he played it safe and forgot to mention that we might not all make it back alive."

"How do you feel about that?"

"You sound like a therapist, Rick."

"I'm just asking questions. So, what *do* you think about it?"

"Dying?"

The question was not the sort of thing you asked lightly and yet here they were, two guys deep in the woods speaking of it anyway. Rick nodded.

"I'm up for anything."

Rick looked at him, then winked and patted him on the back. "Good man! That's why you'll be fine."

Life can sometimes pivot on single decisions, and here they were on a one-way journey they couldn't turn back from.

Chapter 24

Despite the awful smell, she was hungry, but that was the least of her problems. Her arms were pulled up above her head and tied with something. Her shoulder sockets aching, she'd managed to pull some slack to take the pressure off. She couldn't see them but she was sure her wrists were cut deeply from where she'd done her best to tug free. Gently at first, then harder with frustration.

This wasn't the first time she'd been tied up like this, however the previous time was with an ex-boyfriend who thought it might be fun to try. She'd agreed, but had soon grown frustrated when it was clear he had no idea what to do with her other than prod and poke her randomly. She'd had more pleasure having a smear test, and at times the similarities had been uncanny.

But he'd never made her bleed. Nor wrenched her arms like they might've tweaked her ligaments. She'd never understood people who enjoyed pain, and assumed them to be fraternising with the devil.

She could make out shapes, and she knew she was underground in some cool, damp place. Her vest was ripped, and she could feel one breast hanging freely. She no longer wore trousers and her panties had been soiled an hour or so ago when her bladder eventually gave way to the urge to pee. In the past after a night of drinking she'd found herself in some poor situations, but this took the fucking biscuit.

Eloise bucked as she heard the door open; a slice of light shone into the room and flashed on the corpse of an unfortunate other.

She screamed as she saw the red-caped figures shuffle in repeating words that sounded Latin, but in all honesty, it could've been Welsh. The one in front held a staff with the skull of a ram's head on it. Not a real one, that would be silly, but a tiny replica carved into wood and mounted. Had it not been for her unfortunate situation, it would've been fine craftmanship.

"Nooo! No!" she yelled in desperation kicking up her legs and pulling hard on her wrists. She felt pain from everywhere.

They stopped in front of her. The one with the staff looked up; instead of a face, the person wore a mask of red with a snarling face painted on it.

"Who are you?!" the deep voice demanded, slamming the staff down three times.

"Wh-Who are you?" She sobbed, her fight quick to drain from her body.

"Answer us, witch!"

"I-I am not a witch. M-my name is E-Eloise! I-I'm here for the weekend!"

Another of the figures stepped forward, and under the hood they wore a similar mask. “She was caught in the wood. Only witches creep around there at night!”

“No! No! You must be mistaken! I-I was just going for a walk… I… I shouldn’t be here!”

“Get her down,” the first person demanded, and two others from behind were quick to walk to her. One grabbed some rope and untangled it, whilst the other cranked on a wooden handle. The sound was loud and complaining; wood and rope working against each other.

The rope slackened and in unbelievable relief Eloise fell to the floor, her legs unable to take the impact, and her knees buckling in pain.

Behind her was a large water butt. Inside it under the green scum floating on top was stagnant water mixed with blood and bits of human waste.

“Grab her head!”

“W-what?” Eloise managed through the pain of her knees. She thought she was being let free.

“Witches don’t drown,” the deep voice boomed. Others joined in with the chant.

“Witches don’t drown! Witches don’t drown!”

Her eyes were wide open, and she began to hyperventilate. The whole situation was bad. Really bad.

Hands grabbed her armpits, the grip so firm she was sure her arms might pop out of their sockets, and pulled her up so she was hanging onto the top of the large coffin sized water butt. A hand grabbed her head and thrust it down into the water. She didn’t have time to take a breath, and she kicked her legs, and did her best to flail her arms as bubbles of her air burst from the water. Her lungs soon burned like they had been set on fire. She thought she was going to die.

She was pulled out.

Eloise gasped for air and gulped in as much oxygen as she could manage. The foul taste of the liquid made things worse and there were things in her mouth she didn't even want to guess at.

"Why are you taking the children?" The voice demanded of her.

"I don't know what you're talking about!" she screamed, desperate to make them understand her. "I was just□"

Down she was forced once more into the water. The shouts now muffled as her ears were submerged too. The metallic tang wasn't the first thing on her mind, but it was something that stayed with her as she made noises and acted like she'd been plugged into an electrical mains unit.

This time, along with the burning, it hurt in her chest. Hurt in a way she had never before experienced. When she was finally released, she spluttered great coughs of water, and began retching before throwing up. She had inhaled a lot and her eyes were streaming, as she coughed over and over again.

"Witches don't drown," a voice from behind them stated in a deep voice.

It was repeated with one of the others joining in. And then they were all chanting it like a mantra once again.

She managed to take a breath before she was forced into the water again, and the repetitive voices became muffled and she wondered whether she'd ever be let out alive.

She'd been forced to do a lot of things she regretted but this was by far the worst of the lot.

Chapter 25

The stage was an amazing sight now it was completely covered with flowers, coloured paper and balloons. It was obvious to the work colleagues that this celebration meant a lot to them, but as they walked up to where people were already gathering, Jarrod knew that later that day would be even more important.

He could feel something in the pit of his stomach. Was it fear? Was it excitement? It sounded daft that he wasn't sure but really this was one of the most important things he had to do in his life for a long time. He concluded it was probably anxiety, twisting his stomach and mixing up the two emotions he was trying to differentiate between.

They'd worked hard filling up several bags, which had been dragged back. The area was nicely cleared and looked cared for.

They were given fifteen minutes to get washed up before meeting at the stage. Will couldn't keep still as his excitement for what he perceived to be a game later on was building inside him.

Jarrod could smell the cigarette smoke before he saw Di. When she appeared through the crowd, she waved her hand holding the cancer-stick at them. They politely smiled and nodded but silently agreed that absence didn't so much make their hearts grow fonder as much as make them thankful she wasn't around to moan, complain and force second-hand smoking like it was a thoughtful offering.

Verity followed behind with a Monday-morning face on. She looked like her fun had dried up and now she wanted to kill somebody.

"Greetings," Iain said before either Keely or Martin could speak. He was clearly missing his interactions with them, even though the three barely spoke together when in the office.

"Hello," Di said, and took a huge drag like the socialising was that much of an effort she needed the nicotine to cope.

Soon cups of drink were handed out, and the group all stood together looking at the stage and wondering just what was going to happen. If nothing else it made a nice break from the hard work, although most of them found it to be quite therapeutic compared to their normal lives.

Dan and Will looked hot and sweaty, and despite the break, were somehow still covered in greenery. It wasn't something that Verity couldn't help but notice.

"Have you two been wrestling in the undergrowth again?" she said completely seriously. If anyone else had uttered the line it would've been comical, and no doubt with sexual undertones, but for her it was completely literal.

"I bet you'd like that?" Will winked, which only brought a disgusted look to her face and a retching sound from the back of her throat. She didn't like any talk of a sexual nature and it was widely assumed she was religious, until that question was asked and she'd given a similar response. It appeared she had zero interest in any sexual activity at all, be it participation, watching or even acknowledging its existence. The very act should be quick and an annoying process to maintain the population, and nothing more.

"Leave her be," Keely scolded, although she had commented many times she thought the woman was just plain odd.

Jarrod had his back to the stage taking in the commune and talking with his work colleagues, but when he glanced behind, he noticed the grass area had really filled up with people, and when he looked again one of the elders, soon followed by a couple of others, were appearing on the stage. He turned back ready for whatever was going to happen.

"Welcome to Woden; welcome to our visitors; and welcome to all the spirits that still inhabit this wonderful place!" He stood tall and proud projecting his voice in a way that held nobody in any doubt he was the figure of authority there. Once again, Jarrod thought he recognised him, which he knew was odd.

Edwin glanced around the crowd catching as many eyes as possible and engaging in a way only he could, and continued, "We celebrate our community and everything that has been achieved□" He held aloft his arm and pointed above, then turned it around his head like an invisible lasso. "We are not the first community, and we are by no means the last. You should all know that others are growing and thriving all over the country…" He paused, and delivered the next line with much punch. "And the world!" The strange single beat clap began and he stood like some sort of messiah and nodded his head to each clap. The others stood behind in brown capes joining in with the clapping.

Jarrod and his colleagues couldn't help but be a part of it too. With everything they'd done, and how they'd been welcomed how could they not? Despite whatever long-term feelings they had for the community and their ways none of them could say they'd been treated with anything but respect and hospitality.

Edwin raised both hands and when he dropped them, and the clapping ceased.

"We have our house band to play throughout the celebrations, and for the rest of the day you can all continue to drink, eat, and be merry!" He pumped his fist and the clapping began again, but this time the tempo was quicker.

The ragtag musicians gingerly appeared in the background with their instruments and soon kicked into a fast tempo foot-tapper that was a cross between bluegrass and rock. The elders smiled, waved, and disappeared, before the first verse kicked in and a troop of teenagers appeared and danced a simple but effective choreography of movement as the crowd clapped to the beat.

It was hardly a rock gig, but it was better than any country fair Jarrod had had the misfortune of attending, and he could only step back and look at it for what it was. A week ago, he'd been sat in a meeting he didn't understand. He'd been nodding his head whilst Francis, a prematurely bald-headed guy of thirty, tried to explain the complexities of a project Jarrod couldn't care less about. Jarrod never needed to know about what else was going on around the building. It didn't matter. His job was to report data, and produce trends and analysis. The project might affect how the figures changed, but ultimately was irrelevant to Jarrod's job. Whether or not the project was a success still meant his own job would remain the same. He was happy to switch off and dwell on the more important and pertinent areas of his life, like: why his ex-girl-fiend had dumped him; why he fantasised about his boss but fucked the team slut at any chance he got. He never would've expected he'd be standing in a field listening to some folk/rock, drinking moonshine and talking about killing a witch!

And yet here he was.

He picked up his mug again as the woman he'd seen serving breakfast walked around with a huge jug and refilled mugs. Not that she could do many, before she returned to where another woman was placing full jugs on a table, but everything was geared to keep people there in the field enjoying the sun and the happy atmosphere.

The song turned into another one of an equal tempo, before the next one slowed down. Couples decided to take the opportunity to dance together which only made those who weren't couples feel more awkward.

"What d'you think happened to Eloise?" Jarrod asked Rick so the others couldn't hear. Rick just shrugged in the non-committal way he often did. He was happy to leave it at that until Jarrod pushed further. "No, really? You know more than you're letting on, Rick."

Rick glance up at the stage and then all around where much merriment was going on. He looked back at Jarrod, shrugged once more but this time added, "I don't imagine Eloise ran away in the night."

"No, I don't think she did either."

"There are a couple of scenarios though both I fear are bad. She might've gone off in a huff, and somehow got injured and lost." Rick didn't look like he believed that for a minute. "Or perhaps she ran off into the dark forbidden woods. We know people should stay away from them, but Eloise…" he pulled a face like 'you-know-her' and said, "She thinks she knows better."

"You think she's dead?" The words were more shocking as Jarrod said them out loud.

"I have no way of knowing."

There was more dancing, and this time Will was jumping around and giving it his best shot although he looked like he might be having a psychiatric episode.

"Oh, Jesus," Keely said, wondering why he felt the need to do the things he did. The large ungainly guy trying to do a dainty two-step was a bit more than she could take.

Then something was wheeled in. Or rather someone.

The body had long blonde hair and appeared to be wearing Eloise's clothes. Even as the body was lifted and placed against the wood of the bonfire it seemed to be very human-like.

The music stopped.

There was a beat from a drum and everyone clapped to the sombre beat. And then the wood was on fire and the flames licked around the body.

"Whoa! Hold on," Martin was the first to point this out. "That looks like Eloise!"

And all that any of them could see was the full-figure of their missing colleague resting against wood that was now alight like some poor woman accused of witchcraft.

"Shit, it does!" Keely said, and they jumped into action. Martin ran like the hero he was with Keely, Will and Dan in tow. Jarrod and Rick wandered behind in the space they'd created parting the crowds in front of them. The others, unsure of what was happening remained where they were. Locals gasped at the blasphemy of outsiders shouting and causing a ruckus.

"Eloise!" Somebody shouted.

"Stop this!" Another voice.

The hooded figure of the elder stood before them with his hand held out in a silent sign to halt.

Except Will was having none of it. From out of nowhere the huge bulk of the man dove into the elder's mid drift with everything he had, sending them both to the floor.

Martin ran up the steps with Keely behind. They could smell the smoke and feel the heat lapping against them as they got nearer.

Martin grabbed at the body and pulled just before the flames engulfed it. The body fell to the floor.

The arms and legs falling apart with the straw that was stuffed inside.

"What the□?" Martin managed as somebody grabbed him. He turned and saw the angry face of Noah.

"What the fuck, Martin!"

Martin looked at Noah, then back at the dummy's head with straw stuffed clothes. He looked out amongst the crowd and saw faces that were once smiling and welcoming towards them, now pinched in hatred.

"I-I'm sorry," Martin stumbled over his apology. "I really thought it was Eloise!"

Noah patted him, and said, "Okay, this is bad, but we might be able to make it better."

"Really? How?"

"The other job I have. I'm afraid I really must insist on you all coming now."

"Into the woods?"

Noah nodded. "To kill the witch."

Chapter 26

It was a special day for everyone no less for Star and Leo as they struggled not to let Benny out of their sight. That was standard when having a child but increased exponentially when your child had gone missing.

"Are you looking forward to the music, Benny?" Star asked in the slightly childish voice she used with her son. No matter how big and broad he grew up to be, he would always be her baby boy. She'd remember him as being the little boy she had to care for and would continue to do so long after he towered over her and lived his own life.

It was sunny outside. Not quite as warm as the previous day, but enough for a mother to worry about her son getting a chill. One of the strange, and constant blows of cold air mothers warn their children about. The type that single out those foolhardy souls who assume a thin layer of cotton will keep them warm.

"Why don't you get your hoody?" she said to him. He nodded and walked off quickly. But now out of sight, she was overcome with worry.

What if the witch is hiding in his room? Her mind conjured up the question. Swirling her anxiety until she looked around with panic. Anything and everything was a danger to her baby boy.

"Hey Star?" Leo called. "Don't fuss. He'll be fine."

Except she wasn't. She knew it would take a while before the trust could ever be back. She'd forever become beside herself when she couldn't see her son.

She glanced over to him and tried to reassure him with a smile, but she couldn't fully commit to it, and her eyes could never lie.

"I can see your anxiety, love," he tried to say in a soothing way. This had been one of the reasons for them to come out here away from the outside world. Her panic-attacks of city life were too much, whereas here the world was a simple and kind place.

Until the witch appeared.

At first, she was but a legend. Something to discuss after meals and fill out the hours before bedtime. What first was assumed to be the well-constructed story from an elder, suddenly became a dark slice of reality when she began to show herself.

And take people.

Then children.

"I'm just going to check on him," Star said, as if she had no other choice, and as she stood up, she ignored her husband sighing.

She walked out of the room and up the stairs, noticing she couldn't hear Benny walking around the room above on the hard, wooden floors.

"You okay, Benny?" she called as she walked up the stairs.

There was no answer.

Her pace quickened almost as quickly as her heart-rate as she took the steps two at a time.

"Benny?"

At the top she turned left and went directly into his room.

She couldn't see him.

"Benny?" Worry and panic had set in and her heart was once again being squeezed.

She heard movement behind her. She turned and at the last moment saw the small body dive at her. She was caught by surprise that not only was it Benny diving at her, but that it came with a slicing, sharp pain in her lower legs. She fell to the floor before she knew what had happened to her. The knife had cut the calf muscle of her left leg and part of her Achilles tendon on her right.

"Arrgh!" she screamed, unable to take the full scene in as Benny plunged the knife into her stomach. Once. Twice. Three times. And as her arms went to her stomach, Benny swung the knife with an expertise a boy of his age should never have and sliced her throat. Blood began to spill as noise from below suggested Leo was coming to see what was going on.

But he was too late for her.

"Is everything alright?" he questioned, unable to hide the anxiety in his voice. He was scared, though he didn't want to admit to his wife, that something was wrong.

When he turned into Benny's room, all he saw was Star lying in a pool of her own blood, and a horrific injury to her throat that still expelled crimson in a way that it was obvious she could no longer be alive.

"Star!" He was on his knees in desperation, slipping around on the wooden floor.

"Daddy?" the small voice said from behind him, and then Benny clamped a hold of him.

"Benny? What happened?"

"Is she hurt?" The small arm hugged his back tightly and he felt tears well up in his eyes.

And then the other little arm slipped around and when he felt his son had something in his hands, it was too late. Benny whipped back his arm, slicing deeply into Leo's throat. The shock of the situation and the pain hit him at the same moment. He tried his best to turn around to get his son, but Benny continued to stab and stab as if he had no other choice.

Leo swung an arm half in defence, and half out of anger. He didn't have time to fully process what was going on. His energy, as was his life, drained in a shocking speed as he lost more blood. He made a final, half-hearted lurch before collapsing onto the dead corpse of his wife.

The life they'd brought into this world had been the one to end theirs. The irony.

Benny smiled at what he'd done and knew *she'd* be happy.

He left his dead parents to go and meet with her.

"I'm coming home," he muttered to nobody but himself.

The Last Weekend

Chapter 27

The celebrations on the stage halted abruptly, and a few heckles and boos were heard.

This was bad. Really bad.

They had stormed the focal point of the celebration and the whole commune hated them. It was hard to see a way back from here.

At first Noah was silent. Then through supressed anger he'd ordered them back to their house, and was seen standing like a naughty schoolboy nodding as Edwin shouted at him.

"They were scared," he pleaded, but Edwin was enraged.

"I've a good mind to kick them out; or better still banish them to the forbidden woods!"

All Noah could think about was how his chances of becoming an elder were in doubt.

"What if I take them into the woods and we kill the witch. What if□"

Edwin was already shaking his head, though it wasn't clear whether he was telling Noah not to bother or that anything he did now was futile. He'd allowed his guests to cross a line, that was clear. Crystal clear.

"Go then! If you all make it back alive, perhaps we can look at forgiveness, but Noah?"

Noah looked up hopefully, "I am very disappointed."

"I know. Once again, I can only apologise."

"I sometimes wonder about these little stints of having people… You're lucky this group is special." The last few words softened and Noah wondered whether he was going to be forgiven after all. "Now go!"

"Yes, sir." Noah turned and was gone. Bad leg or not, he couldn't bear to be around the faces of the locals who looked at him like he was the one to have brought great shame to them all, and he gritted his teeth and jogged as best he could back to the house.

When they got inside, they headed for the lounge area. Many snatched glances were shared between them.

"Shit bricks," Verity said first, but no one else spoke again for a long time.

When Noah came in, he looked panic stricken, like the whole weight of the situation was on his shoulders alone.

"I'm sorry," Keely was the first to speak. It was no surprise she was apologising on behalf of the whole group. "It was a mistake."

Noah was about to respond when Martin jumped in, quite literally. He moved in front of everyone and spoke through a pained, but highly cultivated and practised sombre face. "I feel I owe the group the biggest apology! I was the first to jump to the very naïve conclusion that the dummy was Eloise… Look, Noah, how could I not? You have all been extremely hospitable to us, but we are a different set of people and we don't honestly know everything about you and your beliefs. It was wrong to think what we did… *what I did*, but I'm afraid I did. I cannot take it back, so all I can do is apologise profusely and hope we can move on from this."

Noah had been nodding, and perhaps was accepting of the words, but he still wrestled with the long-term effects of what had happened. "I see," he began, keeping his cards close to his chest. "The Celebration Day is a big event here. It should be a time for us to be thankful of what we've achieved, to… dare I say, show off a bit to outsiders." He paused as everyone stood around fidgeting with hands, pulling or twisting of hair, and biting nails. "You've let yourselves down. I hate to also say this, but you've let me down! Do you really think we'd burn a human-being? And right in front of everyone?" He was animated, his face contorting into all ways of displeasure, his arms flapping and gesticulating, and he moved from one leg to the other.

"I apologise, again," Martin said.

"We *all* do," Keely interjected. There was a Mexican wave of nods around them. The jokes had disappeared.

Noah held up his hands. "I understand. I get it, truly I do, but now you have to prove your worth. Your ability to be trusted once more."

"Yes. Yes, of course," Martin said and reached out to touch Noah on the shoulder. "We will do anything required of us." He looked around at everyone. "Won't we team?"

Noah held up his hands for them to stop. "Okay. Come and take a seat. Everyone. Come. Come. Sit down and I will go through how we can make this right."

Verity and Di sat together with Iain squashed in next to them. Rick, Jarrod and Will sat in single chairs, and Dan sat on the armrest of the smaller sofa that Martin and Keely now sat on. To Jarrod they looked like a couple. He noticed the sideways glances and the brushing subtle touches masquerading as accidental. Corporate networking at its best. Though who was he to point fingers? He'd been beating off in the shadows like some sort of freak, too.

"We shall be participating in the activity in the woods sooner than we had anticipated."

"Woods?" Verity quizzed. "I thought we were going back to our jobs?" She looked around with an expression on her face that clearly didn't understand the severity of the situation. She didn't storm the proceedings like some lentil-loving activist.

Noah shook his head. "Look, er, Verity, is it?" She nodded. "Things have changed a bit now. The schedule has now, er, been rescheduled. Your colleagues who were with me cutting down the plantation were advised of something we were going to do□"

"A training exercise," Martin jumped in with. Classic director mentality. He had to be the one to have the final word, and to leave nobody in any doubt he was a leader *and* decision maker – even though everybody knew this wasn't his jurisdiction and so had no authority. Martin was hating that. He never wanted to be just one of the crowd, following someone else's orders. He had to be the cream of the crop. He'd felt the breath of the ginger bully forcing him to do things, and he was never going to have that again.

Noah looked at him ready to scold him for his interruption but then did something he wasn't used to doing. Lie.

"Exactly. I am going to take you all out into the woods for an exercise on survival. It was meant to be later, but now… er, considering recent events, I think it's best to remove you all from the celebrations and do this little task this afternoon. How does that sound?"

It was Keely's turn to throw in her penny's worth not wanting to be upstaged by Martin. He may have a higher status in the company and a swinging cock, but that didn't mean she couldn't stand shoulder-to-shoulder with him here. She also knew if it came to it, he'd fall for her charms. She liked him to a point, but if push came to shove, she'd boot him over a cliff to save herself. That was the standard corporate mentality.

Besides, she had a bigger plan to execute.

"And we are *all* doing this now, right?" Said as a statement to be confirmed rather than a question. Classic managerial psychology. If their statement is wrong, they will critique the information presented to them as being weak, vague, and easily misinterpreted. If it's right, it's because they are quick to understand with their superior intelligence. Genius.

"Yes. *Everyone*," Noah confirmed. A confession almost tumbled out of his mouth. He should really advise them of the risks involved. There was a high likelihood some of them would get injured or not make it out alive. These were details he should really be forthcoming with; except he knew he couldn't – not if he wanted to make things right and have a chance at becoming an elder.

He glanced around them again. They were all soft-faced, and pale-skinned from hiding inside when a drop of rain came from the sky, or the wind got up. Even the men that blustered out their boasts of conquests could not be trusted to stay and fight like true men. He'd experienced men like them before. Loud and cocky until the shit hit the fan…

He added, "It's a bit like paint-balling without guns."

"In what way?" Martin was first to ask the questions again, but Keely was hot on his heels. Noah took a deep breath and hoped they fought as strongly as they asked questions.

"Are we getting something? Like a flag?"

Noah made a non-committal face. It was neither a confirmation nor denial. "Well, through the woods is a house. In that house is a witch. We have to hunt the witch."

"Like someone dressed up?" Dan questioned.

"Exactly." Noah waved this off but couldn't look into the faces of any of them. He really didn't like how this had come together. It was nothing like he had envisioned when speaking to the elders. He was a good man at heart. Raised with principles he was now jamming into a sack and throwing away. He looked at the little lambs he was about to take to slaughter and felt tremendous guilt.

Noah couldn't admit it, but he was scared. Bordering on petrified. Earlier he'd been caught up in the notion of becoming an elder. He'd recognised a problem and had confidently suggested the solution – except it involved a host of innocents he probably should give the full disclosure to. The facts were that virtually nobody had gone into the woods and come out alive. The only ones who had were Star, Leo and the two children Rosie and Benny, although Rosie was now missing and now that he thought about it, Star and Leo had been absent from the celebration. With so many people it was always easier to see who was there rather than who wasn't.

But the bottom line was if you went into the woods, you either never returned or had a timebomb ticking over your head.

But how the hell did you tell people they were going to kill an actual witch? Or die trying?

"I would suggest you layer up and return here. If you have any torches, bring them. It sounds daft, but from the stories I hear, even though it's a bright day, once in the woods everything changes."

"What d'you mean?" Di asked. "Like it's different weather in there?"

"It might be snow!" Will jested but nobody was laughing. The narrative had been vague but question marks hung in the air and there was an unspoken hysteria beginning to build.

"Fog," Noah said almost quietly. "People have spoken of a thick fog that suddenly appears like in that movie."

"*The Fog*?" Will grinned.

"Yes," Noah said, and whilst he did his very best not to sound annoyed it was obvious that if Will was half the size he was, and not in his plans for heroism/sacrifice, then he'd show the young buck exactly what happens in the community when people step out of line.

"It's exciting, isn't it?" Martin said, still convinced it was going to be a fully immersive role-playing exercise. "Right up your street, Dan, huh?"

Dan looked at him like he wanted to tie him up and punch him in the face until he cried for his mummy. Instead, he simply uttered. "I'm prepared for whatever is thrown at me. Marines are trained to be ready for anything."

"Good stuff, soldier!" It was a sarcastic jab although Martin never realised how it sounded. To him he was motivating and rallying the troops.

"Right. Ten minutes and meet back here."

They all filed out at a sombre pace, leaving only Noah, who was quick to find a chair. He collapsed into it with his head in his hands. He was overwhelmed with emotion and was surprised he felt that way. He'd not felt like that since he was last in the city. His job was high-pressured and high-powered. Great big highs, but plunging lows. The whole time he was on an emotional rollercoaster.

He took a deep breath, turned his head all the way right and then all the way left, doing his best to free the tension built up at the base of his skull. He closed his eyes and massaged his neck, gulped, and looked up.

Rick stood there staring at him.

Noah cleared his throat. "Right. Ready then?"

Rick grinned at him. "You don't have to put the act on for me," he said, a sly, lopsided grin appearing on his face. "I know what's out there. Some of us will probably not make it back, right?"

Noah remained silent. He didn't want to say any more than he had to.

"Those kids have come back evil. You know it. How many others have ever made it back out alive?"

Noah was sizing him up, unsure of what he was all about. He couldn't understand whether or not he was there to cause trouble or help. "The odds are not great," he said evenly.

"Because they were scared." It was a statement.

"Probably. Who isn't?"

"I'm not scared," Rick stated. "Dan is ex-marines and Will is young, dumb, and full of cum. Jarrod is like me. You don't need to worry about Keely."

"The others?"

Rick shrugged. "Good talkers and making up the numbers, but ultimately useful distractions."

"How do you know what's out there?"

Rick smiled. "I've known for years. I'm not afraid to die, *Gar-ret*." He grinned.

"How'd you know my *real* name?" Noah's stomach dropped. He hadn't been Garret since the financial escapades in the city. He changed his whole persona when he appeared here. He ditched the ties and grew his beard. It was why he'd had such a soft spot for this group. They weren't exactly the high-fliers he was, but they were caught in the corporate web like he'd been until he broke free.

"I know a lot." They heard footsteps approaching. "They don't need to know."

Noah was left with a lot of questions, but also something else. A feeling that perhaps having an ally would be a good thing.

When everyone appeared in sombre silence, Noah nodded slowly towards them. They were hardly an army of warriors but sometimes you had to make do with what you had.

“Let’s go,” he said, and out they went.

“I love working for Uncle Sam!” sang out Will.

“Not appropriate,” Dan huffed loudly, and when Will noticed that no one else was amused he ceased.

It felt different leaving the house. Some of them for the last time. All of them would be forever changed.

Chapter 28

There was a murmur through the undergrowth. The sound of a loud whistle blowing from the treetops. The people below grew wide-eyed as there, out in the field, was a troop of *them* walking with purpose towards *their* world.

They normally stayed away. They were fearful of what may lay here within the trees. But now they walked without fear and trepidation but worse than that: with a warrior's strut.

The largest of them stood there and growled. The sound of anger was used in the wild as a warning. He was ready to fight, but still bearing his sharp teeth, he turned towards his fellow man and woman, and nodded for them to run back and tell the others.

A woman with long scraggly dreadlocks held his gaze for a second. An admiration of the brave, until he nodded forcefully, and she knew he wanted her to leave, too.

A small giggle played out. Benny, with blood-stained hands and crimson drops surrounding his mouth like a cherry sweet, grinned manically. Now orphaned, the child would grow to understand the true ways of the world. The side with the power and not the façade of some hippy commune.

He caught Benny's eye and shot out an arm pointing in the direction of the house. Benny wasn't interested and instead looked out at the gang that grew larger as they got nearer.

"Go!" the man now roared. Benny frowned defiantly, bunched up his fists, huffed and stomped off after the others. His thirst for death was insatiable after murdering his parents, and he was desperate to have more bloodshed.

Outside it was sunny, but behind him, the guy was used to the dark fog that lived around. It was the cause of many an inquisitive villager coming to a sticky demise. The whispers of the fog were there to confuse. It threw voices and disoriented until the person didn't know which way to go. Instead of running for the freedom of the fields they often ran deep into the eye of the storm.

Once you saw the large house, it was already too late.

The Last Weekend

Chapter 29

Martin walked confidently ahead with Noah. He had a stupid shit-eating grin on his face like he was off out on the tiles rather than towards a forest that people rarely came back out of. The guy thought he was fucking John Rambo.

"So, what's the plan?" Martin asked leaning in slightly to Noah like they were co-conspirators. "We run around for a little bit? Maybe put on a bit of a show and then come back out? See how we get on?"

Noah knew it was hard to explain. He'd tried to but this guy didn't get it. He thought this was one big game. How do you make someone understand that this game was real. Maybe this was the way to go? He'd certainly put in more effort if he thought it was a game, rather than life or death. People often did. They were strange like that.

"We have to locate the witch," Noah said deliberately vague. He was frustrated that the importance of the mission was being missed and that nobody else seemed to be as nervous as he was. Nerves were good for some people, but others - and looking around these were probably the others he'd spoken of – would freeze, piss themselves and cry. That was the last thing he needed. Witch hunters rarely had to deal with grown-up toddlers.

"Ahh, yes," Martin continued. "Someone dressed up, huh? A bit of makeup and a few groans, right?" He winked. "What do we do when we get her? A bit of the old-fashioned rough-housing?" He nudged Noah, who calmly considered smashing the guy's nose flat across his posh face. Killing a witch was hardly the rough and tumble of this guy's public-schoolboy upbringing.

"We kill her."

"Nice! That'll do it!"

Noah sighed, "I sincerely hope so."

"The forest does look spooky, to be fair," Keely observed with a mild hint of surprise. "How the hell d'you manage that?"

"Woods," Noah corrected her. "They cover a smaller area and the trees don't provide a canopy. Forests house more wildlife, too."

"There's a difference?" Will muttered like this was some great revelation that had been kept from him. Noah just looked at him like he might be forced to do him some harm.

"He's literally just told you that," Di muttered exasperated.

"Kids." Verity's catchphrase was back.

"We never enter the woods," Noah said, looking out at the dark trees and then back at them all. He noticed the lad Rick looking serious. He thought back to their brief conversation in the house. If he knew what was happening, then perhaps he truly knew about the witch.

Looking off into the woods it appeared dark and hazy. It was like the mist of an early morning floating over a lake. The warm breeze coming together with the cool water producing the tiny droplets in the air.

There was a crudely made fence that surrounded the wood. Only the brave had stood with wooden stakes and rolls of barbed wire, quickly erected the barrier without so much as a glance within. Neither strength nor aesthetics were of importance as they banged in nails and hightailed out of there.

"You want a gate, mate!" Will smirked as Noah carefully bent to squeeze through the hanging wire.

"Don't be a dick!" Di said with an eyeroll.

"Kids," Verity muttered again which was getting more than a little annoying.

Rick looked at Jarrod and nodded. "Ready?"

"Sure," Jarrod replied, but he really wasn't sure. He was entering an unknown world and the woods looked ominous. He was staring his possible death in the face and instead of running he was embracing it.

Despite the fence going along the perimeter of the trees, an orderly queue formed in a true British way. Only Will tried stepping over the fence out of the line and in a comedic way got his combat shorts caught, and in yanking them fell over onto the other side. He had a tear in the material that showed way too much leg.

"What the fuck are you doing?" Dan goaded, as an embarrassed Will struggled to his feet. "You wouldn't last ten minutes in the army." It was his typical response to anyone making a mistake.

"Whatever." Will was wounded and would probably try something heroic before the day was out to prove his manliness – even if it was for his own benefit.

When they were all through the fence, they walked with careful footing behind Noah, going deeper and deeper into the woods. The trees loomed overhead and the branches moved very slowly as if reaching out towards them. The grass was long and dark threatening to house blood-thirsty animals that might jump out with sharp teeth ready to sink into their throats. There was a magnetic pull that kept them moving as sunlight struggled to get through.

The leaves were thick and in the snap of fingers the sunlight dulled until it felt like it was dusk. More than a couple of them were questioning again why this wasn't a forest.

"Shit," Di suddenly said, her voice tinged with fear. She was looking back behind them. "Where is the fence?"

Verity and Iain were the first to look. "It's…" Verity began and soon realised she wasn't sure. Iain pointed behind them but looked unsure, as well. His arm was moving a little right and left too unable to remain in one place.

"There somewhere, I'm sure."

That's when the mist thickened. It crawled along the ground like dry ice, and this some 80s music video or slasher video nasty. At some point a scantily-clad woman would appear screaming and finding a reason to show her breasts.

"What's happening?" Di said, looking all around nervously. They all remained still.

Noah was about to speak when Martin jumped in with a huge grin on his face. He still thought he was part of some theme park attraction.

"Wow! You guys sure know how to immerse yourselves into the full role, don't you? This is really impressive!"

"This isn't an effect, is it, Noah?" Rick stated, although positioned as a question for the benefit of the others.

"It's not?" Verity said. No longer calling everyone kids, and with a distinct worry creeping into her voice. When the bitches of the group mellowed to softies it was a worrying time.

"No. Of course not, right?" Keely added. She understood it was real but seemed less worried than Di and Verity. Will and Dan remained silent, but they were looking all around and things appeared to be more real.

The fog-like wisps covered their shins and began to grow, climbing up as if it was water filling up around them.

"It does this," Noah said in a slow, careful manner. He was conscious his voice might quiver if he wasn't careful. "These woods are haunted. It's not a tale. It's true."

"I don't get it," Iain spoke up. "The temperature hasn't changed so there's no reason for this to happen? The atmosphere should dictate the mist, mixing the warm and cold but… I dunno." He'd started off confidently spilling some scientific narrative but soon lost track of what he was trying to say and gave up.

"I don't like this," Di repeated as the fog moved up their bodies and fully engulfed them.

"Let's stay together," Noah said. "Maybe hold hands."

"What?" Dan said like it was a direct shot at his manhood. "I'm not holding hands with a□"

"Shut up!" Di said, grabbing his hand whether he wanted to participate or not.

"Fine," he conceded, but had little choice, as her vice-like grip was causing his fingers to go numb.

Martin's initial cockiness had begun to drain as they stood together in a huge circle, the thick air around them clearing just enough to allow them to see each other alone with a few feet ahead.

That's when they heard the child cry.

The shock of the sound made the circle fracture in a number of places.

"Hello?" Di called, her breathing loud, like she was on the verge of a panic attack. Her lack of calorie intake, coupled with the excitement, was causing an adverse reaction to the dire situation she found herself in.

"Help me!" the child-like voice responded moving quickly from right to left.

From the other direction was a call from a familiar voice.

"Guys! You're here!"

"Eloise?" Will said, then called out in response. "Where are you, Eloise?"

"Help…!" her voice then appeared to move from left to right.

The child was still sobbing, it was growing fainter.

"We're here!" Verity called, turning round on the spot.

Without warning, the sound of wind bellowed around them. The mist swirled as it was whipped up by a force nobody could see. The absence of a breeze made it even more bizarre.

"Will?" The voice of Eloise called once more but this time there was a desperation to her voice. "Help me? *Please?*"

"I'm coming!" Will called and blindly set off.

"Will!" Dan called to him. He was experienced to know you couldn't allow emotions to take over your common sense. You had to stay on track; understand your mission and the end goal. But he was a civilian now and his stone heart had softened a touch. He followed after Will.

"Where are you going?" Martin said and walked half-heartly behind them.

Verity, Di and Iain were walking quickly, their pace bordering that of a lumbering jog. Neither had run much faster than that in years, and they were never going to make the track events in the Olympics to represent Team GB.

"Hold on!" Noah was saying not sure which group to follow. He stood like a scarecrow, arms outstretched to the side calling all around. It was a time when they needed to stay together and listen to him and yet here he was, herding fucking cats.

The pea-soup atmosphere still moved around them and soon only Rick, Jarrod, and Keely remained with Noah who seemed shellshocked.

"Come back!" he hollered in each direction but it was futile. Soon the sound of their plodding footsteps disappeared away from the remaining group members; they were gone.

"Shit," Keely said. "Imagine trying to manage them?" It was meant as humour, but Jarrod wasn't sure how to take it.

"This place is dangerous," Noah warned. "Together we had a fighting chance. Together we were strong…"

"Against the witch?" Keely said the line like she didn't believe it.

"She will pick people off one by one," Rick said evenly.

Despite the mist, and the fact they all stood within a 4ft radius of each other, Noah narrowed his eyes and said, "What do you know?"

"I listen to what you say, that's all." Rick held up his hands and looked away, not in guilt, but almost dismissing any accusation coming his way. "Look, I've spoken to a few people whilst I've been here. I believe what you say. My mind is not as closed off as others… it's nothing more than that."

"Are we just going to wait here?" Jarrod asked. He also suspected Rick was hiding a lot more than he was admitting, but the group had suddenly split into three and Noah was right, the safety in numbers had now dropped to four.

"Follow me," Noah said with a huff. "I should've warned them." He was mumbling to himself.

"What?"

"It's the witch," he said, throwing back a glance before continuing. "If you cannot see the person's mouth moving, don't believe a word you hear. She's a great manipulator."

The path, of sorts, appeared to be beaten into the ground. The question of who walked the trails to keep them marked was on Jarrod's lips but he didn't ask the question as he was too scared of the answers he might get.

"Jarrod?" It was a voice that didn't belong to anyone there. "I'm lost. Are you there?"

Jarrod stopped in his tracks. "Paige?" He couldn't see her but he could see her the way she looked in the picture on his phone. Stood topless and looking at him with sadness. The image coming alive with hands reaching out to him.

"Jarrod!" Noah demanded. "It's not her!"

Jarrod looked at Noah. "Paige?" he spoke again.

Noah turned and with real anger stamped down. "Listen to me! It's not her!"

"I know what you're thinking," the voice of Paige now taunted him. "I'm not her, am I?" Now it turned sad as it continued. "I could never be her, could I? In fact, what reason do I have left to live! What reason, Jarrod? Aaargh!"

The voice shouted and began to choke, and splutter before stopping.

Silence.

They stopped and Rick just shook his head. "It's not her," he said in a voice a little more than a whisper.

"But…" Jarrod began. "I know…"

Noah pulled Jarrod forward. "Come on we have to keep moving. Ignore the voices."

How quickly the group had dissolved into smaller, more vulnerable groups. Noah felt stupid. Why did he think he could lead a bunch of strangers into the eye of evil and come out victorious? This was a battle they had no chance of winning.

He was nothing but a fucking idiot who wanted to be an elder. His stupid pride had got in the way of what he knew. And now, barely able to see a few yards in front him and getting ever farther into evil he knew there was no turning back.

This was nothing but a suicide mission.

He'd die a failure.

Chapter 30

Di realised all too soon she'd made a huge mistake. She was met by two tall trees and a huge thorny bush but there was no child in sight. Verity and Iain were soon joining her and breathing heavily.

"Jesus, Di," Verity began. "Don't just run off like that! I forgot how painful it is to run with big boobs!"

Iain was pretending not to be looking at her chest as he, too, was struggling to catch his breath.

"You heard it too, right? The child?" Di was worried she was going mad. This was a million miles away from her comfort zone. *Bloody team building shit.* It's the sort of thing that could only be conjured up in the mind of a male. She was surprised there wasn't the insistence to do the challenge topless, or end up wrestling at the end. There was still time.

"I heard something," Verity confirmed, looking at them with worried eyes.

"It might've been an animal," Iain said trying to be logical but seeming unconvinced by his own words.

"It wasn't an animal, Iain."

With his head down he muttered, "I guess not."

"Shit. What now?" Di was flapping her arms and beginning to panic. That only made Verity more annoyed. "Where are the others?"

"Let's go back the way we came," she said, but turned around unsure where that was. Then added, "I'm not running though."

They turned in circles trying to gauge forward and back, and walked slowly in a direction they assumed to be retracing their steps. All the trees and vegetation surrounding them looked the same.

"I've a good mind to keep walking out these bloody woods. This is breaking every type of health and safety rule in the book," Di continued to talk, feeling the comfort in her own voice, and Verity let her. It was marginally better than silence in the spooky woods. They all knew she had no idea which way was out, anyway.

Iain dropped back a step and stopped. He thought he heard something again. He turned his head, assuming it would make it easier to catch the sound.

And that's when arms grabbed him and pulled him over.

He opened his mouth to shout but foreign fingers stuffed a leather strap into his mouth, and with a swift yank cranked his lower jaw with a loud crack. He felt the bright-white pain in his jaw as it broke. Then a figure was on top of him, and another was grabbing at his tongue. There was a snap as his glasses were stood on, and tears dripped from his eyes when he felt the awful sharp pain of his tongue being liberated from his mouth as something sliced through it.

Only at this moment did Iain realised this wasn't a drill. It was not an exercise. He would never get out of these woods alive.

Dirty, scruffy people were all over him. The stench of stale body odour was thick but soon masked by the overwhelmingly metallic taste in his mouth. Blood bubbled from his mouth as he struggled to breath and not swallow the gushing liquid. Through the pain he was becoming light-headed. He was panicking, bucking around like he was possessed.

Somebody smashed something hard against his head and his world exploded into nothing. He'd never need to do a VLookup in Excel again.

"Iain!" Di shouted when she saw he was no longer behind them. She couldn't believe he'd disappeared without them realising. It spoke to how thick the fog was.

"He was just here!" Verity was visibly shaking. Her body jiggling and her arms wiggling like she was loosening up the muscles. She was turning circles on the spot scared of something coming up behind her.

"I don't like this!" Di said, her walking now getting faster. "I don't like this at all!"

"Are we not going to go back and look for him?" Verity showed some compassion, something neither of them were used to.

"Fuck no. Let's get out of here!" She broke into as fast a jog as she could without losing her balance. The visibility in front of her was down to ten feet, but at jogging speed that reduced her reaction time greatly.

"Not more… running!" Verity complained. One arm on her chest to reduce the bobbing of her boobs, the other pumping to keep up with Di.

"Stick with me!" Di called back, and turned just in time to see something on the ground that tripped her.

"Oomph!" the wind exploded from her as she hit the ground hard.

"Di!" Verity saw the bundle of Di just as something was swung hard at the back of her head. She saw a bright-white light and her world went black with unconsciousness.

There was crazy laughter all around and despite their lost memories of a time before they were living in spooky woods, someone was singing a truly awful rendition of 'Another One Bites the Dust' by Queen.

Chapter 31

Will stopped after a while and bent over, hands on his thighs, gulping in large breaths of air.

Dan was quick to scoff, "That's the problem with you rugby lads. All bulk without the athleticism to use it." Dan was puffing slightly but nowhere near as bad.

"It doesn't matter," Martin said, which was a lie as he was grinning ear to ear and for no reason but to show off, was running on the spot.

"I've been out with an injury," Will whined by way of an excuse.

"Broken fingernail?"

"ACL."

Dan scoffed like the knee injury was nothing. "Doesn't matter. Your muscle mass might get you pussy, but it needs to produce more energy than your body can cope with." The pissing contest was starting again. They both stood posturing with invisible dicks ready to swing back and forth.

"You're hardly Mr Universe."

"Lads, lads," Martin cut in. "Let's keep going and win this challenge!" He began to grin as he leant in like he was about to whisper some huge revelation to them. "They deliberately set this to split us up. We're the alphas of the group, so they think we'll cause too much friction and be too distracted arguing for them to waltz in and get the *"witch"* from under our noses!"

That got their attention. "You think?" Will said. His breathing had just about come to its normal level.

Martin nodded and ushered them to continue walking. "Of course! I've been on hundreds of courses that use these very tactics – in fact, gentlemen, I've run courses on them too!"

"So this is just a game?" Dan said, and there was something in the way the words came out that suggested he wasn't sure.

"Of course!" Martin grinned again. His perfect smile had to have been manufactured through a private dental practise. At times they were the clearest, and whitest part of him. He knew the theory of a lot of things and bullshitted his way through his lack of experience.

But Martin stopped for a second as he heard something.

"Marti! Marti!" It was Trevor. Big Trevor, the bully from his youth. He'd recognise the voice anywhere. It had taunted his dreams.

"That Noah guy looked a bit spooked back there. I'm not sure how much of a game it is?"

Martin was suddenly looking all around.

"You alright, Martin? You got the willies?" Will laughed.

Martin shook his head. "No. No. I thought I heard something that was all. What were you saying?"

"About Noah. I'm not sure he knows what's going on."

Martin was back and fully focused once again. "Ah, you see what they've done here, is keep Noah out of this. So that he knows something is going to happen but doesn't know when or where. It's like that movie…" he clicked his fingers. "Blair Witch□"

"Great time to bring that movie up," Will huffed.

Martin chuckled. "Oh, I see…haha! Anyway. The actors knew something was going to happen but didn't know what, so when they're lost in the woods and hearing noises, their screams of fear are real. The crew were creeping around to scare them."

"At least there's nothing in the trees," Dan said, but sounded like he was just humouring him. "No freaky stick people."

"Right," Martin said, now picking up the pace. "Let's continue how we are going. I think we're coming around the side to whatever is deep in these woods. The others are going to be all scared, so us men will show them how the big boys roll, right?" But he could still hear the voice taunting him. Just like back then, he did his best to push it to the back of his mind.

"Hell yeah!" Will shouted.

"Big boys?" Dan muttered. He fucking hated people who watched a few 80s Vietnam movies and thought they were Chuck *fucking* Norris. He didn't have a clue what was going on, but these two idiots were going to get him killed. One was young and full of testosterone and the other should know better.

Dan moved to the side to try and get a better angle on things. You had to understand the area you were going into before you walked blindly into an ambush.

Dan was still shaking his head when the sticks and leaves below him gave way and he felt himself fall. He hit the ground with a thud, feeling a jolt of pain in his left ankle.

"Dan!" Will shouted.

Dan felt around for broken bones but was quickly satisfied it was only a sprain.

"I'm down here!" he shouted, feeling slightly embarrassed. It was typical it was him who fell into a trap. It was then he noticed the spikes and realised just how lucky he was. The spikes were placed on beds of wooden crates and were sharp, metal and designed to give you more than a tickle. It looked like at one stage they'd all been lined together, however a couple had moved, leaving a large space in the middle. A few of them looked to be covered in something dark, that may or may not have been dried blood. He sat staring at this and knowing it was real.

"I don't think I can get out!" he shouted, realising the sides were too steep, and the hole too deep.

"Will! Leave him! We aren't going to lose this because GI Joe can't watch where he's going!"

"We can't just leave him!" Will was saying shocked Martin was even suggesting leaving a colleague behind.

"Military code!" Dan shouted. "You don't leave a fellow soldier down!"

"Wrong!" Martin shouted back. "You're the weakest link. Goodbye!"

"Fuck you, Anne Robinson!"

"Martin!" Will was shouting as the guy walked off.

"You fucking idiots!" Dan shouted.

"Sorry, Dan!" Will called back.

"Fuck you both! I hope you die!" There he sat wondering whether he would ever get out of the hole alive.

Will caught up with Martin. "That was really shitty, mate."

"It's a game. Only the strong survive. The least amount of us the better, right? We can continue to go around in a surprise attack."

"You think?" Will glanced back, which was futile because he couldn't see more than ten feet behind him, let alone the hole where his abandoned colleague had been left.

"I do."

The trees parted, and in front of them was a small shed. That wasn't the strangest part though. There were very few trees now and the air was clearer. The sun still wasn't exactly bright, but there was enough light to see the huge building in the background. It was a grand house, and hardly the small cottage they envisioned when they thought about a witch's lair.

"Shit," Will said. "The witch looks like she's got some cash!"

But that wasn't the only unexpected thing.

A small plane sat on a flat piece of land to the side. Even from where they stood, they could see it was abandoned, the white paint bespoiled with a green moss-and-algae combo.

All they could do was look and stare. That was no fucking broomstick.

The Last Weekend

Chapter 32

Jarrod didn't know what to think anymore. It was all like a dream. He looked around at where they all once stood and tried to take in the fact that only a small number of them remained. He'd made peace with the knowledge of never going back to Thornhill again. He was even, to a point, okay with never seeing Paige again, even though she was the one regret he knew he could do nothing about. But all of this was after seeing the community and how the place ran. He loved the satisfaction others seemed to have, constant smiles finding their home on optimistic face. He was pleased to hear nothing about mental health, stress, self-help, social-media, influencers – all of those things that had become regular in his every-day life that he no longer cared about. Yes, mental health mattered, and he was a victim of it as much as anyone, but now it was no longer a millstone you carried around your neck, but a badge of honour made fashionable by people who knew nothing about it. Those who did suffer were normalised and made to feel like all that was required was positive mental attitude and determination.

But this all seemed a lifetime away from the strange, and slightly supernatural atmosphere of the woods – or as named The Forbidden Woods. Did he really want to get caught up in entering a place that would most likely kill him? The stress-free off-the-grid living clearly had nothing to do with witch hunts and murder.

"How are we meant to kill a witch?" The words had slipped out of Jarrod's mouth before he realised he'd uttered them.

"We have to catch her off guard," Noah said, as if it was a rodent they were hunting and not something of another world. Still, they trudged on. The response did nothing to make Jarrod feel any better. It was hardly a master plan to go by, and whilst his knowledge of haggard old biddies, with pointed noses and warts, was limited to whatever the Brothers Grimm had depicted, he wasn't aware of any specific weaknesses they could target. In fact, now thinking about it, they were a powerful force to be reckoned with when they wanted to be.

"We need to locate her first," Keely said, marching in front with a newfound confidence.

"Everything will become clear," Rick said and momentarily threw a glance at Keely. She looked with the dismissiveness Jarrod had become accustomed to.

Jarrod realised both Rick and Keely knew a lot more than they admitted. Their whole confident demeanour was uncharacteristic of normal people. Jarrod was taken back to the office at the beginning of the week when Rick had been summoned before him. His cards had been kept quite close to his chest and these two both had seemed to act the coolest since they'd been on this mission. Even Noah appeared to be feeling the pressure. He followed behind them both, and just in front of Jarrod with his head down. He was almost resigned to his fate.

"Do you know where we're going?" Jarrod asked, but his question wasn't aimed at Noah, but at Keely.

"Sometimes you just have to look at the signs, Jarrod."

Jarrod looked around. The fog was clearing, and above he could just make out the sun but there was little to suggest a sign, unless he was missing something. All he saw were trees, until ahead he finally saw a break with land behind.

But that was when he felt a deep pressure in his temple. His vision blurred, and he suddenly felt light-headed like his blood pressure had plummeted. As his legs gave way, his vison completely black, he crumpled to the ground and lost consciousness.

When he opened his eyes again, Jarrod could see a lot further in front of him. He noticed Noah sat on the floor massaging his forehead.

"Noah!" The scream sounded like Keely.

Noah got up but when she shouted again, Keely's voice could barely be heard. Somehow, she'd been taken off deep into the forest.

"What happened?" Jarrod said, and he could feel the fear around him. Keely and Rick were missing.

"The witch," was all Noah was able to say. "She's taken them!"

Jarrod felt paralysed. It only underlined his concern. How were they supposed to defeat a witch when she could knock them out with such ease? Was she toying with them? Tossing them around like a cat before eventually getting bored and killing them?

"How has she taken them?"

Noah glanced behind himself, doing his best to Linda Blair his head all the way around. "I heard Keely screaming. She has them."

"Rick, too?"

"I guess. I don't know about you but the last thing I remember was us all walking, then suddenly I woke up."

"I'm finding it hard to think about a witch. I…I mean. I thought they were made up? How does she take bodies?"

"I can't be sure about witches. I only know the stories, but how else would we fall unconscious and them both be missing?"

It was possible. They were talking witches, and evil woods, so anything was possible. There was probably Bigfoot, dragons, and little green men, too.

"I guess," he said and slowly got to his feet.

"And then there were two," Noah said in a slight attempt at humour. He dusted himself off and they continued to walk forward, both having no clue how long they'd been out.

"I don't like this," Jarrod confessed.

Noah looked over for a second with a serious look fixed upon his face. "If I can be honest with you, Jarrod. I don't like it either."

"Be straight with me. Do you think we have any chance against the witch?"

"There's always a chance. Wherever there's hope, chance is walking by… we have to grab some luck, use our hearts and hope for the best."

"That sounds like optimistic bullshit – no offence. Our chances aren't great, are they?" Jarrod said, unsure whether or not he liked Noah being so honest. Maybe he preferred it when he was shouting out the rally cry, and verbally pounding his chest rather than conceding the possibility of defeat. And this wasn't a game. This was real, and losing meant much more.

If they lost they would die.

The Last Weekend

Chapter 33

Troy couldn't help but wonder what had been going on. Earlier he'd helped take the bodies to the church. He'd been entrusted with hauling them down the steps into the cellar, and along to the part no one else knew about.

It made perfect sense to him. They couldn't just go and dispose of the bodies within the grounds. Nor could they dig graves as it posed to many questions that needed answering. Troy was given such tasks because he carried them out efficiently, and because, more importantly, he did it without question.

This was not the first incident he'd had to cover up, and he was beginning to question life in paradise.

Everyone was enjoying the festivities. After the disruption from the city slickers, which he personally found highly amusing, things had stalled, but soon the moonshine was flowing and the band was up going hell for leather, aided by the devil's water.

He was the only one to notice the elders slip away. Often they watched and celebrated from afar, but it was also not lost on him that when the music and alcohol was at full swing, they used the time to disappear. Nobody questioned it, or at least not out loud.

But he'd been watching. Just where the fuck did they go?

One by one they slipped behind the building and into the backdoor of the church. Troy stayed in the shadows, observing.

He slipped inside, quiet as a mouse, and saw them descend into the cellar. After a few minutes he went down there too, his feet making nothing but a whisper on the stairs.

The bodies were gone.

The secret door called to him. It invited him to take a chance, to cure his curiosity.

He was expecting a tomb. Or a large area with candles where the three might be seen chanting and slaughtering virgins. Okay, perhaps not the latter.

What he didn't expect to see was a tunnel. A long tunnel made from stone and heading out in the direction of the Forbidden Woods.

Was there really a witch? Was the whole thing made up?

Troy was questioning everything he'd ever known. Maybe now it was time for answers.

He looked behind him to make sure he was alone, and disappeared into the tunnel.

The Last Weekend

Chapter 34

The last thing they expected to see was an aircraft and a huge manor house. Granted the woods were a very bizarre experience that defied all logic but once you got through that, here was something else. Something quite unexpected.

"Don't you find this a little strange?" Will quizzed, glancing from the abandoned private jet towards the well-kept hedges that bordered the grounds of the house. "Back there is a community living off the grid and going back to nature, and a short walk away is some millionaire's paradise?"

Martin shrugged and continued walking ahead. "Country folk are strange. They don't understand the real world. Anyway, come on! We've got a witch to get!"

Will pushed on even though his legs were beginning to feel heavy. He couldn't understand how Martin had got where he was without having an inquisitive nature. Will was no expert but the woods were definitely a lot more than special effects. Why would a community of pagans waste money and resources for some stunt? It didn't make any logical sense.

"Hey, Martin?"

Martin looked frustrated he was being called. "What?"

"Shouldn't we think this through a bit? Your plan so far is to storm the building without looking at the best entrance to get inside? Also, we don't know she's in there, do we?"

"Where else is she going to be? She's not going to be in the plane, is she?"

They were on the outside of the grounds, following the manicured hedges towards the left side of the building. The sun was peeking through the mist, which was slowly lifting the closer they got to the house.

"I'm not comfortable with this," Will admitted. "If this is some sort of challenge then why would we be allowed to just walk up to a door and get inside? Where's the challenge in that?"

Will couldn't see Martin's face, but the pause had him thinking Martin had probably rolled his eyes.

"This a bit of fun. We fucked up their little gathering and we've been sent away to play in the trees until they've got pissed enough to allow us back."

Will couldn't help but think that somewhere along the line they'd switched roles. Like one of those stupid Hollywood movies were two unlikely people changed bodies, and viewers were entertained by their idiotic escapades. Martin had taken the role of foolhardy, and will found himself being cautious and sensible.

"I can't help but think about Dan in that hole, though."

"He's been in worse situations. He tells us enough about them! Sitting on his arse in a hole is hardly nuclear warfare, is it? He'll see the funny side later on when we're knocking back moonshine with the others!"

Will wasn't so sure but Martin's confidence was infectious so he went with it.

As the hedges ceased, they could see a huge orangery extending out along the left side of the house with tables inside like some boutique restaurant. Over to the left of that they could see a large lake with a small island in the middle. It would be a beautiful scene to gaze at while eating brunch and sipping wine.

"Uh-huh," Martin said walking up to a door at the side. Will looked through the many panes of glass to see inside. The tables were set for meals. Silver cutlery, wine glasses and napkins were set out ready for guests.

"It feels like we're burglars," Will muttered.

"Only if we steal something."

"It's still breaking and entering."

Martin pulled the sleeve of his hoody over his right hand as he grabbed the handle and turned it. Will was impressed that Martin was thinking smartly about not leaving fingerprints but it also went to show he was now worried about what they were doing, and on some level was covering the risks.

Martin thought the door was locked, but as he pulled a little harder, the top of the door opened; it appeared caught at the bottom. The wood of the door slightly warped with the changing weather.

"Here, let me," Will said, nudging him out of the way. He did an efficient grab and tug manoeuvre, and the door came open.

They slipped inside feeling completely underdressed.

Each step on the terracotta tiles seemed incredibly loud, but the place was so large that unless you were in the same room it was unlikely you'd hear it.

Was this a hotel? Or a wedding venue? How strange would it be to find out that people paid to be within a place that a community had considered to be forbidden? Or was it all a ruse? Was the talk of a witch a euphemism for capitalism? Whilst the place called Woden lived off the land and embraced minimalism, a stressful walk through the trees, a world of wealth and high-society capitalism was evident. A world most professed to escaping from was so close. The abandoned jet and well-maintained grounds - was this the witch?

"What is this place?" Martin said thinking the same thing. Martin walked towards the large double doors, Will following behind. Martin determined where they were going, pulling rank wherever possible, and soon they were creeping out into the main section of the house. The place was draped in darkness, but to the left the corridor snaked around to the side, and a reception area could just be seen through slivers of light, whereas to the right everything seemed dark. Clearly shutters were pulled across the windows at the front of the house blocking whatever sunlight was left in the day.

"I'm thinking either right at the top of the house or at the bottom, right?" Martin acted like he wanted confirmation from Will, but they both knew that wasn't the case. The vague nod at democracy was nothing but a ruse for Will to think he had a choice.

"Sure."

"Let's go up. Witches wish to be high up, right?" Martin was still thinking of old women casting spells, and suddenly Will had visions of the movie called *The Witches* – the adaptation of Dahl's book filmed in a large Newquay hotel. What if there wasn't a witch, but plural. A whole coven of them? Bald heads, pointy features and a penchant for turning children into mice! He fucking hated mice.

"You don't think there's more than one, do you?" He mentioned his fears out loud. "Witches, I mean?"

"I bloody hope not," Martin said but in a way that said he was now thinking about it. He pulled out his mobile and used the torch. Along the walls were portraits of people probably no longer living. Will could tell Martin was less confident now they were sneaking around the house, and Will suddenly felt like they'd fallen into a Netflix horror movie.

"To think, I was in a board meeting this time a few days ago, spinning a yarn about overheads and the roadmap for next year. Now, here I am creeping around Amityville." Martin added a false laugh to it. Both not wanting to admit to the other they were far from okay.

And that's when the child appeared making them both jump.

"Hello?" The small lad walked forward into the beam of the light. "Are you going to help me?"

"What the fuck is that?"

"It's a child."

"I can see that! What's it doing here?"

The child held up a hand against the light and Martin was quick to point the beam away from the child's face.

"Sorry," he said. "Who are you?"

The child looked scared. He was probably about eight or nine with floppy blond hair, and baggy, denim dungarees. He had on a striped T-shirt underneath and looked like a knock-off version of Chucky.

"Help me?" the child said, but it was in a confident voice as a statement rather than a question.

They walked tentatively towards the child, who smiled slightly and pointed towards a door.

"Where are you taking us?" Martin asked as Will looked all around. He didn't like it. It felt all parts of fucking weird.

"Will? Come on!" Martin said. When he turned back the child stood in front of a large door and gently rapped his knuckles against the dark wood. It was more than weird.

There was a click.

And the door opened slightly.

Martin grinned at Will. "See! We're first here!"

They wandered at a saunter into the room. Everything was dark but they could just make out shapes. The door slammed behind them, and they knew they'd made a huge mistake!

The Last Weekend

Chapter 35

Dan tried again to climb out of the hole. He grabbed a vine, which turned out to be something spiky with thorns. He had to get out, so he ignored the pain and gripped it tightly, whilst he tried to step up onto a rock. At first, he felt it was going to work, but as his whole weight pushed onto the rock, it was evident that not much more of the rock was in the side of dirt wall and it slipped out. He tried again but this time tried to kick his toe into the divot where the rock had been, but the dirt crumbled.

He remained looking up, hoping someone would come. He had more chance of a unicorn appearing.

This was not how it was meant to have turned out. All of his army training he'd endured; from a wet-behind-the-ears eighteen-year-old choking up on his own when missing his mum, then throwing up from death-drills in the heat, to carrying his fellow solider on his shoulders out of the range of a sniper in battle. His stories were vast and in-depth, and he knew it meant fuck all to those office pricks who'd been pulled kicking and screaming from their mother's nipples much later than normal. The likes of Martin had no idea what risk and danger were all about. He'd bought risk-free experiences and paraded them like he was a hero. The others were nothing more than whining babies. Even Will, who tried to masquerade as a big brave guy was a fraud. He ran into people smaller than him in a sport that stopped the match for an injury. He didn't see friends with missing limbs, speak to parents of fallen squaddies, the awful aftermath of a village massacre.

Those two pricks were walking freely above him whilst he was a laughing stock, lost and forgotten in a hole.

You never left a man behind. That mantra was beaten into them. It didn't matter what you thought of your squadron, their quirks will still remain, but for the most part your experiences moulded you into similar men. You quickly became family, and nobody would ever walk away from a family member.

Subconsciously, his left hand touched the sleeve of his right arm where his tattoo marked his past. The ink had begun to fade, the black now slightly dark green as the pigmentation of the old ink began to break up slightly and bleed. It was still legible, and more importantly a stamp of honour.

He was full of pent up aggression that he longed to release. He shouted in a way that was primal and close to a roar.

That's when a head appeared above him. And then another. And another.

Children grinned down at him. Almost mocking.

"Hey! Can you help me out of here?" he called. "Get some help?"

He could see the outline of their heads and just about hear grunts and whispers, but he had no idea what they were saying. Just his luck to be chanced upon by some fucking thick inbreeds.

Then he saw an arm move. It swung and he felt the pain as he realised he'd been hit with a stone.

BANG! Another.

The kids were laughing as Dan covered his head, and the stones still rained down upon him and with a lot more force.

He felt them on the backs of his hands as they laced behind his bowed head. The humiliation of this was even worse.

The stones were getting bigger and the force seemed harder. He did his best to move to the side, and rolled himself into a ball, making himself a smaller target.

"Stop!" he shouted. He couldn't believe that after all the horrors he'd seen in the Middle East, he was now being stoned by kids in the woods. The embarrassment turned to anger, but as the stones turned to rocks, his hope disappeared more and more with each painful hit.

His hands were bruising and he felt blood trickling, but it was after the first flash of white light where he was struck on the back of the head, that he knew he was in trouble.

"Get off me!" he shouted, and looked up just as something really big was hefted by two people straight at his head.

A war veteran, an explosives expert, and a master at hand-to-hand combat, Dan had fought for his country and survived, only to die at the hands of pure evil in the form of kids. How fuckin' typical.

Chapter 36

As soon as the door slammed behind Martin and Will lights flooded the room, and loud carnival music blasted out.

In front of them was a merry-go-round, and a number of small tents. Like a funfair inside a large ballroom.

"What the fuck is this?" Will said, and Martin had huge wide eyes and a twitching smile that couldn't make up its mind whether this was amazing or just fucking creepy.

The jolly organ music with its scales tune was quick in tempo, and it was easy to imagine this being outside with children laughing and eating popcorn and candyfloss.

Machines to the side flashed colours to attract people to spend cash, and the entrances of the tents flapped to beckon them forward and within.

The music slowed. The happy tempo dramatically dropped and the lights began to flash. At first the bright colours remained like it was just another effect, but then they switch off and were replaced by red.

Just red.

Speakers throughout the place pumped out cackling laughter. It jumped from speaker to speaker giving the illusion that someone was all around them.

"This is fucking weird, Will," Martin took a step back. If he wasn't ready to embrace it before, he'd completely U-turned now.

"This is not right." His face was scrunched with worry as he added. "The lights are red." Surely that was a bad sign.

Martin's mind went back to Noah on that first day, asking them to remove all red clothing. If it was so bad, why would it be flashing now?

The lights stopped and for a beat they were plunged into darkness. That was a petrifying few moments.

A single red beam highlighted one of the tents and the flap of a doorway opened.

"Roll up! Roll up! Come inside and beat the witch!" a voice sang out like a ringmaster.

Both Martin and Will began to move forward, but their steps were tentative.

"Beat the witch! Win a prize!" the enthusiastic voice continued.

Martin puffed out his chest and was first to enter.

He stopped.

In front of him sat a figure in a red robe. Lit candles were all around them.

"You've survived the forest, and stayed away from red! Grab the bat and beat the witch dead!"

A cackle came from the hooded figure, then words were formed in a very witch-like voice.

"Hit me, if you can!"

Martin stumbled, kicking over two bats. He looked down, then back up at the witch.

"Go on you pussy! Hit me hard!"

Martin picked up one bat and nodded to Will to do the same.

The figure remained still, but as they picked up the bats they suddenly felt heavy, like a force was pulling them towards the ground. It didn't seem possible. It was an invisible energy fighting them.

"Whoa! What the fuck!" Will said, then the bats shot up as they felt their natural weight again.

"Pus-sy! Pus-sy!" goaded the witch, her back to them still.

They took another step forward, then another, until they stood behind the witch. There was a flash and unexpected movement as the figure turned round, but Will and Martin weren't waiting for anyone and swung as hard as they could.

The hood and cape fell away as the person turning was hit from both sides and fell backwards onto the floor.

Martin couldn't believe it. The naked figure of Eloise lay there, the hood open, and fanned out underneath her.

"Eloise!" Will shouted trying to ignore the blood on the side of her face.

Martin was taken back to the night before and the last time he'd seen her looking like that. His guilt was unbearable and he didn't know what to do. Then he saw the smoke and realised her red cape was on fire. It had fallen on to a candle and was clearly not flame resistant.

"Shit!" he called and jumped on the smouldering material, but it did nothing to take away the dead eyes of Eloise staring back at them and the frozen look of horror on her face that was now broken and bloody.

Suddenly everything flashed red as through the speakers rang out *"Ding-Dong! The Witch is Dead!"*

"No!" Will said picking up her wrist to test her pulse.

"Turn your hand around!" Martin said. "Your thumb has a pulse you won't get a proper reading!"

Will switch his grip but was struggling. It wasn't something he'd ever done before. "Nothing!" Will said, then despite how it looked placed his head on her ample boobs to listen for a heartbeat.

"What the fuck, Will?"

"Shut up!"

The music seemed to be getting louder and flashing lights made them both more agitated.

"Fuck! Fuck! Fuck!"

Then it went quiet.

"Let's get the fuck out of here!" Martin said, grabbing at Will, both thankful they could no longer see her body.

What the fuck was she doing there? Had they really killed her?

They scrambled out of the tent, knocking into things. They finally found the door, and as they opened it they heard a clown-like voice giggle and say, "Y'all come back now, ya hear!"

They fell out of the room in a tumble of limbs and found themselves back in the corridor. They went to turn right but saw the strange child again.

"Fuck no!" Will said, and they turned and headed deeper into the house. They didn't wait to hear what the little shit had to say.

Chapter 37

Noah was looking increasingly more nervous as they walked along the well-maintained gardens. He seemed almost apologetic when he said, "I'm sorry for getting you all involved in this." He stroked his beard as he spoke.

"Believe me this is the most excitement I've had in years."

"But you know this isn't a drill, right?"

Jarrod nodded. "I know this is real. Am I scared? Sure? But fuck, Noah, I feel alive. Really, for the first time in a long time I feel like I have a purpose!"

Noah seemed to struggle with what to say to that. They headed past a stone statue of a Greek goddess. She stood proudly posing topless.

"You're quite unique," Noah replied. "Most people don't understand our ways and soon long for the normality of their lives. But you… forgive me for saying so, you appear lost but you look more at ease as each hour passes."

"That's fair," Jarrod agreed. "My life consists of make-believe. Can you understand that? I dream of having sex with my boss but know it will never happen. My ex left me long ago and yet I pretend it was only recently. My best female friend is in love with me after I fucked her in my kitchen… and my job is boring as shit."

Noah was amused, and his beard twitched with a hidden smile. "Your mind is fixated on sex… You ever think that might be the problem?" He stopped walking and threw his hands up. "Sorry. It's none of my business. I apologise. I used to be a psychologist before working in finance, and… well, it's easy to slip back in."

Jarrod shrugged. "You going to ask me if I'd fuck my mum, or something?"

"Not quite."

"I get it. It's all about affection, trust, close bond… blah blah blah. I've seen a shrink. I don't get it. He let me speak like I knew all the answers myself. Is that really meant to work? I pay a guy a hundred quid and he just listens to me? Is he silently leading me to my own conclusions?" Jarrod looked at Noah, who looked back with kind eyes and remained silent – not to mention annoyingly neutral.

"Ah, yes," Jarrod said. "You have that look. The silent gap that forces me to fill it. Is that it? You ask me how I feel, and why I think I do things?"

"I'm not here to analyse you, but yes, the point of your therapist is to help you to understand your issues without leading nor through any coercion. That's not always easy. Often patients are hugely influenced by subtleties, as they grab around for labels to hang their issues from. They want to know they're not crazy, and they want something to blame if they do something wrong, and finally, they want to know that they can get better."

They climbed up some steps and alongside a path decked with a wooden trellis covered in large pink roses.

"Did you know this place was here?" Jarrod asked Noah, no longer wishing to be a patient.

"I had no idea. I don't know whether this makes things better or worse. We… or I, at least, expected some small house. Perhaps a stone cottage with a thatched roof, but this huge place? No way."

Faintly they could hear fairground music, which blew Jarrod's mind.

"What the fuck is that?" They were in the middle of nowhere, standing in front of a huge house that looked dark and empty, yet the sounds told a different story.

"I dunno," Noah said, as they walked towards a doorway.

Jarrod had an epiphany. He thought about the drive out of Thornhill, and Edwin's face, and he came to a conclusion that made him stop. Pieces of a puzzle falling into place.

"He's a pilot," she'd boasted on many an occasion.

But something magnetic pulled at Jarrod, and he turned around and looked behind them. What he saw had him grabbing at Noah.

"What?" Noah said and turned around himself.

There in front of them and walking like soldiers were people and children, except nobody was smiling. They looked dirty, feral and had they been holding out their arms and dragging their limbs, then for all the world they'd have looked like zombies.

Except zombies didn't exist.

"Shit!" They pushed against the door but it was closed. In a panic they broke into a run and moved along the side of the house, all too aware these people were getting closer. And they looked angry.

In front of them was a wall with an archway. It led to the service area of the gardens where there were outbuildings, and gardening equipment all out of sight from the rest of the rolling landscaped gardens. Here they saw another entrance and this time the door was ajar – a can had been placed in the gap to stop it from closing.

Noah pushed open the door that had an emergency exit push bar on the other side, and they burst inside and pulled the door up behind them with a clunk.

"What the fuck, Noah?" Jarrod said, as they both felt for a light.

"I have no idea who those people are! They are not part of□" The place flooded with light and his sentence was snatched away with his breath. Jarrod may've considered he'd received all the shocks he could within the past twenty-four hours but this trumped all that.

The once-white walls were splattered in blood, and there hung up were the naked bodies of his two colleagues Di and Verity. He swallowed and went to speak but couldn't. His eyes uncontrollably drawn towards the macabre scene as if he had no other choice. Di's deflated, scrawny body was in sharp contrast to Verity's rounder, chubby physique. No one should be displayed like that in life or death. Their intimate parts on show for all to see. Both were covered in blood, although it wasn't obvious whether or not they were still alive. Neither had moved and both had eyes that were open and vacant. If these weren't dead bodies, Jarrod didn't know what they were.

"W-we have to move," Noah said, glancing back at the door expecting it to swing open at any stage.

"Shit, Noah… I thought…" he slowly shook his head and in a half-hearted attempt, tried to point at the obvious, but his arm no longer had the strength and his finger remained half-curled, unable to fully extend.

"I didn't know, Jarrod. How could I?"

Jarrod turned and grabbed Noah by his shirt. "How could you *not*?"

Noah accepted the attack without defence, realising Jarrod was angry, and scared but not really directed at him. "We knew people were disappearing. People will wander not matter what we say… but we didn't ask questions. That's not what we're about. Can't you see that?"

"You thought they just left? Are you really that naïve?" Jarrod's whole perception of the place had suddenly changed. He'd been drawn in by the romantic notion of a community that was drama-free and where everybody looked out for each other.

"You've seen Woden, it's nothing like this place. Here is… I really don't know. We have trust and… this? I don't even know what it is?"

"And the witch? Is there even such a thing?"

Noah looked beaten. He stopped, unsure of what to do anymore. "I don't know." The words were said with a disappointed sorrow. Everything he knew and believed was now questionable.

The door at the far end was shut, but they headed forward, unaware of what they'd find behind it. They both held silent reservations, knowing they were heading deeper into the house, and that only served to cut off their means of escape further.

Momentarily, they looked back to the door they'd entered and then at the bodies still lifeless as a degrading example of what could wait for them. The first of the bangs began on the backdoor and it boomed out within the silence in a deathly rhythm.

That was enough. Jarrod grabbed the door handle, pushed it down and swung open the door.

When Jarrod looked to the left all he saw was two children stood still like statues with one arm behind their backs. Their heads were down slightly but evil eyes looked up and they were grinning.

They began to march forward at the same time their arms whipped around clutching the sharpest knives Jarrod had seen in his life.

The Last Weekend

Chapter 38

Martin realised something was very wrong when he saw the underwear in the corridor. He knew right away what it was.

"Marti!" The familiar voice floated around with a slight distortion to it. It sounded like Trevor again. Big Trevor, the monster from his past.

"What's wrong?" Will was asking when he saw Martin stood rigid. It was as if his words were silent. They did not register with Martin at all.

Martin saw the panties discarded. Bright in colour like they were bikini-bottoms, but familiar with the spots of blood. Martin's blood.

Martin heard a voice calling him again, "Marti! MARTI!"

He turned, and what had been Will was now the hulking mass of Trevor. His bulging belly and man-boobs obvious under a polo-shirt clearly a size or two too small. His shocking ginger curls bobbed as he grinned through teeth that had gaps wider than average. Then the smell came from nowhere.

The greasy sweat of body odour mixed with a hint of garlic-breath took Martin back to those days in the halls. A fat hand wrapped around his throat as the garlic and sweat scent turned his stomach just as much as each thrust of pain from behind.

"No!" Martin screamed, swinging an arm round, and catching Will off guard. He fell to the floor, unsure of what had suddenly possessed Martin. He was just as freaked out but something had triggered Martin further, and now the guy was there with tears streaming down his cheeks.

Will went to speak as he pushed himself up, but just as his hands were on the bristly carpet, Martin kicked him full in the face. Will was blinded by the pain and he felt light-headed as his head whipped back, and his brain made contact with his skull.

Martin looked down at the naked body of Trevor with pure hatred. The fat, unattractive male with uneven wisps of ginger hair covering his body grinned back at him and it only made him madder.

"Leave me alone!" Martin shouted as loud as he could and kicked him hard in his genitals. Then again and again, knowing how much pain both physically and mentally that swollen member had caused him. He wished he had a knife. He longed to castrate him once and for all. To stop him from ever doing the awful act again.

Will passed out on the second kick to the nuts. The pain was too much for his body to take.

Martin stopped for a second when he saw something. The thing he wanted more than anything.

A knife.

It sat lonely on the long rug that ran the length of the corridor. A foreign object now felt right at home there. A gift from God, willing him to take revenge on the evil man.

Martin grabbed it and looked back at Trevor. Somehow, Trevor was now wearing clothes. The detail didn't register as peculiar as Martin grabbed at Trevor's jeans, popped the button like a randy teenager, and as the zipper lowered with motion, he yanked them down. Without further thoughts of what he was doing, he tugged down the underwear and took the knife to the small growth hiding in a mass of public hair.

It wasn't easy. He tried to slice, then saw. He stabbed the bag of testicles and yanked the knife hard to rip the skin open. There was blood.

A lot of blood, but Martin didn't care. He was no longer a corporate director in his late forties, but a teenager again. One who had been abused one too many times by this prick. This was what he'd dreamed of doing. Not so much grabbing the cock of another man, but slicing off that fucking thing so it could no longer invade his rear end any longer. He'd cried into a pillow too many times to understand that this was an act too far.

Will briefly came back round, but his hands received defensive wounds as Martin continued to go to town on his nether regions, and the wounds continued to squirt blood. Will collapsed back into unconsciousness once more, his body becoming weak. Very weak. The blood loss was too much.

When his knees began to slide, and Martin almost fell onto his own knife, he stopped. He looked over what he'd done and sobbed. Really sobbed. Like he'd not done in thirty years. The flood of repressed memories overwhelmed him. Lost in the horrors of years gone by Martin was no longer there in the hallway of a strange house but back as a teenage victim of rape.

"Marti…" the voice was back whispering to him. "Marti! Marti! Mart! Mart!"

"No!" he shouted, waving the knife into the darkness. Threatening a voice that had no body.

"I will always be here!" the voice taunted. "I will never die!"

"Go away!" Martin said. Bloody hands against his ears. The slick blade of the knife touching the side of his head.

"I'm inside you. Just like I was at St Alberts! Ha! Ha! Ha!"

"Go away! Leave me alone!" His arm swung out with the knife even though he knew nobody was there. When he went to pull it back, he couldn't. His arm was strong and now he couldn't control it. That's when it stabbed the air to the left and pulled back quickly to the right. The blade quickly slicing his own throat. He had no control. It wasn't him. He'd lost all control. He went to speak, then scream, but the blood choked back his words and by the time he was able to fathom out what he'd done it was too late. His body crashed to the floor and the blood of two men joined in some external hemorrhagic marriage.

The years of life had not prepared either of them for pure evil and that is exactly what found them that day.

Broken and lifeless, two men who'd previously barely spoken to each other now lay centimetres apart. Their souls reluctantly leaving their bodies as their deaths became official.

The Last Weekend

Chapter 39

There is something distinctively scary about children with knives. It might be the knowledge that they think it's a game and therefore might not know the difference between reality and make-believe, or it might be that to defend against them and willingly inflict pain on a child still seemed wrong – even if they are knife-wielding.

Neither Jarrod nor Noah were taking any chances, even when the two children in question were known to Noah. Rosie and Benny held hands and looked like they meant business.

As their walk turned into a jog, then a run, Noah grabbed the last door at the end of the corridor, and they spilled inside. A safety light glowed but gave off only a small amount of light. Two metal doors could be seen. It was a lift.

Jarrod was quick to press the large button on the wall, and Noah glanced behind them. With a click and whirr of mechanics the door opened, and they both frantically stepped in just as they saw the door they'd come through, opening.

There was only one button. And that went down.

The door took an age to close. The two kids sprinted at them just as the doors shut.

"We're going down." Noah observed.

"What the fuck is down there?"

The lift stopped with a clunk and a sudden jerk making them both stumble. The doors opened and in front of them they saw a short corridor in the same dim light, with draped curtains covering the end. A strip of light could be seen through the gap.

"I've got a bad feeling about this," Jarrod was saying and Noah just looked like he was walking to his death.

Jarrod didn't even realise he was making an involuntary murmuring sound as they got closer to the curtains. Noah tentatively reached out where they crossed over and pulled them apart.

The room was huge. A light was overhead but it was what the rest of the room held that shocked him.

"What is it?" Jarrod hissed, but expected nothing back as Noah had turned mute. Jarrod almost barged Noah to the side, which was a mistake as with them swapping places Jarrod tripped over Noah's retreating foot and fell forward, straight through the curtains.

He looked up and saw the huge circle of people dressed in long red hooded robes. Around them were hundreds of candles. Another pair were knelt in the middle of the circle and on the outside were three thrones, and beyond that what appeared to be a cross between and old-fashioned phone box and an up turned coffin with a veil over the doorway.

Everyone looked up at them.

"No," Noah gasped.

The thrones at the front were occupied by the elders of Woden. They all had staffs of gold with small animal skulls carved on top, and their eyes were fixed on them – the intruders.

"Noah!" the guy with the long beard exclaimed. It was Edwin. "Come in! Do join us!"

Noah sheepishly came through the curtains. He tried to take it all in but was overwhelmed. These were the people who had forbidden them all to enter the woods and now he knew why. It was all lies. Everything he knew was made up.

"What is this?" he said, his voice faltering. "The woods are evil, that's what we were raised to think."

Edwin nodded and held out his arms like he was some sort of messiah. "The woods are indeed evil. You've seen it with your own eyes. You think that fog is natural? And those poor lost souls residing there? Well, they're like human piranhas! They eat your flesh clean off, given half the chance!" He turned to the others, who nodded in agreement. "Their eyes glow red..."

"But I don't understand. I..."

"You don't need to understand, Noah. We do not ever enter the woods. Those that do are entering into a challenge with the witch."

Slowly, other heads had turned round, but the hoods hung so that faces couldn't be seen.

"Is the witch even real?" Noah did his best to keep his words strong and to the point. Inside he felt like this was his last speech. His *Butch Cassidy & The Sundance Kid* finale.

"Very much so," Edwin said, his tone measured and deliberate. For all the people in the large room, the place was incredibly silent. The hooded people allowed the new entertainment to continue.

"If that's the case make her show herself." His fists were balled up when, completely out of character, he shouted, "Show yourself, you old hag!"

And that's when he felt his throat constrict ever so slightly. A Darth Vader moment. That was all it took for him to drop to his knees with both hands around his throat, his face going red.

The veil over the large box moved as from behind it appeared a woman dressed in a robe as red as blood. Edwin nodded to her and took his seat.

"You want to challenge me, you fool? You think you can storm in here and demand me to show myself?" The figure was bent over slightly but her face could still not be seen. Her arm raised, then dropped dramatically. And with the movement, Noah felt the air gush into his lungs.

Jarrod stood behind him not knowing what to do. He was part of this no matter what side he took, and he might not even have the choice.

The witch struggled to walk for a second, and Wilfred was moving out of his seat. The witch swung her arm in his direction, and hissed, "No! I'm fine!"

The old woman straightened up, moved her arms in a circular fashion and before their very eyes levitated off the ground and moved slowly through the air.

"Fuck," Jarrod gasped.

She dropped down behind the two hooded figures in the middle.

"What are you?" Noah said the words that his brain struggled to comprehend, because he didn't know how to process it. Was it smoke and mirrors? Was this a ruse? Elaborate parlour tricks to fool the masses?

"None of those!" the witch cackled reading his mind. "You came here to kill me, right? Then why don't you try?"

He'd been sent here as a trap. The elders were never going to promote him to be one of them. His sand had fallen through the hourglass. Only a few grains remained and everyone knew it.

He stood up proudly and began to walk purposefully towards her.

"You cannot scare me!" he shouted putting on his bravest face.

There was a loud crack, coupled with Noah screaming in pain as his leg gave way.

"How's the knee?" the witch's voice was full of sarcasm and she laughed at the end.

"Oh my God! My knee!" He was grabbing it as the joint throbbed with pain.

"I am real, No-ah. I am here." She defiantly pointed to where she stood, then up to her box as she continued, "I am there! I am in fact everywhere!"

It was at that point that Jarrod looked at Edwin. Really looked at him. He knew him. He'd always known him. Each and every time he'd been in that room he'd subconsciously looked at him. In her picture.

He was Keely's husband. The one she rarely spoke about. The pilot who was always overseas. Complete bullshit. He was here at Woden. She was going to join him. She'd held tightly to his balls so he'd follow her.

It all made sense now.

The witch cackled loudly looking directly at him, and laughed. "Hahaha! You have got it!" She turned from Jarrod to behind her. The two figures in the middle turned and pulled back their hoods.

Keely and Rick.

"I'd like you all to welcome my daughter, Keely, and her son, Rick!"

"What?" Jarrod's legs went weak with the shock of it all. He looked at them both and only now saw how there was a resemblance. But aside from that Jarrod felt betrayed. All the times he'd spoken about Keely, from slagging her off to talking about his fantasies, and not once had Rick ever admitted to the true relationship between them.

That's why Rick had said he wasn't interested in Keely. She was his mum!

And Keely, he wasn't sure why but now everything felt strange.

"You knew Rick was never going back, didn't you, Jarrod?"

He found himself nodding. "I thought about staying too… but… What about everyone else?"

Rick grinned. "Like who, *Jarrod?*" There was sarcasm now, and his friend seemed to have been replaced by someone he barely knew. But then, did he ever truly know Rick?

"Eloise? Everyone! Will… Dan… er, Martin? Where are they?" He looked at the hooded people. Were these them?

"We saw Di… and Verity… I just... I don't get it. What's it all about?"

"What do *you* think, Jarrod?" He smiled, and glanced over to Keely, who took over.

"Poor Jarrod. Poor sweet Jarrod! Your fantasies about me were your downfall. It was so easy to coerce a person with those desires. You were my first project. My training into taking over here."

"Taking over?" Jarrod was unsure what this all meant but he knew nothing was positive for him. He knew too much.

The witch cackled and pulled back her hood to reveal a gruesome face that could never be replicated by a Halloween mask. It was sharp, and disfigured, and looked like a freshly dug up corpse.

"My body will soon die," she stated very matter-of-factly, "and I will only remain in the whispers of the damned! I need a replacement with a body that's strong!"

"Ahh!" Noah, sat clutching his knee making a noise so everyone remembered him.

"Shut up, fool!" the witch shouted.

Noah looked up with a face that was contorted between anger and pain. "If I could get to you, I would do my darndest to kill you!"

"Shut up!" the witch screamed and there was an awful loud crack as Noah yelled in excruciating pain, and his other leg jerked into an unnatural position. "Come and get me now!"

Noah pawed at his legs but he could no longer hold himself up and fell on his back with his legs still at impossible angles.

"Stop!" Jarrod shouted with raised arms. "What are you doing? He's done nothing wrong but follow your demands!"

"He's a traitor!" shouted Edwin. "He has been communicating with the outside world!"

"I was doing nothing wrong!" Noah pleaded through gritted teeth.

"You know the rules!" Herti was quick to add. "No communication after people have been here. Unless it's for donations or future bookings!"

"It was!" Noah said, after a deep breath. "They… wanted… to… return." Then he screamed as his left foot twisted with a crunch.

"Liar! You were getting personal and there was no talk of her returning, just you talking about sneaking out!" Through the pain, Noah's stomach dropped and he knew he wouldn't get out of there alive.

"I'm sure he's sorry," Jarrod interjected. "He's sorry, and won't do it again, right Noah?"

Noah's eyes were rolling around as he struggled to maintain consciousness. His body was getting too old and weak for such pain.

"Of course he won't!" The witch laughed louder than she had done before. It was like a mad, drunken woman.

Jarrod's eyes shot open when he realised all too late what was about to happen. He looked down at Noah, whose eyes flickered to try and stay open, when just as suddenly, with great force his neck shot to the right with a crack and he went rigid.

"Oh, my god! Rick? What the fuck?"

"Join us, Jarrod," Rick said calmly, but Jarrod was anything but calm about everything that was happening.

He'd hoped this would be the retreat from real life that he was looking for, but he was far from comfortable with threats of death. It took that laid back, community vibe and shot shit all over it.

"They'll come looking for us," Jarrod said. "What then?"

Keely took over from there, forever looking to take charge. "They are already looking for you. *For us*, in fact. There are helicopters and search-parties…" She smirked like she knew the punchline and was itching to drop it.

"What, at Woden?"

She glanced at Rick, and he was equally as amused, then they turned towards the elders.

"Edwin?" Keely spoke struggling to contain her amusement any longer. "My darling husband, are we about to be swarmed by SWAT teams?"

"Jarrod, you will not be found. No doubt you saw the plane outside, right?" Jarrod nodded. "That is what they are currently searching for, except not here but over the English Channel. Every detail about your weekend points anyone to a small island between Guernsey and France. That plane is registered to me, and I am the missing captain of the plane.

"Over the fields is an old RAF base which is now a private airport for small aircraft. That is where my plane is registered to, and the flight was logged as having taken off yesterday. But it never got to its destination, so I, and all of your work colleagues are missing. Soon to be presumed dead."

"But… surely they won't just give up looking?" He snatched at the invisible straws but knew in the bottom of his heart that after a few days the search would be called off and they'd be presumed dead.

"A replica portion of the plane's bodywork with the aircraft number was dropped by another plane yesterday, and when that is retrieved the authorities will be only too pleased to draw a line under it."

Jarrod stood up. He felt railroaded and now with all these people in front of him he was exposed and at risk.

"What's wrong?" Rick asked, but his usual sincerity was lost. Everything in front of him felt like a trap. "We hated work, and we hated our colleagues, so stop being such a pussy. You'll get a robe!" He laughed at that like it was a funny joke.

"But Woden… are these people here part of it? Are they the ones sat drinking and dancing together?" It seemed unlikely.

Edwin spoke up. "No. No, the two communities are different and kept apart. Woden is exactly what it looks like. It's for the fucking hippies. The free-lovers and eco-warriors."

"And this place?"

"This is the future!" Edwin boomed. All the while the witch was moving around in front of him. She was almost like a pacing tiger. Looking at him and waiting to pounce.

"Woden is the worm on the fishing line," he continued, "attracting people in, but this is the place that will eventually take over the country."

Rick cut in almost before Edwin had finished. "Remember when I told you about other places across England that are like Woden? Well, that's true, except it's more like here. Each has a set-up next to a large Manor House. These have become available more and more with ancestors unable to finance the upkeep. We move in and take over backed by powerful people!"

"What people?"

"You'd be surprised. They are out there watching us grow, then when it's time they will join us."

Jarrod found it hard to take, and realised they enjoyed boasting about their triumphs as so rare was it that they were able to do so.

"Come on, Jarrod. What have you got to lose?"

If he'd not been worried before that it was a cult, he really was now. All heads were turned towards him but he was unable to see their faces. All he saw was the naked and discarded bodies of Di and Verity hung up as if they were on the menu for the visitors to the restaurant…

He stopped. No, that couldn't be, could it? Were they changing the tastes of rich people to eating human flesh? It seemed obscure.

But suddenly very, very likely indeed.

Then from behind him came a noise. He thought he'd seen it all. That is until Dan burst through the curtain with a large stick on fire like some medieval torch!

Chapter 40

The walk along the underground tunnel went on and on. Only small safety lights were there hooked in a long line along the side of the tunnel wall. At one point Troy looked back behind him and for the first time in many, many years felt nervous. Both forward, and behind him looked the same. Neither way could an end be seen.

He had no idea what he was going to find when he got to the end, but the elders had taken this route and it stood to reason it was going under The Forbidden Woods. But then what?

What was there?

He kept going. He was obsessed now and needed to understand what it was all about. The elders had lied to them and that really wasn't okay. The residents of Woden trusted them, but here they were going where they preached not to go.

He came to a slight turn and a wooden door. When he got near he pushed it open and the tunnel became a freshly designed structure. The smooth edges of the new corridor continued for as far as he could see, and ten minutes later he came to another door.

He looked through the window in the door, and was taken aback by the hoard of caped people sat round in a huge, sinister circle. There was a great light dangling from the ceiling, although dimly lit. Most of the light came from candles that flickering around the room.

The elders were there with huge elaborate thrones but it was the character in the middle that made him stop and stare. The person in a blood red cape that at first levitated whilst in a standing position, then later pulled back the hood to reveal a monstrous looking human that could only be the witch!

Not some made up story to scare the locals into not wandering off, but the honest-to-God mythical person with powers. He was here bearing witness to it. He saw her float up and around, and he heard Noah scream in as she inflicted pain upon him.

But worse than that, if indeed you could consider it to be, was the revelation of the words Edwin, and the others were saying. The truths they hid behind. They were in charge of Woden, but as a cover; they were actually in charge of something a lot more powerful.

And then someone burst in behind Noah and Jarrod and the whole world went to hell!

He turned to make his escape, but instead felt pain flash through his brain and he was struck by someone.

He should've known there would be cameras and security there.

He should've known, but he didn't.

The Last Weekend

Chapter 41

His face was covered in blood, and he had a large welt on his cheek but he still looked like he could wrestle a bear and win.

"Fuck this lot, Jarrod! Come on!"

Jarrod didn't need to think any further and turned towards Dan. Dan touched the curtains with the flame and watched as it smoked, then slowly began to burn.

"Follow me!" Dan shouted, side stepping the lift as a doorway could be seen. Jarrod realised that when closed it was almost invisible. It made sense, any power cut would stop the lift and without a staircase you'd be trapped.

"What happened to you?" Jarrod shouted as they ran up the stairs as quickly as possible.

"We'll talk later. Our mission here, soldier, is survival. Lucky for you it's something I do well!"

Jarrod really wished he'd used the gym membership that he still paid for despite not having entered the place for over twelve months. Living was a good motivation and he pushed on.

"Come on!" Dan barked. "The flames should hold them for a while."

"The flames?"

"Stop talking!"

As they got to the top of the staircase, Dan burst through the door. As Jarrod got there, Dan was picking up a bottle and splashing the contents against the door. He touched it with the torch and the doorway lit up in flames.

They turned to run and saw the two kids – Rosie and Benny – armed with knives once more.

"Fuck off!" Dan shouted but they just began to march towards them.

"Let's go this way!" Jarrod suggested backing towards the opposite direction.

"No. This is the way out." He took a deep breath. "Fuck-sake." He handed Jarrod the torch, and walked towards them. Just as Benny swung the knife at him, Dan kicked out some ju-jitsu-type shit and kicked the kid so hard he hit heads with Rosie. It didn't stop them though, and they scrambled for their knives again. Rosie sliced his arm, as Dan punched Benny straight in the face with a swift jab. It momentarily stopped the boy, and Dan slapped the knife from Rosie's hand and punched her straight in the face too. He didn't give a shit. In the Middle East it wasn't uncommon for women and children to be used as decoys, and when soldiers went over to them to help, the supposedly innocent would attack.

Benny made an unsuccessful grab for Dan's leg, as he turned and punted the kid straight in the face again.

There was a loud bell as the fire-alarm went off throughout the building.

Jarrod felt useless and crept up, slapping Rosie as hard as he could. Dan kicked her feet from under her and stamped down on her leg.

Dan took back the torch and then they ran.

"Thanks for your help," Dan said sarcastically, as they ran hard towards the end of the corridor.

"You're welcome."

"That was a joke. All you did was slap a girl."

"Well you beat up two kids. Great work marine! Your mum must be proud!"

"If I hadn't, they would've sliced you up like vegetables… or something." Dan wasn't too happy. "Through here."

"You've been here before?"

"Whilst you were down there chatting, I was planning your release. It's what we do. If you fail to prepare, then prepare to fail."

"Always be prepared. That's your motto, right?"

"That's the fucking scouts."

"You say tomato and□"

"Maybe don't speak until we are out of here."

They passed the other door Jarrod had entered and followed down another corridor. That was when they saw the dead bodies of Martin and Will, laid out in pools of blood that had become sticky and congealed.

"What the fuck happened there?" Jarrod exclaimed, stopping to take it in.

"Keep running, they will soon be on our tail!"

"Hey, why has the witch not…"

"Are you fucking stupid?" They turned a corner and the place opened into a reception area with huge doors that allowed light to flood in, even if it was beginning to get dark.

When Jarrod didn't answer, Dan said, "Fire. Did you not see all the signs warning about fire in Woden? It's the one thing that stops the witch!"

They burst through the doors and were met by a group of people looking like extras from *Day of the Dead*.

"Fuck-sake!"

Dan held up the torch, then pulled something out of his pocket.

A gun.

"What the fuck. Why didn't…"

"Let us through or I will shoot!" One guy nudged him and Dan placed the torch against him, which made him scream as his shirt caught fire. The gaggle of people parted as Dan pushed through, swinging the torch back and forth. It appeared to be a lot more powerful than the gun.

There were a couple of cars that looked expensive, and of a similar value to his house, but next to them, almost hiding was a battered old Land Rover.

"Why are we going for the oldest, slowest, and shittiest vehicle?" Jarrod didn't get it.

"Well, I can start that thing in seconds, whereas the others I can't even break into. Plus, Land Rovers are the most reliable vehicles around. A lot better than those poncy fucking things. Back in the army□"

"Alright. I get it. You're fucking Rambo and I'm the fair-maiden you've just rescued."

"I'm beginning to think I should've left you," Dan said half under his breath as he jumped into the driver's seat. He lobbed the torch which rolled under another car. He grabbed some wires from under the steering column and after a spark, the engine kicked in. Easy, just like that.

"Shit. You're good!"

"We used to race at doing it in the Middle East. It was that or playing Human Minesweeper."

The wheels spun as they skidded out of the car park and along the drive, behind them a host of people stood watching.

That was until the heat and the flames from the torch exploded the fuel tank from the car it had rolled under. Jarrod jumped, but Dan just kept driving.

Jarrod looked back as Dan handed him the gun.

"Hold this."

Jarrod held it, scared shitless like it was a hand grenade about to go off.

Relief washed over him and suddenly his energy drained from his body, and he felt like crying. There was a lump in his throat and his hand began to shake.

"You're in shock," Dan said. "It happens."

Jarrod nodded, not trusting himself to speak. Dan would probably punch him until he stopped if he started to blub.

"I dunno where the fuck I'm going, but if we get to a main road then I can see from there."

Jarrod wanted to close his eyes and pretend he was anywhere else. He'd happily be in Keely's office whilst she verbally laid into him threatening him with dismissal again.

He glanced behind expecting to see men in red robes or even witches, chasing them with speeds faster than Usain Bolt. But there was no one there. They were in the clear.

"Fuck," Dan said slowing down. Jarrod looked forward and saw a child sat in the road.

"Keep going!" Jarrod said, his voice trembling. "Keep going. Keep going." He couldn't stop the mantra, but Dan wasn't listening.

"We have to," he said and slowed right down.

"Dan, no."

Dan got out and walked over to the child. "Hey! Are you okay?"

The child looked like she was crying. Her blonde hair was unkempt, but the closer he got the older she looked.

Jarrod didn't like it. He looked around and saw a sign: Tall Trees Camp Site. It rang a bell.

Dan held out his hand then heard a sound off to the side, deep in the hedge and looked up. The child pulled out a large knife from behind her and thrust it up into his groin as he immediately fell to the ground.

Jarrod grabbed the gun and pulled the trigger. Once. Twice. Three times.

Each time a small flame popped out. It wasn't a gun but a fucking cigarette lighter.

The girl, who looked a lot older than Jarrod first thought, was on top of Dan and stabbing him repeatedly.

Jarrod hopped over to the driver's side, yanked the cumbersome gear stick into first and sped past them and off into the darkness. The girl, covered in blood, was grinning at him in his rear-view mirror.

He was crying. When he came to a road sign pointing him in the right direction, Jarrod was bawling his eyes out, all the way back home to Thornhill.

The Last Weekend

Chapter 42

Paige stood there like he was her popstar crush. Her hand slowly moving to her mouth, which was open in shock.

"Jarrod," she gasped. "They said you were missing!" Her arms were outstretched and he was falling into them. He was crying and so was she. The emotional overload hitting its heights.

"There was never a plane," he began, but she pulled away and planted a kiss on his lips. He didn't know how much he really wanted it until it happened. He kissed her back.

"Shh!" She said, gulping and wiping her tears. "You want to take a shower…? Oh my God, is that blood?"

He glanced down and through his deep regrets he saw splatters of blood, though he couldn't be sure whose it was.

He shrugged. "I guess." She grabbed him by the hand and took him off to the bathroom. He stood there like a child as she turned on the shower, the spray loud against the bathtub. After a while the steam began. He was still in shock, so she was helping him to undress, but there was nothing romantic nor erotic about the whole process.

"Thank you for coming back," she said, and perhaps she knew he'd been close to not returning. Had things turned out differently, and had the world not gone to shit, he'd be far away, with her soon to be forgotten. He felt guilty, but it was one of many strong emotions suffocating him.

When he was naked, she helped him into the shower. He closed his eyes as the water soothed him. She may have rubbed soap on him but he couldn't remember it.

He felt lost, and lonely. Of course he had Paige, but he felt like he'd seen a life that suited him and that had been snatched away just as he thought it was his.

"Come and see me when you're done," she said, but the words were lost in his thoughts. "Mary is out…" the last bit was said as a tease which was lost on him.

He saw the broken bodies of Martin and Will like some horrific game of Twister gone wrong. Flashes of other things caught in his mind as he felt guilty remembering Verity's drooping breasts and Di's shaved pubic area, like his eyes were drawn to the places they shouldn't. Then he thought about the room below with all those people, silent but powerful. He still didn't understand it all, but he could piece together enough to know that good and bad lived side by side, and like everything it was the evil that called the shots. Was that any better than his corporate job, even as tedious as it appeared to be? Keely, nor the rest of the idiot team would be there anymore. He'd have a lot of questions to answer and he'd have to decide pretty soon what line he was going to take, but right now he was emotionally exhausted.

Should he feed them the lies they were already snacking on? Wait a day and say he was found in the water? Could he say he'd been locked in a room at the small airfield and never made it onto the plane? He knew he could never explain the truth, and that was what scared him the most. If somebody applied any pressure, he couldn't trust himself not to crumble.

He set about trying to wash away his troubles, but knew it was an impossible task. He scrubbed and scrubbed until his skin felt sore but the residual pain tattooed his skin.

Eventually he got out and dried himself down with a black towel that had a skull on it. He looked for his clothes but Paige had already taken them. She'd jumped at the chance to act like a wife and he'd been in no position to stop her.

He stepped out of the bathroom and walked towards her bedroom, hearing her moving in there anticipating him.

"Better?" she asked, and grinned at him. She pulled back the covers of the bed to show she was as naked as him. He wanted this to be as exciting as it should be but he struggled for the first time to compartmentalise it all. It wasn't her fault, she didn't know.

He dropped his towel anyway and laid down next to her. She snuggled into him and rather than it being sexual, the feeling of skin on skin just felt nice. Before he knew it, he had fallen asleep.

Light cut through the curtains and he saw her sitting up nothing but contentment in her eyes. Finally, her breasts were here in the flesh and not on his phone. It was still with his stuff back at Woden. His heart beat fast with the flooding memories but he'd survived the night.

He tried to relax. It was all too much. He felt exhausted. But the touch of her hands on his body felt soothing, and then they were touching him more intimately and he was growing hard. They were kissing, and he felt her smile as her lips grew wide, and she was pushing him with two hands on his chest and he got the full view of her on top of him. She was so happy as she straddled him, and he reached behind her. She grabbed him with a delicate finesse, and after a few false starts, guided him inside her and made a contented face he'd never grow tired of seeing. He reached up and cupped her breasts as she moved slowly, back and forth, up and down slightly squashing him, but it was bearable. This was what he missed with his ex, and dare he say it, what he lacked those times in the alleyway bending Eloise over a barrel. Here he was with a woman who wanted more than sex, she wanted him. All of him. Forever.

But then the smile dropped. Her arms shot up, and her eyes grew huge.

Something was wrong.

"Urgh!" she said as one arm, and then the other clicked into an impossible position with a loud and ugly crack.

"Paige?" He gasped at what should've been in pleasure but now was horror.

"My arms!" she screamed and fell backwards onto the bed. His member popped out of her comically but soon withered into nothing.

Her left leg shot out to one side, and the right leg did the opposite until there was an awful crack. A yoga position he was sure was barely possible. He scooted up into a sitting position and felt helpless. She was hysterical with pain and fear until invisible hands twisted her neck with a huge crack and she became still.

"Paige!" he shouted, then his world turned black.

When he opened his eyes, the hessian sack over his head made it impossible to see anything. The smell was strong and organic and it was disorientating. The bag was whipped violently from his head and sunlight burned his eyes.

He felt a breeze over his naked body and knew he was outside.

He was standing up on a stage. A rope was around his neck and he was in front of a crowd. It wasn't Woden though; he was back at the manor house. The people held flutes of champagne, with hundred-pound haircuts and thousand-pound accessories. This was high society. The untouchables who needed more from life.

"You fucking, useless cunt!" a familiar voice screamed at him and he recognised it as Keely. He turned his head as best as he could and was shocked to see her standing naked with a rope around her neck, too. The other side, he was shocked to discover the naked and well-chiselled body of Troy swinging. His face plumb-red, his tongue stuck out and bloated.

"I thought you were a witch?" His words were monotoned, and really, he didn't care about the answer. It was more a statement as he conceded his fate. How did he get there?

He struggled to turn as he was on tip toes and the rope tightened around his throat when he strained, but he saw her stood exactly as he was, but her face contorted in complete anger and hostility. He gained a tiny bit of pleasure that she, a woman with such power had, because of him, lost it all and was now standing there with her well-toned stomach muscles and perfectly maintained pubic area ready to die in the same way he was.

"I hate you!" she blasted back. "I was meant to be the one!"

A cloaked figure appeared in front of them. Hands grabbed the hood and pulled it back and the monstrous figure of the witch stood before them.

"You do know that witches are immortal, right?" She laughed loud and hard and the crowd joined her, some pointing at them.

"Drop 'em!" someone jeered.

"Where's Rick?" Jarrod asked, realising he was nowhere to be seen.

Another hooded figure appeared and took its place next to the others.

"I'm the new elder," the familiar voice of Rick said.

"No!" Keely screamed. "I'm part of this family!"

"Silence!" the witch shouted. "You're nothing but a self-centred harlot! It was Rick that got everyone here, and Rick who got this escapee back! What did *you* do?"

"I put out the fire!"

"*I put out the fire!*" the witch mimicked her voice. "This isn't about family. This is about power and you will be more powerful dead! Believe me!"

Rick lowered his hood. "She's right. I know it doesn't seem it now but your evil spirit will live in those woods and will stop people from getting through again! Those woods are yours forever!"

"But I don't want that," Keely was hysterical and began to wriggle but her hands were tied behind her back.

"It is as written, and the time is now. Let's all count down and let the celebrations begin!"

Jarrod's eyes began to dart around. What celebrations? The figures once again pulled up their hoods and they all stepped back from where he and Keely stood. He knew what it meant even in the primitive way it was set up.

The countdown was loud and haunting as the whole crowd joined in.

As the countdown hit one, he glanced towards Keely but couldn't focus as the floor gave way and his body dropped and violently jerked to a stop, his neck breaking instantly.

The crowd cheered like a goal had been scored by the home team.

For the next hour the rich mingled around the swinging bodies and took selfies with them. A drunken lout did his best to fuck Keely, but was swiftly asked to refrain from such disrespectful behaviour.

Later that day, the bodies were cut down; eventually they would be cut up and transported, under the woods, through the tunnel and up into the church, all for preparation for supper. Woden would have a special feast.

Edwin nodded to Rick; they'd both enjoy eating Keely. The beautiful corpses were often the best. Isn't it funny how that's often the way?

Epilogue

It had been a long journey. The close proximity of a bunch of models was always going to be testing. Felix had done his best to make sure nobody had scratched anyone else's eyes out yet, although Charise was about ready to bear her teeth when they began their walk.

"Why don't we know where we're going?" the blonde with famously long legs complained. "Not to be funny, but I thought it would be a little more exotic!"

"Like me?" the mixed-race woman with dark chocolate skin, and eyes that were slightly Oriental purred.

There was a series of eyerolls, and a pale-complexion women with stringy hair tutted loudly. She felt she had the most natural beauty even if she secretly wished her skin had more colour and didn't rash at the mere mention of sun.

"Girls!" Felix shouted, and turned to Joan a middle-aged woman who'd been a model when these girls were at school, now put out to graze as a modelling agent. She was one of the best but it didn't matter, to her she was still the wrong side of the camera. These prissy bitches didn't realise these were the best days of their lives. They could do whatever they wanted, and more if they gave enough blowjobs to the right people.

"We have a short walk," she stated with frustration, and waited for the groans.

"Seriously?"

"In heels?"

Joan turned around and threw her hands up in the air. "No heels," she said. "We have the clothes you need to wear, *including heels*. You should have on flats, or trainers. We've been through this like a hundred times!"

"Urgh! Trainers!" the strawberry blonde spat with her fingers pointing down her throat. "They are hardly going to show off my calves, are they!"

"Who cares, Fire-Crotch!" a tall woman with Farrah Fawcett hair shouted back. She was the big-mouth, and what she lacked in beauty she made up for in bitchiness.

"Fuck you, Slag!"

"Girls!" Felix shouted again, though secretly he enjoyed it. For an average, middle-aged white guy with a paunch and scant body hair, he was privileged to be in a position where most of these women had sucked his balls on more than one occasion. He loved his job. Good money and even better perks.

It was another fifteen minutes of arguing, and slagging each other off before they came to the large gate among the trees. No one was excited about this assignment and all assumed they'd failed having achieved it.

"What is this place?" Anastacia muttered curling up her lip in distaste.

"I hope there's a shower, I can smell your sweaty flaps from here!"

"Fuck you, Flat Chest!"

"Girls!" Felix shouted, just as the gate opened and a young-looking guy stood there grinning.

"Welcome to Woden!" said Rick, and beckoned them in.

They all smiled at him, and Rick couldn't help but grin to himself.

"Let me show you around!"

All these beautiful women will taste fantastic, he thought. He was licking his lips and salivating as he followed them through the gates for their first, and last, time.

The end

Acknowledgements

A big thank you to my family and friends. Your support it massive.

Thank you to my wonderful editors Heather Larson and Shelagh Corker for their hard work.

Thank you to Matt Rayner for your friendship, motivation and support with Question Mark Press. Cheers to everybody else at Question Mark Press: we are a great family!

A special mention to Elli Toney for her wonderful design direction. You certainly got what I was after!

Thank you to my ARC readers for having the stomach to read early versions.

I'll finish with a high-five, fist-bump, or hug to you the reader. You are, and will always remain, incredibly special to me. The journey is far from over so sit back and enjoy the ride!

ABOUT THE AUTHOR

Jim writes horror and dark mysteries that have endings you won't see coming, and favours stories packed with wit. He has written ten novels and well over a dozen short-stories spanning many genres.

Jim has a very strange sense of humour and is often considered a little odd. When not writing he will be found playing the drums, watching football and eating chocolate. He lives with his long-suffering wife, three beautiful children and two indignant cats in Swindon, Wiltshire UK.

Connect with Jim Ody here:

www.facebook.com/JimOdyAuthor

hyperurl.co/JimOdyAuthor

: jim.ody@hotmail.co.uk

@Jim_Ody_Author

@jimodyauthor

https://www.pinterest.co.uk/jimodyauthor/

https://www.bookbub.com/profile/jim-ody

Want to read more books by this author?

Here are details of three more books for you to get your hands on!

Camp Death

The place had a gruesome past that nobody wanted to talk about...

Camp Deathe is now a great place to spend the summer. Ritchie soon finds a group of outsiders like himself. Teenagers who ignore the organised activities, and bunk off in the old abandoned cabins deep in the woods. The cabins that have a history.

The campfire monster stories were meant to just scare them. Nobody expected them to come true. Then one of the teenagers disappears in the middle of the night.

Something is watching them. It hides in the woods and hunts at night.

Ritchie will have to uncover the secrets of the camp, and understand his own problems in order to survive.

Little Miss Evil

There's nowhere to run
But plenty of places to hide...

Tall Trees An Idyllic Campsite, situated on a picturesque lake, and surrounded by woodland.

Three Groups Of Strangers:

All meet for the first time, each one of them with something to hide. But someone knows all of their dark their secrets and now they want to play a game...

PLAYTIME JUST GOT DEADLY

Little Miss Evil 2: Evil Returns

Years after the murders, Tall Trees Campsite has been refurbished. The bodies removed, and the bloodstains painted over.

A group of people have been given free accommodation to enjoy the lake, activities and food. A PR stunt to show how great the place is. And safe.

Except not everyone is happy to see the Campsite back open. The murders couldn't happen again... *Could they?*

After a hard week at work they're dying to relax at Tall Trees!

Question Mark Horror

A new series of YA Horror books. All standalones.

Are you ready?

1 – Camp Death

2 – The Brood

3 – My Friend Peter

4 – The Ghost Club

Printed in Great Britain
by Amazon